Bankers Hours

Second Edition

Bankers Hours

Second Edition

Mike Faricy

Library of Congress Control Number: 2023913116
paperback ISBN: 979-8-9880826-4-4
e-book ISBN: 979-8-9880826-5-1

	MJF Publishing books may be purchased for education, Busi-
ness, or promotional use. For information on bulk purchases,
please contact the author directly. mikefaricyauthor@gmail.com

Published by

MJF Publishing
https://www.mikefaricybooks.com

Acknowledgements

I would like to thank the following people for their help and support:

Thanks to Cheryl, Roy, Steve and Julie for their creative talent and not slitting their wrists or jumping off a bridge when dealing with my Neanderthal technical capabilities.

Last, I would like to thank family and friends for their encouragement and unqualified support. Special thanks to Maggie, Jed, Pat, Schatz, Pat, Emily, and Av for not rolling their eyes, at least when I was there. Most of all, to my wife Teresa whose belief, support and inspiration has never waned.

One

It was exactly one week before Beau's attempted bank robbery went down the tubes. One week before he was taken hostage, shot, had his face splashed across the evening news, and was written up as a hero on the front page of the local newspaper. One week before all of that happened, the body of Thor Lunquist was found.

Thor Lunquist was the bank president and Mayor of Henderson, Minnesota. His body was found seventeen miles from town out on Minnesota State Highway 19. He was found face down on the kitchen floor of an abandoned farmhouse. The late Mr. Lunquist had been held overnight with the idea of coercing him bright and early the following morning into opening the vault of the Henderson Bank. There was only one thing wrong with the plan. It didn't work. An untimely breakfast coronary left Thor very dead on the kitchen floor, which was an oddly ironic demise since he'd foreclosed on the place back in 2009.

His three abductors, brothers Mendel, Elvis, and Lucerne Ditschler proceeded to do the only sensible thing. After finishing breakfast, they rifled Thor Lunquist's pockets, grabbing seventeen dollars in cash, his credit cards, and cellphone. The Ditschler Brothers promptly fled sixty-one miles east to the saintly city of Saint Paul in their spray-painted, rust-encrusted Fleetwood Brougham Cadillac. Lucerne was behind the wheel. They made the journey in near-record time, leaving a trail of blue exhaust across four counties.

TWO

eau's real name was Anthony DiMento. In his early years, he had been Tony to all his friends. At least until the infamous Beaujolais wine incident some years back. From that point forward, he'd been Beau. This applied to just about everyone, with the exception of his mother, Rita, to whom he would always remain Anthony.

Beau was just leaving his mother's home, having dropped off his laundry and picking up six ironed shirts. Actually, six shirts along with the pile of jeans, socks, T-shirts, and boxers. They were all waiting for him, neatly folded and stacked in a laundry basket next to the pan of lasagna and a dozen chocolate chip cookies.

"Ma, look, I wanted to cut the grass," Beau groaned. He clicked the remote and rose off the couch. "But I'm out of time. I've got a meeting to go to tonight, so I better get moving. Maybe Michael next door?" The suggestion seemed almost as good as doing the task himself.

"Oh, Anthony, you work so hard. Just like your poor father did in that bar. Now, don't you overdo it. You're always working. Working all the time. How do you ever hope to find a nice girl to settle down with and raise a family?"

"Thanks, Mom," he said, ignoring the question. He threw the Ziploc bag of cookies on top of the laundry basket and lasagna, thinking a *nice* girl was the last thing he wanted. He gave her a hasty kiss on the cheek, gathered everything, and spun out the door before she had the chance to remind him for ten minutes that a mother looked forward to becoming a grandmother.

The night's important meeting was actually a poker game with pals. He barely had enough time to unload his laundry, check-in at the bar, and grab a hundred from the till before dashing over to be dealt in for the first hand.

Three

Across town at Rudi's Bakery on Saint Paul's East Side, a well-dressed gentleman held the door for an elderly woman as she was leaving. He gave a subtle nod to his gargantuan companion, who promptly locked the door and turned on the red neon 'CLOSED' sign.

"Hey. Hey, what the hell do you think you're doing? You can't be doing that," Rudi yelled from behind the refrigerated counter of cream-filled pastries. He was a rotund little man with a shaved head, a naturally whiny voice, and dark beady eyes that darted back and forth as he stared at the two men, suddenly horrified he hadn't recognized them sooner.

"Oh, Mr. Osborne, sorry. I didn't realize it was you," Rudi stammered as he backed away from the cream puffs. "Gee, umm, long time no see. Is it that time already? I guess you might have caught me just a little short. Course, you know I'm good for it," he shouted and attempted to waddle away quickly. In his haste, he knocked a tray of cream puffs to the floor, making traction difficult. He slipped, fell, and split his white baker's trousers. As he clawed and grabbed for balance, he pulled a tray of chocolate éclairs and raspberry compotes down on top of him.

The well-dressed gentleman seemed bored by the whole affair and casually turned to his large companion. "Milton," he said and nodded toward the kitchen area as whipped cream and raspberry covered Rudi attempted to escape through the doorway on all fours. His split trousers revealed the unfortunate hint of a pink thong.

"No. No. No, Mr. Osborne. Please, I promise. I'll have the money for you. I just got a little behind. You understand. Come on. Please. You know I'm good for it, please. Please."

Milton stepped behind the counter, grabbed Rudi roughly by the ankles, spun him around on the floor, and dragged him through the whipped cream, raspberry, and chocolate slime. Rudi's fat fingers clawed at the worn wooden floor in a desperate effort to avoid the fate he knew was waiting. In one seemingly effortless motion, Milton hoisted him up and slammed him onto the oiled wooden worktable. Metal bowls scattered, and Rudi let loose with a loud "Uff" as the wind was knocked out of the cream slathered baker.

"Oh, Rudolf," intoned Osborne. He brushed a dusting of powdered sugar from the sleeve of his otherwise spotless navy blue coat. "I think I've been more than generous with the time I've allowed you. I fear I'm beginning to sense a lack of resolve on your part. Which leads me to believe that, most unfortunately, some instruction appears to be necessary at this juncture. Milton, if you would please." Osborne nodded at a shiny steel cleaver sitting in a rack at the end of the table.

"No. No. Oh God, please," Rudi screamed.

In one swift motion, Milton grabbed the cleaver and, with a practiced downward stroke, sliced off the fingertips on Rudi's pudgy left hand. The fingertips tumbled into a vat of rising dough. Milton turned on the industrial mixer, and the fingertips quickly disappeared.

"What? You maniac. Not my cinnamon rolls. Ahhh, my God," Rudi screamed.

"That might be a health code violation," Osborne advised. "I'll see you in two weeks, and I'll be expecting payment in full. Come, Milton. Not to worry, Rudolf, we shall help ourselves to some pastry on the way out."

Osborne took up a flattened, white cardboard box and handed it to Milton. Milton quickly assembled the box and proceeded to fill it with the various mouthwatering pastries Osborne pointed at. He closed the lid on the box and took a step towards the door.

"Really, Milton. Aren't we forgetting something?"

Milton gave him a blank look.

"The red elastic band that keeps the box closed and therefore aids in the stability of the treats inside? We can't have things falling onto the floor. Oh, and mind the mess. I don't want you tracking things into my car. We'll be leaving now, Rudolf," Osborn called into the back room. "Not to worry. We shall return in two weeks' time. Bit of a mess to clean up out here."

Rudi, covered in whipped cream, chocolate, and raspberry preserves, held his bloodied hand and sobbed.

Four

Patti the bartender called, "Hey Beau," as he escaped from the stifling heat into the dim light of his air-conditioned bar. She was filling a half-dozen beer glasses from behind the bar and wiggled her finger in his direction.

He winced inwardly at the memory of a gloriously wild weekend with Patti three or four months back that raced from torrid to horrid over the course of forty-eight hours. He'd done his level best to dodge her ever since.

"Beau," she called again, adding a hint of disgust to her tone.

He nodded, gave her a slight wave, and continued to talk to a couple of guys at the far end of the bar. They were neighborhood regulars. Retired guys just grabbing a beer before they cleared out once the younger crowd began to ooze in the door.

"Beau!" This time she was louder, and there was a definite edge to her tone.

"Excuse me, guys," he said, laughing as he walked away. "Yeah, Patti. Look, I don't really have the time to—"

"Relax and save it. Thought you should know. There's a couple of creeps waiting for you up in your office. Didn't look to be all that pleasant."

"Creeps? What kind of creeps? City inspectors?"

"Got me," she shrugged her shoulders. "I just figured it would be okay with you if they waited up there. Wouldn't want them chasing customers away," she said and brushed against him as she squeezed past.

He caught the scent of sexy perfume as she pressed against his back. She seemed to linger an extra second or two. Just long enough for a hot breath against his neck and a soft moan in his ear. Long enough to remind him what he'd be forever missing out on.

"Gentlemen!" Beau sounded full of bravado striding into his occupied office thinking, *'Oh shit.'* "Shoulda let me know you were going to be in today. I would have arranged dinner. We've got the best prime—"

"We're not here for any free dinner!" The larger of the two men sneered. Large was an understatement. Hands the size of ten-pound hams, one long, abnormally heavy eyebrow, and a low forehead that gave him an overall Neanderthal appearance. His gigantic frame spilled out of the green Naugahyde chair across from Beau's desk. Beau couldn't help but notice, was it foam or possibly even whipped cream on his shoes and around the cuffs of the giant's trousers?

"Mr. DiMento, Milton means no real offense." The gentleman smiled, revealing yellowed teeth. He brushed dust or powder from an otherwise spotless navy blue suit coat. "But there is the matter of a rather sizable payment coming due in just a little over a week. Payment in full, I hasten to add, in the amount of—"

"Sorry to interrupt, Mr. Osborne," Beau interrupted, holding up his hand, all smiles and not at all sorry. "But according to my figures, the payment in full is two hundred and fifty thousand. Not to worry. I just thought I'd let the money work for me for another week before paying off your loan. On time, I might add. Of course, I'm looking forward to paying you and getting it off my books. Sorry you had to make the trip all the way over here for nothing."

"Sounds like a bunch of bullshit to me," Milton growled and stood from his chair, towering over Beau.

"Please, excuse my associate for responding in kind to your rudeness, Mr. DiMento. If you think there might be a problem, we would be willing to work with you at this juncture to facilitate an equitable and painless transaction for all parties. I'm sure you can understand our concern in this matter." Osborne brushed more flecks of white powder from the sleeve of his coat. "Yeah, painless, sure you would. Like I said, sorry you made the trip for nothing. I've already got your money. I'm just letting it work for me for another week. That's all."

There was just a hint of something in the air. Not aftershave. More like disinfectant mixed with something sweet. Was it a hint of raspberries?

"Very well, Mr. DiMento. We shan't keep you from your appointed rounds, as it were. We'll look forward to seeing you next week. In the meantime, should anything not go as you planned, you know how to reach us."

"Yeah, right. That nine-hundred phone number you gave me. Thanks. I get charged four dollars a minute when I want to talk to you."

"I am a businessman, Mr. DiMento. That's why I'm successful, and that is why you came to me for financial help."

"How can I ever forget," Beau said, wishing to God he could.

On closer examination, the almost too lean Osborne appeared transparent. His skin took on the appearance of parchment paper. His close-cropped blonde hair was almost translucent. Red-rimmed, ice-blue eyes appeared eternally bloodshot. His eyelids seemed to be permanently set at half-mast. His spotless hands featured glossy manicured nails. He wore a heavily starched shirt, and his trousers were pressed to a razor crease. Not exactly what one expected from a dangerous mobster.

Declan Osborne controlled a major portion of the 900 number businesses in the nation, along with online interactive sex sites plus a stable of outcall services. All of which provided him with a license to print money. Money that Beau had desperately needed to stay afloat after being turned down by every conventional lender within two hundred miles. Now, one year later, Osborne and his trained ape Milton sat in Beau's office, reminding him payment in full was due in one week.

They stood to leave, and Beau moved quickly to the door babbling something nonsensical about how happy he was to put their mind at ease.

"Shit, shit, shit," he cursed once they departed, swinging a fist in the air to punctuate each word. He wasn't sure he could get two hundred and fifty dollars, let alone two hundred and fifty thousand, in a week's time. He had signed over everything to them. The bar, the restaurant, the lounge, the backstage, and dance area. They'd get it all, every square inch, if he didn't find a way to pay. There was a simple enough solution to the problem. He just had to find two hundred and fifty thousand dollars, a quarter of a million bucks, and find it fast.

Driving over to play cards, Beau was thinking, *If I break two hundred and fifty thousand dollars down into smaller pieces, it might sound better. Stop thinking of it as a quarter of a million-dollar lump sum and, instead, break it into a piece for each of the remaining days before payment was due. Which makes just thirty-five thousand, seven hundred and fifteen dollars I'll have to come up with each and every day...* which didn't seem to help very much.

Five

On the short drive into work the following morning, Beau attempted to rationalize the hundred and fifty bucks he had lost the night before. He convinced himself it didn't really seem so bad if he broke it down into seven pieces and just added another fifteen plus bucks to his daily total of thirty-five thousand seven hundred and fifteen dollars.

As he drove, his hangover seemed to grow even worse, and his headache was now throbbing nonstop. He suddenly had a vague recollection of an old girlfriend hanging up on him, at least twice, sometime after midnight. It had seemed like the thing to do at the time. To call her and apologize for his behavior the last time they had been together. After which, he planned to tell her he felt like talking and wondered if it might make sense for him to stop over. When he called back, suggesting he'd been cut off, she hung up on him again. He groaned inwardly as the memory grew a bit more clear.

He'd already received a couple of calls from work. He figured since he was only a few blocks away, work could wait ten more minutes while he swung into the coffee shop for his morning latte and doughnut.

"Hi, Chrissie, I'll have a double latte and one of those French doughnuts," he said to the sinful looking blonde behind the counter.

"The bagels would be better for you, honey. A lot less cholesterol."

"Give me two French doughnuts," he said. "Here, you should stop in and see me tonight or some other night," he quickly added, handing her his business card. "I'll buy, and we can see where things go from there."

"Gee, thanks, Beau. I don't know. Can you even be trusted?"

"Hopefully, not. That's part of the deal."

"Hmm-mmm, sounds fun. We'll have to see. Anything else I can get you?" she said as she slid his coffee across the counter, followed by the bag with two French doughnuts.

"Yeah, as a matter of fact. You got any aspirin back there?"

"Oh, Mr. Party," she said, smiling, and set two aspirin on the counter.

Beau tossed the aspirin into his mouth and washed them down with a mouthful of scalding hot latte. "Ahh," he groaned and headed out the door.

"Hope you're feeling better," she called after him, tossing his card in the trash once the door closed behind him.

"Beau? Didn't you get my calls?" Patti whined at him as soon as he entered the bar.

"Look, Patti," he started with a mouthful of French doughnut then washed it down with a swallow of latte to buy time. "I don't know exactly how to tell you this, but your kids…"

"My kids? Oh my God, Beau, is that why you've been giving me the cold shoulder for the past damn months? Don't be stupid. My kids? I don't want someone like you around my kids. No offense, but they're really impressionable. Believe me, I am not looking for a relationship. Actually, I have a doctor's appointment this afternoon, and I'm going to have to leave about thirty minutes early. I just wanted to let you know."

"No problem. Thanks for the heads up." Thinking, Doctor? He quickly counted back the time that had passed since their weekend together and concluded no. It couldn't possibly be him.

Up in his office, he continued to obsess about Osborne and his loan. Christ, he'd have to rob a bank. He gradually recalled bits of a drunken conversation last night with his card-playing pal, Dickie.

"Ahhh, man. Sorry, guys, I gotta run," Dickie had said and raked in his winnings.

Dickie's name was really Hans. Hans Ulmbacher, about as German as it gets. Five feet seven inches tall, blond hair, blue eyes, and close to five feet seven inches wide. Dickie weighed in at just about three bills. It was why they called him 'Dickie.' Apparently, Dickerchen meant fatty in German. Dickie worked in IT for a large bank.

"Look, fellas, I'm really bushed. I told ya, this is State Fair week. One of our branches handles all the cash from the fairgrounds. I mean, this little dinky branch. They do next to nothing for the rest of the year. But during the fair, they've got the cash literally stuffed into trash bags. The courier guys go nuts. We bring in a half-dozen extra counting machines just to handle all they have. Once it's counted, we haul it to Central, where it's a hell of a lot safer."

"Aren't they worried about getting robbed?" Beau asked.

"Frankly, it's kind of amazing they've never been hit. They literally wheel the bags of counted cash in a shopping cart out to the armored car. All this cash, it's sticky from cotton candy and smells like pronto pups or worse."

"Should you even be telling us this?" Victor asked.

"Yeah, like you guys would tell anyone," Dickie snorted.

Beau placed a call to Dickie then waited until someone finally answered on about the twentieth ring. "Hans Ulmbacher, please," he said into the phone.

"One moment, please, while I connect you."

He waited for close to five minutes before Dickie picked up.

"Beau, sorry to make you wait, buddy. What can I do for you? Don't need a loan, do ya?" Dickie laughed.

"Dickie, you got time to stop in on the way home? I got a couple of things I want to run past you."

"I could. It might be a little late. Maybe eight or so. Everything okay?"

"Yeah, fine. Just looking at a couple of different systems here and wanted your input."

"Not a problem. My fee is dinner. Payment in advance."

"Perfect. We got a great prime rib. We'll go back into the kitchen, and you can pick the one you want. No rush. Just ask for me at the bar."

"Now you're talking, man."

Step one taken care of. Beau figured he had enough time to run over and see the physical layout of the bank. Maybe begin formulating some sort of basic plan while he looked around without being too obvious. *Note to self,* he thought, pulling out of his parking place. *I'll need a set of disposable, untraceable wheels for a getaway vehicle.*

Six

The staccato synthesized beat blaring across the mirrored stage and the naked redhead on the brass pole were lost on Milton as he helped himself to another plate at the early bird breakfast buffet. From six-thirty to eleven every morning, Cheaters served a 'Brunch and Buns' special, featuring scrambled eggs, bacon, and ten different strippers. Milton returned to his usual place at the bar and ignored the naked woman stuffing dollar bills into her garter.

Brunch and Buns had been Osborne's clever idea. He skirted the city restrictions by offering only non-alcoholic fresh juice drinks before eleven in the morning and thereby conforming to city code.

A naked woman stepped on stage. A large rattlesnake tattoo emerged from her backside and coiled seductively around her waist a couple of times before barred fangs poised to strike a surgically enhanced right breast.

Mary Alice Mahoney, dancing under the stage name Serpentina, had attempted to create an element of mystique when she got her tattoo two years ago. Unfortunately, her thought process had been somewhat clouded by three days of tequila shots and cocaine at a Las Vegas golf cart convention. Her sponsors, a bunch of sales guys from Coral Gables, had been pushing the idea of charging a hundred bucks to chip plastic golf balls off her breasts. She fled Vegas with her new tattoo that night.

Along with dancing, her Brunch and Buns duties consisted of getting things for Osborne. The mail, the phone, his chair, a pen, anything and everything he wanted. She would be decked out in a starched white nurse's uniform while wearing surgical latex gloves. Everything that might come in contact with him was to be slathered with a liberal dose of hospital disinfectant.

Once upon a time, she'd been a promising nursing student until her fondness for Darvon and nitrous oxide had been discovered. Now, when she wasn't dancing, dispensing disinfectant, or getting the mail, she monitored Osborne's pulse, temperature, and blood pressure. She issued various pills to him throughout the day for his contrived ailments and, in general, helped to feed the man's neurotic hypochondria.

She ignored the furtive looks from the other girls in the dressing room. She kicked off her silver stiletto heels, pulled the plastic bag off a freshly starched nurse's uniform, and pinned her nurse's hat in place, ready for another germ-free day with Declan Osborne.

"Good morning, come in, my dear," Osborne said a few minutes later. He sat behind an expansive polished mahogany desk and rolled up his sleeve for the blood pressure cuff.

Serpentina was forced to take very small steps due to her uniform being two sizes too small. It was probably just as well since Osborne had her wearing white stiletto heels, and she hadn't seen her feet ever since her breast augmentation.

"Let's get the day's preliminaries over with, shall we?" he said and opened his mouth for the digital thermometer. After taking his temperature, blood pressure, and checking his pulse with a stopwatch, she quickly misted the phone and desk area with disinfectant.

"And begin," he instructed. He shut down his computer and signaled the all-clear for her to cleanse his keyboard.

Once finished, she quickly reached under his desk and rebooted the computer while he sat in his office chair with arms outstretched, palms upward, not unlike a surgeon waiting to be handed the proper instrument. He kept one eye on the digital clock to ensure she completed her appointed tasks within the prescribed timeframe.

"Excellent, excellent girl." Never once did he ever call her by her real name. "Now, on your way out, there is a box of pastries I happened to pick up late yesterday. Please, take them up to the Phone Farm and then return." He turned back to his computer and began typing frantically.

The Phone Farm was located up on the third floor of the building and consisted of cubicle upon cubicle of women responding to 900 number calls. Each woman was armed with a headset, a sexy voice, and all day to keep the caller on the line. Working as independent contractors, they were paid a ten percent commission on the four dollar and ninety-five cent per minute fee advertised on late-night cable. This was different from the Internet sites located up on the fourth and fifth floor. They billed out at fourteen to thirty-nine dollars per minute, depending on the activity. Next to the school system, Declan Osborne was one of the largest female employers in the state.

Seven

Note to self, Beau thought. *When planning the robbery, allow for traffic conditions.* He was sitting in traffic, having not really moved more than thirty feet in the past ten minutes. Eventually, he was able to see the bank up ahead. It was a single-story brick building sporting weathered cedar trim and double glass doors.

It took him another ten minutes to inch his way to the bank, park on the street, and wait in line at one of the teller windows. Dickie had been right. The place was jammed. Lines of customers holding two and three business deposit bags stuffed to overflowing. One guy carried a paper shopping bag full of cash.

Glancing out to the parking lot through the teller windows, he saw two armed guards wheeling a grocery cart toward an armored car. The grocery cart was piled high with green trash bags, just as Dickie had described the night before. The back doors on the armored car were open. As they approached, one of the guards climbed into the back while the other proceeded to toss the bags to him.

"Hello, there," the bank teller said. The nameplate on her window read Erma, but her name tag read Cindy.

"Are you Erma or Cindy?" Beau asked.

"Right now, I'm crazy," she said.

"Pretty busy, I guess. What with the fair and all?"

"Been like this all day. It will get absolutely insane the last hour before we close. It's like a sauna in here behind this glass. We've got a half-dozen extra people and equipment just to try to keep up. Let me tell you, six o'clock tonight can't get here fast enough. There might be a wine cooler or two in my future this evening. What can I do for you, sir?"

"Yeah, well, I'd like to get two fives for this ten, if I could," he said and slid a ten-dollar bill under the thick glass.

"Long wait for two fives. Anything else I can help you with?"

"No, thanks. Well, actually," he said, folding the fives into his wallet and pulling out a business card, "if you're serious about that wine cooler, stop in and see us tonight. DiMento's Bar and Restaurant. We're up on Snelling, corner of Selby. Our address is on the card. Prime rib every night. I'll spring for your dinner, and—"

"Ahem," an elderly woman behind him cleared her throat in an agitated manner.

"Hope I'll see you there." He winked.

"Thank you, Anthony," she said, reading his card.

"We've all been waiting," the woman said as she stepped to the counter.

Eight

Mendel groaned and said, "Will you look at all this state fair shit?"

Lucerne was driving the three of them past a crowded little bank. Elvis snored in the backseat of their '94 Fleetwood. Back when Bill Clinton was president, the car was originally Dark Adriatic Blue, but it had since been two-toned with the help of some white spray paint and Elvis's lousy aim. It was a poor attempt to disguise the car after a particular incident. In point of fact, it only served to draw attention.

"Mercy, hello there, city gal," Lucerne yelled at a woman standing on the corner, holding the hands of two small children. The young mother looked up and quickly pulled her two little girls closer. The Fleetwood proceeded to engulf all three of them in a noxious blue cloud of exhaust that seemed to hang in the humid air.

"Take us around the block, Lucerne, and let's just see what all the fuss is back there. I just might be gettin' me an idea. We could maybe make up for that damn Henderson banker pulling the plug on us too soon," Mendel said.

Lucerne drove around an elongated residential block, passing fairly pricey looking homes. He slowed as they came alongside the bank parking lot and the drive-up teller windows. They arrived just in time to see the final trash bag get tossed into the back of the armored car and watched as the uniformed guard closed the rear doors.

"Well, will you just look at that?" Mendel said. "So much cash they have to bag it and wheel it out in a grocery cart. Seems to me, fellas, we maybe just struck gold. Might not be a bad idea to help ourselves to one of them cartloads of cash. You know, just take it off their hands and help 'em out. Drive around the front again, Lucerne. I want to take another quick look. Get me a little better idea about this."

Nine

Dickie swallowed the mouthful of prime rib he'd been chewing, chasing it down with a large swallow of beer. "Umm, thanks. Like I was telling you guys last night, Beau, that branch is bringing in millions. Literally over a million a day. All of it cash. You'd lose your mind if you were working there, man."

He paused to swirl a doughnut-sized onion ring through a puddle of catsup. He stuffed the entire thing into his mouth, dribbling catsup across his tie in the process.

"We actually went up to the Indian casinos. Saw how they were handling all the cash and got some general ideas. Although, to tell the truth, during Fair week, that little bank is about a thousand times busier than those casino folks."

"So what do you do? Put a machine gun on the roof or something?"

"Naw, I mean, the cops can be there in about two minutes. That's probably the best defense we've got right there. Well, and you know, keep a low profile. Hell, we got insurance, and the couriers are in there on an hourly basis, hauling away as much as they can. Tell you the truth, we're more concerned with electronic theft, you know transfers, passwords, identity theft, hackers. All that shit you always hear on the news. Whenever some bank gets knocked off, it's no big deal. Those punks only get away with a grand, maybe two if they're lucky. And, if they're stupid enough to be repeat guys, they're bound to get caught. The real dirty little secret is that just about any fool can rob only one bank and get away with it. But the dumb shits never do that. They rob a second and a third because it seems so damn easy, and that's when they get caught."

"You're kidding," Beau said.

"No. The electronic stuff, everything I'm involved with, you don't have to be at the bank to rob us. Hell, you don't even have to be in the country. It gets really spooky, man. You'd be amazed, absolutely amazed. Course, your deposits are always safe with us. Ahh, I think I'll have the cheesecake," he said, looking up at the waitress as he grabbed the last onion ring. "And, well, since Beau's buying, I better have another beer."

They chatted on about vague things. Beau started to feel somewhat upbeat after gaining the initial intelligence from Dickie.

"Beau to the lounge. Beau to the lounge bar." An overhead page interrupted whatever remained of their conversation.

"Gotta run, Dickie. Thanks for the advice. Good seeing you."

"Hey, see you Sunday. Pre-season Vikings game, man. Don't forget."

"Wouldn't miss it, Dickie. Sorry, but I gotta run," he said and headed out to the lounge. "Yeah, Tommy, what is it?" Beau asked his bartender.

Tommy inclined his head toward six figures clustered at the far end of the bar. "I don't know. Something about the dinner, it's the band for tonight, bunch of jerks if you ask me. Anyway, figured you'd want to deal with it. That idiot in the black jacket with all the silver studs and the golf tee thru his nose, he's doing the talking."

Beau sized them up as he headed over. Collectively, they looked to weigh about eighty pounds soaking wet, and that's if you removed all the metal piercings. Beau wondered for half a second if they ever had to pass through airport security. The four with hair had it dyed a variety of different colors, none found in nature. They had an odor about them, not necessarily unpleasant, but definitely not aftershave, more like incense.

"You're the band, right? Kiss of Death?" Beau said. Tommy was right. The kid's nose piercing did look like a golf tee.

"It's about the dinner," the kid with the golf tee said. He was the scrawniest of the group.

"We got the best prime rib in town."

"Yeah, man, that's the bummer. See, dude, we're all vegans. So, like, the prime rib thing is, well, it's just totally bogus."

To Beau's way of thinking, there weren't many things worse than some jerk from Minnesota affecting a soft-spoken California accent. He reminded himself that this band was supposed to pack them in all weekend.

"Sorry about the mix-up. Look, I'll have the kitchen rustle some things up for you. We'll bring it into the green room off the stage. And I'll make sure the vegan word gets passed around for the next two nights. Okay?" It wasn't worth asking why they agreed to play a steak and prime rib place if they were so opposed to red meat.

For one long moment, they stood as one stupid block of pierced anatomy. Eventually, Scrawny said, "Well, yeah, dude. That would be screaming."

"Good, screaming it is," Beau said, wishing at that moment that he could. "I'll go take care of it personally, get things delivered, and you guys can go through your soundcheck, okay?"

The scrawny kid nodded, and Beau retreated to the kitchen before he strangled the night's entertainment.

"Bonnie, Caesar salads, six of them to the green room and mix a little bacon fat into the dressing," he yelled, standing in the middle of the kitchen.

"Huh?"

"Bacon fat, you heard me. Mix it in with the dressing but not too much."

Ten

Beau was back in the lounge area a little after eleven. Kiss of Death was indeed packing them into the back bar area, as promised. It may have been a strange-looking crowd, but their money was just as green. He was chatting with Tommy, the bartender. The lounge served as more of a meat market for the older set. Tommy's eyes looked over Beau's right shoulder and remained fixed, finally causing Beau to turn around.

"Hi, Anthony."

It took him a beat or two to realize the attractive woman with brown eyes was talking to him. Her blonde hair was pulled back. She wore jeans that looked as if they had been spray-painted onto her gorgeous thighs and a tight-fitting top that must have been held in place with industrial-strength adhesive. She looked vaguely familiar.

"Excuse me?"

"I said hi, Anthony. You don't remember me, do you?" She laughed.

"It's just that it's sort of out of context here."

"I'm Cindy, remember, from the bank? You were in this afternoon and gave me your card. Changed a ten for two fives? Ring any bells?"

Yes, it did, alarm bells, which he promptly ignored.

"Oh yeah, Cindy, nice to see you. Wow, thanks for coming in. Like I said, it was just a little out of context. You know, the dim lights and you not on the other side of bulletproof glass. Been here long?"

"No, we just got here, Anthony. This is my friend, Karen," Cindy said, moving back half a step as a way of further introduction.

Karen seemed like a nice woman, attractive enough, but Beau knew from bitter past experience that she had but one function. She was the third wheel. She was here to make sure Cindy didn't end up in bed with Beau. For some reason, certain women felt they had to make sure their girlfriends weren't tumbling in and out of bed. So they remained ready at the first sign of a loud laugh or a slurred word to apply the brakes to any late-night enjoyment.

"Nice to meet you. Please call me Beau," he said and extended his hand.

Karen nodded, dutifully playing her role.

"Beau? You mean like Beaujolais wine?" Cindy asked. She took a half-step forward, returning Karen to the background.

"Yeah," he replied, wisely thinking that would not be a good tale to tell just now. He might have laughed a bit too nervously before turning toward Tommy, hoping he might interject some bartender's etiquette and save him.

"Ladies, what'll it be?" Tommy asked.

"Mmm, I think I'll have a glass of Beaujolais, then," Cindy cooed, all smiles.

"Just a Coke for me," Karen said, staying in character.

"So, Beau? Do you own a winery or something?" Cindy asked.

"How about you just call me that, and I'll tell you some other time. It's a long story and, well, you know."

Actually, the telling of the event itself didn't take that long. Unfortunately, climbing naked out of a second-story bedroom window after throwing up two bottles of Beaujolais wine on a married woman as her husband charged up the stairs always seemed to lead to more questions and usually shed an unfavorable light on the whole first impression thing.

"Should I call you Anthony or Tony?" Cindy said, picking up her glass of wine and raising it in his direction.

"Tony would be fine."

They chatted on and off over the next hour and a half. Karen sipped her Coke and kept a governor on the conversation until, finally, after her third Coke, she left to use the ladies' room, proving another axiom when dealing with women. They always went to the ladies' room in multiples, unless there were only two, and one of them was there strictly in the role as the third wheel. In that case, the third wheel went alone, and the woman you were really interested in got about six minutes of uncensored airtime.

"Gee, Tony, it was really nice of you to invite me tonight. Are you sure I don't owe you something for all this?" As she spoke, she rubbed her index finger briefly across the back of his hand.

"No, I wouldn't think of it. There have to be some perks to working nights and being the owner. Having you stop by is one of them. Really nice of you to drop by," he said as he spotted Karen already making her way back across the room.

"My pleasure," Cindy said and began to slide out of the booth. He was suddenly aware of her breasts taking on a life of their own as they bounced an inch above the tabletop. Ultimately, swaying to rest just above his forehead.

"Really, really nice to meet you both," he said, standing up.

"We enjoyed talking to you. Well, another zoo day tomorrow at work," she said and held out her hand to shake.

He took it, gently pulled her close to him as he did, kissing her cheek.

She turned quickly, gave him a second kiss on the lips. Not a lingering, open mouth tongue stab, but a good beat or two longer than a peck. Something akin to an electrical charge suddenly surged through both their bodies.

"Working tomorrow? It's Saturday."

"Yeah, special hours because of the State Fair, you know. Anyway, thanks again, Tony."

"Yeah, thanks for the Cokes," trumpeted Karen, sort of ruining the moment.

"The pleasure was all mine, ladies. Remember, I still owe you dinner," he said, making a point to address Cindy specifically.

"We'd enjoy that," she said, smiling back.

"You sure you know what you're doing?" Karen asked, driving home.

"What do you mean?" Cindy said.

"I mean, that guy, that Beau character. Listen, honey, not that we want to go into your past, so I won't. But just for starters, the guy calls himself Beau, after the damn wine."

"But I called him Tony."

"Honey, were you listening? He introduced himself as Beau, and he doesn't own a winery, so don't get on that jag. He's either a drunk, a goofball, possibly a loser, but more likely all three. I mean, let's face it, your luck hasn't been all that great the past couple of years."

"Oh, I don't think—"

"Remember your last great love, Sheldon? If I recall correctly, after mooching off you for three months, he drained your bank account. Hey, and what's with the 'we'd enjoy dinner' line? You bragging about your attributes?"

"I kinda like him. He bought us drinks," Cindy said, ignoring her question.

"The way you're dressed, any guy in there would have bought you drinks. Look, I know how it is. Jesus, the last time I can remember being in bed with someone, it was my little nephews sleeping over. They got scared in the middle of the night and climbed in with me. I'm just suggesting that you go slow, that's all."

"Did you see the way he looked at me when we left?"

"Yeah, and I saw the way you gave him that kiss. Saw the way you strutted out of the place turning heads all around. Look, I'm just suggesting you think this through, okay? Just don't get all wound up, fall in love, and then we pick up the pieces a month down the road because he ends up doing what everyone warned you about, and you find out he's married. That's all I'm saying, okay?"

"Well, I don't think he'd ever do that to me. He's too sweet."

"There you go, Cindy. That's three glasses of Beaujolais talking," Karen said.

"This is Beau," he said, answering his phone, wondering what the problem was if someone was calling him this close to midnight.

"Hi, Tony."

He recognized Cindy's voice, and he straightened the moment he heard it.

"I just wanted to thank you again for the really nice night. It was fun getting to know you," she finished with a sipping sound.

"I'm really glad you came in, Cindy."

After too long a pause, she said, "Well, that's all I wanted to say. I had a great time, thanks, and be sure to come to my window if you're ever in the bank again."

"I'll be sure to do that. Appreciate the call. Look, I still owe you dinner. I know you're working tomorrow, but maybe you could swing by about nine after our evening rush here. I mean, if that's not too late. We could have some time to talk. Maybe just the two of us," he added, hoping she'd leave wet blanket Karen at home.

"Tomorrow? Umm, I think I've got something going, but let me try to cancel it. I'll see you at nine," she said.

"Great. Looking forward to it."

"Okay, bye, bye."

The moment he hung up, he thought, *What in the hell did I do that for?'* Christ, he was thinking with the wrong head again.

Mmm-mmm, Cindy thought. She sat crossways on an overstuffed chair and sipped her glass of wine. It was a Shiraz, not a Beaujolais, but she closed her eyes and pretended all the same.

Eleven

The Ditschler brothers fled the fairgrounds later that night, reeking of the swine barn. A mother and daughter had reported their leering stares and rude comments to a policeman standing outside the beer garden, and they thought it best to make a hasty exit.

"Roll past that bank again, Lucerne," Mendel directed as the three of them crammed into the front seat of the Fleetwood and sped out of the No Parking Zone. Mendel had to slam the door two or three times to get it to stay closed, causing the window to rattle dangerously with each attempt.

By the time they had circled the block for a second pass, two more cars had pulled in front of the bank building and dispatched people to make what looked like a pretty fat night deposit. They also spotted a St. Paul police car parked on the opposite corner. Two bored-looking patrolmen sat in the front seat.

"See, what'd I tell you, boys? So damn much money, the cops got to sit there. It's near midnight, and they're here sitting on their ass, making sure everything's okay. I'm telling ya, we hit this place, and we're gonna land on easy street."

"Don't tell me you're fixin' to kidnap another bank president, Mendel. 'Cause, in case you forgot, that last one we grabbed didn't work out too damn well," Elvis said.

"I'm thinking of something a lot better than that."

Lucerne and Mendel were now stretched out on the motel double bed, sipping from beer cans. Elvis was curled up on the floor beneath a closet shelf almost, but not quite, passed out.

"No man, like I told you, there's only one way," Mendel said, sounding more rational after a number of beers. "What we need to do is hit the damn place fast and hard. We plan a getaway route and a backup, in and out in just a few minutes. Do it when the traffic's heavy. Most likely, it'll be five, maybe ten minutes before the cops even get there. Hell, by the time they arrive, we'll be long gone and a hell of a lot richer."

"But how we gonna actually do it? I mean, are we gonna blow it up? Knock out a wall? What?" Elvis said. He remained curled on the floor and spoke with his eyes closed.

"No," said Mendel. "We don't need to blow it up. How 'bout we work on planning. Take our time. Go into the bank at different times. End up with all three of us in there together. We'll just waltz in, scoop up all that money waiting for us. Walk back to the car, and Lucerne here takes us home. Lucerne?"

Lucerne was stretched out next to Mendel, surrounded by empty beer cans and talking on his cellphone. His breathing was heavy, and he was absently playing with the hair on his chest.

"So, what are you wearing then? Something seethrough? Right? So tell me what you're seeing?"

"Lucerne," Mendel shouted, then reached over and swatted the phone from his brother's hand. "Damn it. I told ya before, them gals ain't worth the time it takes to call. She don't know your ass from the next stupid bastard. She just talks to fools like you so she can take your damn money. Dumb ass."

"Well, then that's gonna be pretty hard to do, Mendel. See, that there phone belongs to that old heart attacked banker back in Henderson. I charged the damn call to his damn phone, so I ain't gonna have to pay one red cent. And for your information, I'm getting to know Tracey. We're building one of them relationships. I seen her picture on TV last night when the two of you was asleep. She's shy and don't like going out alone and all. It even said so."

"That's just about the stupidest God damn thing you've said all day. I was just at the part where you drive our getaway from the bank. So please, pay attention. Damn it." Mendel shook his head and tossed the phone back onto Lucerne's chest.

**** * ****

It wasn't the first time Tracey had been disconnected. Good Lord, that was just an occupational hazard. It happened every day. But she had just finished telling the familiar voice she was wearing a black babydoll nightie and a smile, thinking *she'd have him for at least another ten minutes*. The timing of the disconnect seemed unusual.

She adjusted her headset and brushed the sugar crumbs off the front of her T-shirt. She quickly stuffed the better part of another chocolate eclair into her mouth and clicked onto the next call.

"Hey there, this is Tracey," she said, taking a hearty second bite before cooing. "Well, what do you think I'm doing, baby? I've been waiting for your call. Let me hear your name again, honey. I love the way you say it."

Twelve

It had been a very, very long day at the fair. Sixteen hours, in fact. Otto O'Malley felt like telling the woman at his food stand to drop dead. By the looks of her, she was more than halfway there. He kept that idea to himself and attempted to smile. Always the consummate professional. He took her money and handed her one of his treats, Deep-Fat-Fried-Bacon-on-a-Stick. He knew instantly the old bag had never been the adventurous sort. She didn't go for the hickory, maple, or his new flavor, Cajun Bar-B-Que.

"Thank you, ma'am," he said and smiled.

His smile always came across as a sneer, unless the woman happened to be good looking. Then it came across as a half-sneer, half-leer, with a slight reptilian flick of the tongue across his upper lip. This old bat just got the sneer as his fingers snatched her five-dollar bill, and he turned to busy himself near the deep fat fryer.

"Excuse me, but my change?" She stepped back to double-check the price on the sign above Otto's stand featuring a neon pink pig in a swimsuit roasting in a lounge chair. The swimsuit was pulled down to show just a hint of the pig's butt crack. The kids loved that part.

"Oh, change. Didn't I give it to you?" he stalled, a slim outside chance at this point that he might make an extra buck.

"No, you did not."

"Oh, sorry about that. It's been a long day," he added, not the least bit sorry.

He had a number of Deep-Fat-Fried-Bacon-on-a-Stick stands scattered across the fairgrounds. Each one situated beneath a sign featuring the neon pink pig in the swimsuit.

He had schemed, scammed, and labored for over thirty-five years to get a stand at the fair, surviving some colossal failures along the way. There was the BBQ Cauliflower on a stick. The Turtle on a Stick. And, who would ever forget his poorly received Cone of Sauerkraut? None of them met with the sort of success he was looking for, but he'd learned from his mistakes.

All of that occurred before Otto read a book on simplicity. That got him thinking. Why the hell not? So in the process of simplifying his life, he divorced his wife, sold his house, and came up with Deep-Fat-Fried-Bacon-on-a-Stick. The rest was simple, high calorie, artery-clogging history.

Along with keeping each of his stands supplied throughout the sixteen-hour day, he made all the bank runs. He carried a leather briefcase. He dressed like any other fool at the fair and desperately attempted to blend into the crowd. Which was hard to do when you were a fifty-eight year old, five foot five, fat, red-headed guy with a crew cut carrying a loaded handgun.

Making the bank runs for all his stands had him covering about twenty miles a day on foot. He stuffed the cash into his briefcase and brushed his fingertips across the .45 jammed in his belt. He made his way to the handicap parking area, where he climbed into his pickup and drove three minutes to the bank.

He wasn't a fool. Walking twenty plus miles over the course of any day, it made sense to print up a fake handicap tag and hang it from his rearview mirror. Just to play it safe, he bribed the guard at the handicap lot as a backup plan.

He sat in the air-conditioned comfort of his pickup truck and let the cold air frost his body. It was almost six o'clock, still a humid ninety-six degrees in the shade and Otto hadn't seen very much shade. He sipped a Gatorade with the doors locked, the windows rolled up, and the AC set on 'arctic' blowing full blast. His briefcase was stuffed with greasy cash, and his .45 was tucked in his belt. He relaxed for a moment and let the cold air cool his sunburned skin while Garth Brooks sang about Friends in Low Places.

He gave a little two-fingered wave to the kid watching the gate. The kid waved back and grinned like an idiot. He licked the Deep-Fat-Fried-Bacon-on-a-stick Otto had given him. They were pals now. Just old buddies, looking out for one another. As he drove off, he made a mental note to bring the kid some more of whatever wasn't selling.

He parked in the bank lot, climbed out of his pickup, and strolled to the deposit drop. It was a heavy metal affair he had to unlock with a key before he could drop his deposit down the chute.

It was when he walked back to his truck that he noticed the car. He'd seen them before. All three men crammed into the front seat of a battered, two-toned Fleetwood with the white roof. Even in the half-light of the evening, he could tell they needed shaves and haircuts. He deftly touched the butt of the Colt .45 in his belt.

Come and get it, trash, he thought as he drifted back to his days in the service. Memories of buying drinks for bar girls with the heat, hot, like today only worse. All the strange smells, not understanding the language. He remembered people shooting at him and suddenly took a deep breath, reminding himself to worry about Deep-Fat-Fried-Bacon-On-A-Stick.

"You see that clown?" Elvis laughed. "He was looking at you, Lucerne. Bet he was thinking, *'I'd like to waste that guy.'* That's what he was thinking."

"Guy looked like Porky Pig, all sort of pink and whatnot," Lucerne said.

"Wait for me," Mendel commanded, hopping out of the car. "I want to walk around here. Get a feel for this place."

"You think that's such a good idea? They might be taking our pictures right now," Elvis called. He nervously looked around with his good eye searching the outside of the bank to see if he could spot any cameras.

"All I'm doing is walking past. Ain't against the law just to walk past now, is it? Public sidewalk, after all." He circled the building twice and spun around, walking backward while staring at the entrance to the building, thinking about how they might approach it.

"I think on Monday we'll come back here."

"Monday!" Elvis exclaimed, alarmed.

"Just to look. Get a feel for it when she's open, that's all. Go inside, look around, see how they work when it's crowded. Take it easy, man. It ain't like we're going to rob the place, yet."

Thirteen

Beau poured his second cup of coffee while he looked at used car ads and waited for the meat delivery to finish up.

The two delivery men soon joined him after hauling boxes of meat into the walk-in cooler. They were red-faced and dressed in white juice-stained coats embroidered with their names on the front. Kevin and Larry.

"You guys done already?"

"Yeah, double-check us," Larry said and handed Beau the delivery slip.

"Looking good as always," Beau said a few minutes later, then signed the packing slip, tore off the bottom copy, and handed the rest back to Larry.

"Thinking of buying a used car?" Larry asked, looking at the circled ads.

"What? Oh, no. Not really." The term 'corroborating evidence' exploded in Beau's head.

"Well, why'd you circle all the car ads? You want a used car? Kevin's got a van for sale. Don't you, Kevin? What do you want for that thing? Real good runner," Larry said, not giving Kevin a chance to answer.

Beau didn't really care about Kevin's price. He just wanted the conversation to end. "I was just checking things out for one of my waitresses. She said she was looking for a car. I told her I'd look in the paper, that's all," he said, attempting to move on. "You guys catch the Twins last night?"

"Damn Twins. I can't figure out what they need more. Fielding, hitting or base running," scoffed Kevin.

"Tell him about the wife's van, Kevin. Thing runs like a top, Beau. And Kevin's wife has taken good care of the thing. Hasn't she, Kevin? Changed the oil regularly, no maintenance beyond the normal. No accidents. Just picking up kids. Only about sixty thousand miles. Got it in 2010, but it's a 2011 model."

"I think this gal is going for something a little more sporty," Beau said.

"Well, you had a van circled here, and this one's a van. She got kids, this waitress?"

"I don't really know, but you guys are right about those Twins. They need help in all departments."

"Know what you should do, Kevin? Drive the wife up here for a steak tonight. Show Beau and that waitress the van. She'll buy it soon as she sees the damn thing. What price you got on it, Kevin, that van?"

"Sold it last night," Kevin said, finally able to get a word in.

"Sold? What? Jeez, Beau, it would have been perfect. She just drove it with the kids. You know, picking them up, dropping them off, just family stuff."

"Thanks, guys. I'll see you Monday morning. Have a great weekend. I got a busy day ahead of me, and I gotta fly," Beau said. He hurried through the swinging kitchen door, making an exit before he had to hear any more about Kevin's van.

"Hey, Beau, you forgot your want ads," Larry called. "Jeez, you sold it, Kevin? Why didn't you tell me?"

Great! Beau thought, returning to the kitchen once he watched the meat truck drive away. So much for keeping everything below the radar. At least at this hour, he could swing past the bank. Get another look and a feel for the place. Maybe drive down a few side streets and try to formulate a plan.

* * *

Cindy hit her snooze alarm at least three times before she bolted upright in bed. She ran to the kitchen and gobbled three aspirins. The sight of the empty wine bottle made her head throb. The need to be at work this Saturday morning did absolutely nothing to help.

On any given Saturday, there might be two or three night deposits. But during fair week, there were upwards of thirty, totaling anywhere from five to twenty thousand dollars. They had to be counted, recorded, bound, and ready for the first courier run. She half-toyed with the idea of phoning in sick as she stepped in the shower but knew she'd never make the call. She hadn't taken a sick day in four years.

"Oh my God!" she exclaimed, letting the water run down her shoulders. Had she set a dinner date for tonight?

Great first impression, she thought and scrubbed furiously. She toweled dry as she half-ran to her bedroom to get dressed. Let's see, the guy invites me to his restaurant for a glass of wine. I repay him by calling back drunk, and now I can't remember if we set a dinner date.

* * *

There was a little more traffic on the streets than Beau expected, but nothing like the day before. He had plenty of time to cruise the side streets leisurely. He was making his second run past the bank when he caught sight of Cindy dashing across the sidewalk and slipping into the bank.

Damn it, he thought, reminding himself of their dinner date. What in the hell was he thinking?

57 ♦ Bankers Hours!

It had been his experience that when events started to get shitty, he usually did one of two things. Either he found a way to step in it, or he just plain fell down and rolled in it. This seemed to be no exception. He had arranged a dinner date with a teller from the bank he planned to rob.

On the other hand, what better way, he reasoned, to garner inside information. Maybe, he could just loosen her up with an evening of drinks and dinner and get the inside scoop on security.

Fourteen

"What do you mean they won't dance?" Osborne bellowed into the phone. "You tell them to get their collective hot little bodies back up on stage."

It had always been the policy of Cheaters, the dance portion of Osborne's empire, that the stage temperature be kept somewhere just below freezing. He had set up cold air returns to blow continually across the stage, all day, every day, much to the consternation of his dancers. Despite the potential for enhanced tip revenue, the ungrateful little trollops continued to complain.

Sassie, one of his headliners, had supposedly slipped and fallen near the end of her Brunch and Buns shift. She had slipped on a patch of icy condensation just at the edge of the stage and landed, rather inappropriately, on an ill-placed long-necked beer bottle. The force of the fall on the beer bottle caused some rather unfortunate side effects.

For her part, Miss Sassie, very mad and currently unable to sit down, was pacing back and forth across the stage, indignantly rallying the rest of the dancing crew. She had them conducting a work stoppage. The dancing crew were all sitting down, fully clothed, in the middle of the stage. As if that wasn't bad enough, they were collectively demanding that the heat get turned up, and that beer bottles no longer be allowed on the edge of the stage.

"Milton," Osborne instructed through clenched teeth once he'd sprayed his phone with disinfectant, "get down there and toss that wench out into the street. And get the rest of them back to work."

Milton returned twenty minutes later, sporting a perfect bloodied imprint of Sassie's orthodontia on his right hand.

"They ain't moving," he said, holding his throbbing right hand. The individual teeth marks were already beginning to swell. The overall bite area felt as if it was on fire.

"What do you mean, not moving?" Osborne pushed his chair back and thrust his left arm out as nurse Serpentina wiggled forward with the blood pressure cuff and delicately rolled up his shirtsleeve.

"I reached for her, Sassie, I mean. They were all gathered around her, and that's when she bit me. Someone else grabbed hold of me, wouldn't let go and—"

"What in the hell do you mean, grabbed hold of you? For God's sake, Milton. You're three times their size."

Milton glanced downward.

"Oh, yes. Well, I see. This simply won't do. I can't have a bunch of my dancers just sitting around with their clothes on." Osborne grabbed the bottle of disinfectant and sprayed a heavy dose in Milton's general direction.

"Oh, dear," muttered Serpentina as she released the blood pressure cuff.

"What now?" Osborne growled.

"Nothing to worry about, sir."

"Hmm-mmm, wait a minute. Yes, of course, you could just get down there and dance for the customers while I think of some alternative," he directed.

"Well, that's just it. There really aren't any customers down there. They all sort of left," Milton said, not looking directly at Osborne. He suddenly began to study his hand, caught in the fact that he hadn't lied. But then again, he hadn't delivered all the bad news.

"No cust— what? No customers down there? Why it's— it's two-thirty in the afternoon, and you're standing here telling me there's no one downstairs? No one requesting lap dances? No one drinking? You've got to be kidding."

Fifteen

Beau quickly glanced from the paper on the passenger seat to the road and back again. He was reading the ad he had circled. His last two stops had been completely fruitless. The first was anything but what the ad had described as a good runner. A nondescript old Chevy that wouldn't start.

The second vehicle he looked at was a Plymouth wagon that started but had some distinct bearing problems, which made themselves known on the test drive around the block. He was now on his way to see about a Honda Civic, listed 'as is'.

The four-door faded blue vehicle sat in the driveway of a suburban home sporting a rear bumper sticker that stated *Plumbers Do it Better*. The test drive was acceptable, despite the lack of a muffler, but the guy shut the whole deal down as soon as Beau suggested he would take care of the title transfer.

"Look, no hard feelings, but this belonged to my kid who decided it would be more fun to party than to go to class. I'm just trying to demonstrate to the genius that nothing in life is free, including this car, which his mother insisted we buy for him."

"I'll pay you cash."

"I don't think so. It's a fifteen-hundred-dollar car that's given me too many problems already. If you don't want to go down and do the title transfer with me, then I can't sell it to you. It's just that simple." He took a sip of his coffee and stared in a way that basically told Beau to hit the road.

The next ad on his list was a Saab. It turned out to be a perfectly nondescript olive-drab vehicle that started, seemed to drive well and the seller, Bernice, was more than willing to let Beau do the title transfer for an additional hundred dollars.

"Like I told you," Bernice said. She was talking through the cloud of cat hair that swirled around her while she scratched the stomach of the feline on her lap. "Terry's in the Marines on his third tour. Just loves the Corps. I figured he wouldn't want to deal with this by the time he returns. I'll put the money in a savings account for him. I looked all over but couldn't find that title anywhere. I checked the kitchen drawer, Terry's room, even the garage," she said. She pushed the cat off her lap to make room for the one at her feet.

Beau could feel his allergies kicking in. Cat hair seemed to be everywhere, drifting across the room, settling on him, clinging to his socks and trousers. He figured, by now, he had enough cat hair on him to knit a small sweater. His back was beginning to itch. His nose was starting to run. He prayed Bernice's verbal house tour wouldn't last too much longer.

"I even checked the damn bathroom and didn't find anything there, either. Well, I'm gonna have another," Bernice half-cackled as she struggled to her feet.

She was a large woman, squarely built. Beau guessed she hadn't been out of the house for a number of months. Although tightly permed, her blue hair had an unkempt look to it. She wore a stained house dress, suggesting she may have been cleaning. Although there was no evidence of that undertaking in sight. She ambled toward the kitchen counter and her vodka bottle.

"You want a drink?"

"No, thank you. Look, let me get you paid, so I don't interrupt any more of your day. I can have my niece come pick the car up this afternoon. I'll get the title changed. I want to make sure my insurance is on there, too. You know, before she drives it."

"Sure you don't want a little something?" she asked. She poured a good three inches of vodka into her glass before adding a few drops of orange juice to suggest color. "Time was I wouldn't have to offer a drink to get a nice young man to spend some time with me," she said and ran a hand through her hair. Her glassy eyes seemed to drift back in the direction of the Reagan administration.

"Let me throw in an extra hundred dollars just to give you a little extra maybe to get a present for Terry," Beau said and proceeded to count out eleven hundred dollar bills.

"Oh, Heavens, you don't have to do that," Bernice said, quickly scooping up the cash a nanosecond after he had counted it out. She folded the money and stuffed it inside her bra. She smiled, took a couple of hearty swallows from her drink, and gasped contentedly.

"Bernice, I can't thank you enough. My cousin will be very happy. Now, she can get to school without worrying about where her next ride is coming from," Beau said. He shooed the cats away with his foot pushing a little more forcefully this time.

"I thought you said it was your niece?" Bernice replied and suddenly cast a sharp eye at Beau.

"Well, she is my niece, and my cousin, too. It's an involved family situation," he stammered.

"Believe me. I know how that goes," she exclaimed and drained her glass to prove her point.

He grabbed the car keys from the counter and made a hasty retreat toward the door. He gently prodded cats away with his foot, desperate to get to his car and pop a Benadryl.

Sixteen

By the time Beau returned to his office, his eyes were glazed. His lids were puffy, and his nose was plugged. He was wrapping lengths of tape, sticky side out, around his hand in an unsuccessful attempt to remove cat hair from his slacks and shirt. The problem was, there was just too much cat hair. He didn't have a lot of time to fool with it since getting the vehicle had taken hours longer than he had expected. He could feel a rash beginning to develop on his arms and legs. A prickling sensation was beginning to run down his back, and finally, he just gave up and took off his clothes. He quickly dumped them in the wastebasket and changed into his softball uniform.

"There a game today?" Buddy asked as Beau strolled past on the way to tossing his clothes in the dumpster. Aged somewhere beyond one hundred, Buddy had tended bar as long as Beau could remember. Currently, he was the eleven to three bartender in the front bar. Apparently, Buddy didn't have time to wait for an answer. "Damn it, the schedule they gave me is all screwed up. I didn't know there was a game, or I would have gotten someone to cover for me."

"No, there's no game today, Buddy," Beau said. He was attempting to scratch his back against the end of the bar without seeming too obvious.

"Man, you look like shit, Beau," Buddy continued. "How come you got your softball uniform on if there's no game?"

"Long story, Buddy." Beau was now against the doorframe, rubbing back and forth against the edge, finally able to scratch his back.

"You sure you're okay? I mean, if you don't mind my saying so, you really look like shit."

"Yeah, you already mentioned that, but thanks all the same— no big deal. Just an allergic reaction, so I thought it was best just to ditch these clothes." He nodded at the wastebasket he was carrying. "I'll run home to shower and change in a bit. I took a couple of Benadryl. So I should be okay in the next hour."

"Yeah, well, thought you'd probably want to know you were looking like shit. You sure there's no game?"

"Yeah, I'm sure. There's no game, Buddy. Honest. But thanks, I appreciate the input."

Once home, Beau dropped his softball uniform on the floor, stepped into the shower, and in just a few moments, felt a thousand percent better as the combination of Benadryl and the shower began to work their magic.

He dressed in a pair of dark blue slacks and a starched, long-sleeved white shirt, his standard Saturday night uniform. It was almost six, and Saturdays were always busy. He'd be doing everything from bussing tables to cracking the whip, making sure it all went well.

Seventeen

"Okay, tell all!" Karen said, not for the first time. She was lying on the couch, taking a quick break watching out the window as her nephews ran in and out of the wading pool set up in her backyard. "So tell me again, you called this Beau guy after I dropped you off?"

"Yeah, unfortunately. I'm sure he thinks I'm just a tramp. I had three or four glasses of wine last night, another one or two at home. Suddenly, it seemed like a good idea to call him," Cindy said.

She was finally home from the bank after being jammed all morning without a break. She'd dealt with huge overnight cash deposits and a nonstop line of customers almost out the door until they closed at noon. And this was just the warm-up. They would have Saturday night and all of Sunday's deposits to count on Monday morning. She was scheduled to be in at five-thirty Monday morning to get a jump on things. The perfect kick-off to the week from hell.

"So? What did he say? He must have known you were feeling no pain. I mean, the guy *is* in the bar business."

"He was really nice, I think," Cindy said. She was on her back, attempting to squeeze into a pair of jeans and kicking her legs up and down. She finally gave up and tossed the jeans to the side.

"What do you mean, you think? Don't you remember the conversation? I mean, did he say never call me here or don't come into my bar ever again? Anything like that?"

"No, he didn't say anything like that. In fact, we're having dinner tonight at—"

"Dinner! He's taking you to dinner! I'd say that's something. Quit playing it so cool, Cindy, and give me more details. Thomas!" She suddenly screamed.

Cindy could hear Karen rapping on the window at her nephews. "Thomas, please don't do that to your brother. You share, do you hear me?" Then a pause, "Okay, that's right. Play nicely."

"So give me the details, girl. Come on and don't hold anything back."

"Karen, you've got all the details. I'm just having dinner with him… at his place."

"You're going to his house? That's—"

"No, his bar. DiMento's. He's working. So, I'm going to stop in and have dinner with him. He promised me dinner for helping him out at the bank the other day, that's all. I'll probably never hear from him again after that."

"So, you're having dinner with this guy tonight. You just met him last night. I don't know— Thomas, I'm warning you. Let your brother up. He can't breathe underwater. Thomas, if I— hey sorry, I gotta run here, darling. They're trying to murder each other out there. Thomas," Karen shrieked as she disconnected.

Cindy stood in her underwear, holding up another top against a half-dozen different pairs of slacks, not happy with any of the combinations. She was painfully aware she was due for dinner with Beau in twenty minutes, and it was a ten-minute drive. Since the air conditioning in her car wasn't working, she would be completely pitted out by the time she arrived. None of which was helping her decision making process.

She had wondered off and on what it would be like having dinner with the owner of a restaurant. Would he suggest they order something special from the menu? Or, would he have something completely unique prepared for just the two of them? Would they be eating at a special table? Maybe there'd be a couple of waiters hovering at the edge of the candlelight, ready to take care of her every wish. They'd pour the wine. Maybe he was a champagne guy. No doubt, he would pull her chair out.

A waiter would suddenly arrive and dish up a half-dozen special courses.

It was bound to be romantic. All she had to do was decide what to wear in the next four minutes. With time slipping away, she threw up her hands, dropped the new top on a pile of slacks, and pulled a slinky tight dress out of the closet. She wiggled into the thing, misted a cloud of perfume, and walked through it on her way out the door.

Eighteen

It had been a normal busy night of narrowly averted catastrophes. Beau was sitting for the first time in about three hours. He was sipping a Coke with Tommy, the bartender. He was seated in the lounge, pleased to see the dinner rush extending this late on a Saturday.

"I'll tell you, Tommy. It'll probably curse me once I say it, but with this crowd tonight, I thought for sure something would get screwed up. I mean, no major head-aches other than the usual nonsense."

He had been dogged all night long by the feeling he had forgotten something, but he couldn't remember what until he saw her step into the lounge and search the crowd. She waved and headed toward him.

"Hi, Tony, sorry I'm late. There was an accident on Snelling, and they had it down to one lane of traffic. You didn't invite anyone else in my absence, did you?"

"No, Cindy, no problem. Just catching a quick Coke while I waited," he lied. "Cindy, you remember Tommy?" He introduced the bartender.

"Yeah. Hi, nice to see you again."

"Your usual Beaujolais?" Tommy said.

"What else? Nothing but the best, right?" She half-laughed, wishing to God she didn't always say stupid things when she was so nervous.

"Okay, come on. Let's grab a seat for a minute and take it easy before we sit down to dinner," Beau said once she had her glass of wine. She followed him along a carpeted ramp outlined with runway lighting that led up to a red upholstered booth. There were three separate levels of booths, all sort of loosely facing a small stage area where a Neil Diamond impersonator was busy doing a last-minute sound-check.

"Gee, Cindy, I really can't thank you enough for coming here on such short notice. I know you're swamped at work, and it sounds like you have one hell of a week lined up ahead of you. So, thanks for making time for me."

"My pleasure, it's really no trouble at all." She suddenly felt famished and ready to kill for whatever special romantic dinner he had prepared.

"Beau, to the dining room. Beau, to the dining room, please," a rather urgent sounding page came over the paging system.

"God, I'm sorry, would you give me just a minute? I'll be right back. Can I get you anything while I'm up?"

"No, not to worry. I'm just fine. I've got this wine. You go ahead and take care of whatever it is. I'm fine, honest."

"Okay, back just as soon as I can."

"God, Beau!" Allie, the dining room hostess, sounded more than a little flustered as he approached. "We are seriously overbooked in here, and there's some weirdo really putting the pressure on to talk to you. He's giving me the creeps, and, well, the whole thing is just weird."

"Point him out to me without being obvious," said Beau.

"Point him out? God, no problem! He's at table sixteen, the creepy guy with the mustache. He's sitting with that Neanderthal kind of guy and the slut with the boob job pretending to be a nurse. Little early for Halloween, don't ya think? Look, look, there she is, wiping the menu before he holds it. Some kind of germ nut if you ask me."

Beau immediately recognized Osborne, just as Osborne glanced up and caught his eye.

"Shit! Make sure he gets top service. Anything he wants and no bill. Bring him a bottle of champagne. Some good stuff, with their dinner. Make sure you tell him it was compliments of me and that everything is on the house." Beau smiled and waved across the room at Osborne.

"You're kidding me, right?" Allie said, having known Beau to bitch more than once about having to buy a round of beer.

"No, I'm not kidding. Use every ounce of charm you've got," he said and headed to the rear of the dining room and Osborne's table.

"Thank you for coming," Beau said. "No, please. Please, sit down, Mr. Osborne. You're our guest. The prime rib is excellent, or if you prefer, the lobster tails are great, and I'll gladly pick some out for you myself."

"Thank you, but I think I'll look at the menu if it's all the same. Nice to see you again," Osborne said, making no effort to introduce the nurse.

There seemed to be just the hint of a medicinal scent in the air. The table glistened with a sheen from the disinfectant spray. Beau noticed that Osborne had wrapped his fingertips with the cloth napkin before picking up his menu.

The larger man, Milton, had a swollen right hand sporting a series of small purplish gashes. He rested the hand on the table and held the menu with his left.

"Call me if you need anything, Mr. Osborne. I look forward to our meeting in a few days. Enjoy your evening. Ma'am," he said and inclined his head toward the nurse.

Nineteen

"You want another drink, hon? If you're not going to drink, you'll have to give up the booth. Saturdays are always busy nights."

The cocktail waitresses were dressed in what could only be described as short, velvety black French maid outfits with little white aprons and very low-cut tops. The lounge was filling up with the Saturday night meat market crowd. Cindy felt as if she had a large spotlight shining directly on her. She was dressed to the nines in her slinky dress and sitting alone in the booth.

"Yeah, sure. I'll have another."

"What are you drinking, hon?" the waitress asked, not sure by the outfit if Cindy was a working girl or not.

"Beaujolais," she said, blushing as she said it.

Ten minutes later, and balancing her tray, the waitress said, "That'll be ten-fifty, hon." She almost spilled out of her low-cut top as she set the drink on the table.

Cindy nodded and hoped Beau returned quickly.

"Ten-fifty, hon," the waitress repeated. She smiled sweetly, clearly not meaning it, and then looked bored while she waited for payment.

"Oh, yeah, sure. Here you go, thanks," Cindy said, finding the solitary twenty-dollar bill in her billfold.

"You need change, hon?"

"Yes, I do," Cindy said, flashing a fake smile.

"I'll be right back," the waitress said, sounding like maybe she wouldn't.

Cindy wasn't necessarily pounding the wine down, she was just sipping, but they were big sips. She wanted to leave, but she would be damned if she was going to leave nine dollars and fifty cents of hard-earned cash with a bitchy cocktail waitress.

"How's it going, darling?"

She turned, expecting to look into Beau's eyes. Instead, she feasted her eyes on a lounge lizard with an open collar shirt. Actually, the top four buttons were undone, exposing what looked like wall-to-wall carpeting on his chest. He wore tight iridescent slacks with a large brass belt buckle. The outfit was offset by black and red cowboy boots, she couldn't help but notice since he'd placed one on the seat next to her. His orange-tinted glasses were thick bifocals supported by very large steel frames. He sported a pencil-thin mustache, and if he'd had hair, Cindy figured it would have been combed back in a sort of bouffant style from the early sixties.

It was at that moment that the Neil Diamond impersonator opened his act, launching into a rendition of *'Cracklin' Rosie.'* The lounge lizard immediately began to snap his fingers and bounce to the beat.

"Yeah, baby, yeah. Come on, sugar. What do you say?" he yelled at Cindy over Neil Diamond's alter ego. He took a step back, waiting for her to fly out of the booth as he shook his hips from side to side.

Cindy stared at him wide-eyed, not sure what to do.

"Come on, sugar. Let's shake that thing," he spun around in front of the booth as she sat dumbfounded. "Yeah, let's go, baby!"

That was enough. She wasn't going to wait all night looking like an hors d'oeuvre for some senior citizen sexual feeding frenzy. She drained her wine glass, gathered her purse, and was sliding out of the booth just as Beau slid in alongside her.

"Sorry that took so long. Things just got crazy." He looked at her empty glass. "You should have ordered from one of the girls," he said and waved to 'Bitchy' still standing at the bar, hoping to pocket Cindy's change.

Cindy thought she could lip-read a reaction when the woman looked up and saw who had joined her in the booth. The dancing lounge lizard was suddenly nowhere in sight.

"Heidi," Beau said to 'Bitchy.' "I'll just have a Coke and…" He looked at Cindy.

"Ahh, ma'am." Bitchy smiled weakly. A hint of terror seemed to creep across her eyes.

"The same, please."

"A Coke?" asked Beau.

"A Beaujolais?" Bitchy said simultaneously.

"The Beaujolais. Oh, and you were going to get me that change." Cindy smiled icily.

"I'll be right back," Bitchy assured them.

"Sorry about that. Just a little headache in the dining room. Actually, the right kind of problem. We just over-booked and didn't have enough tables. It's all taken care of." Beau cast an eye across a sea of baby boomers bouncing rhythmically to the Neil Diamond tune.

"Here we go," 'Bitchy' said, returning with Beau's Coke and Cindy's glass of wine in record time. "Your wine, Ma'am, and your change," she said, making eye contact. She slid a crisp ten-dollar bill across the table.

"Thank you," Cindy replied, then turned to give Beau her undivided attention.

"So, how would you feel about dining in an exclusive part of the operation tonight?" he asked. "The dining room is full, like I said, the right kind of problem." He half-lied, not wanting to take the chance of having to talk with Osborne any more than necessary.

"Exclusive part?"

"I was thinking. If you wouldn't mind, we could dine in my office. It would be private, the service will still be good, and the food excellent. Plus, it will give me a chance to get away from all this and have an uninter-rupted conversation with you. I feel like, well, between me running around tonight and, what was your friend's name, Kari?"

"Karen," corrected Cindy.

"Yeah, well, either way. I feel like we haven't really talked yet. To tell you the truth, as long as I'm out here, they're going to keep calling me."

"Your office sounds wonderful," Cindy said, envisioning candlelight and personal wait staff.

It took them fifteen minutes to make their way through the bar. Beau stopped to talk to a number of people. Eventually, he gave the word he wasn't to be disturbed and checked with the hostess, Allie, about some special situation before they made their way up to his office.

Twenty

Whatever Cindy was hoping for, it wasn't what she found. She had conjured up some sort of elegant, romantic private table with a linen tablecloth and a waiter or two. Maybe a cut rose on the table, not to mention candlelight. He'd have a sound system playing soft music, and the lights would be dimmed for some romance.

"Let me just clean this shit off," Beau said over his shoulder as he stacked piles of invoices one on top of the other. He dumped a stack of files on a dreadful green striped couch with torn, duct-taped armrests. He set two coffee mugs on a pile of files on the credenza behind his large black chair. Each mug still held coffee. As he quickly picked up the mugs, they dribbled a small puddle across the desktop.

He grabbed a soiled cloth rag that may have been an old sweat sock and attacked some sort of stain that didn't seem to want to leave. He moistened the rag by dipping it into the trail of spilled coffee and garnered moderate success. He nodded casually at a green faux leather chair. "Just pull that damn thing up here to the desk, and I'll get some food for us. What do you feel like?"

"Ahhh, is there a menu?" Cindy asked, still a little in shock.

"Oh yeah, sure. I'll grab one for you," he said and quickly left the room.

She looked around, remembered the new top she had purchased now lying on her bed and her ridiculous dreams about a romantic evening, and started laughing. The guy runs a damn bar and restaurant, and it's Saturday night. He doesn't have time for a romantic dinner.

He quickly returned with a menu, two bottles of wine in hand, and things began to look better.

"Recommendation?" she asked.

"If it were me, I'm partial to the bruschetta appetizer, and we have the best prime rib," he said, knowing they had plenty of both in the kitchen.

"Okay, you sold me. Is there any more Beaujolais, Tony?" she asked as she slid her glass across the desktop.

He filled her glass, left with the menu, and returned in short order with silverware and napkins.

She attempted to sit gracefully in the green chair and failed miserably. The high arms on the thing kept it from moving any closer to the edge of the desk, and the angle of the chair's seat placed her rear about a foot lower than her knees. With her skirt up at the top of her thighs, she would have killed right now for a pair of jeans. Instead, she had to settle for the napkin, quickly unwrapping her silverware and draping the cloth across her legs. It was a little like having her yearly exam. The only thing the chair lacked was a set of stirrups.

Beau sat on the other side of the desk and just a bit higher in his black leather office chair.

"Who's that?" She pointed at the framed photo on the wall with another refilled glass of wine. It was the only photo in the room, a man with a young boy in a Little League uniform.

"That's my dad, and that goofy looking kid in the baseball uniform is me."

"Is he still alive, your dad?"

"No, but I still miss him every day. We were real pals."

She attempted to wedge her knees underneath the overhang of the desk, but the arms of the chair prevented her from moving any closer.

He seemed not to notice, and he chatted on about work. Her work mostly. Asking what she did in a day? How crazy was it working through the fair week? What were her hours?

"Well, Beau, isn't this cozy," cackled a waitress. She carried four plates and another bottle of wine as she pushed the door open with her hip. She set the plates on the desk and then looked down at Cindy, who still felt on display.

"I'll get some candles, honey. Never enough time for romance."

Beau rolled his eyes and remained quiet until the door closed behind her.

"She's been with us for over thirty-five years. My dad hired her. She's a good worker, very loyal, and she gets away with murder."

"Ahhh, that's so sweet," Cindy said and took another sip. She wiggled down ever so slightly into her chair. A warm glow from the wine began to flood over her.

It was toward the end of the meal. Beau had set the empty bruschetta and salad plates on the floor next to his wastebasket. Candles flickered in the draft from the window air conditioner as melted wax dripped on the worn surface of the desk. From somewhere in the distant background downstairs, Kiss of Death pounded out their final set for the night.

He poured more wine into her glass, not that it was empty. In fact, it hadn't been empty all night. Every time he filled it, she would say, "Oops, not too much."

Eventually, she stopped worrying about getting drunk and cautioned herself about getting too drunk. Although, right now, that didn't seem to be working either. She was sitting sideways in the green chair. Her legs swung freely over the arm of the chair. Her shoes lay discarded somewhere on the floor below. A half-eaten plate of chocolate gateau was balanced on her chest. She gestured with the wine glass as she spoke.

"The money these fuckers bring in, oh Jesus, I didn't mean to say it that way."

"Customers?" suggested Beau.

"Yeah, the fucking customers, Tony. That's what they are, customers. Anyway, you wouldn't believe it. It's really sticky. The bills are all covered with grease, sugar, and fruit drinks. And it smells like all that gunk they have at the fair. By the time I get home, I just peel my clothes off and take a long hot shower."

"There's this one guy, really weird. He's always eyeing us up. Get this. He wears a Vikings jersey, these really baggy shorts, a baseball hat, and hunting boots or something. Oh, he's so gross." She shivered at the thought.

"He's all sweaty, and he's at the bank making a deposit about a hundred times a day, always in a hurry. Know what we call him? Porky Pig. I know that isn't very nice. He has red hair, a crew cut, and a Donald Duck tattoo. I mean, what's that about?" She laughed and took another sip. "I think I'd have to take all my clothes off and just burn them if he ever touched me."

"Sounds interesting," Beau said.

She didn't react. "I smell like the fair after handling all that money, and I haven't even had my butt inside the gate."

"More wine?" asked Beau.

"I'd better not. I've got to be at work early on Monday morning to count weekend deposits," she said and held her glass out so he could refill it.

"Tomorrow's Sunday. You can sleep in," he said as he poured.

She seemed to think about that for a half-moment then sipped. "There's so much of this cash from the deposits we have to balance our drawers about ten times a day, haul the cash into the vault. They separate it into the various denominations."

"You mean like Catholic and Lutheran?" he joked.

"No," she said, not picking up on the joke. "You know, tens and twenties, that sort of thingy. Then they run it through the counters and bundle it in master bundles of one, five, or ten grand, depending. Once that's done, the couriers haul it to Central."

"Sounds busy," Beau encouraged.

"Busy? Oh my God," she said, washing down the declaration with more wine. "You've no idea. We have to hire extra people just to run this stuff through the counters. Ha! That's real glamorous, sitting around card tables with five other people in a vault and no fan. We used to have people supplied by Central, but they've cut back on staff so many times they didn't have anyone to spare."

"So get this," she said, lurching halfway in Beau's direction, spilling wine on her dress, and hiking it well above her hips. "I've got thousands upon hundreds of thousands of dollars to count, and I have to hire temps. You know how hard it is to get good temps? Let me tell you, it's a nightmare. Last year," she continued after a healthy sip, "we caught a girl stealing. College kid. I felt really bad. I mean, it was stupid. She stole, I don't know, a hundred bucks or something. Course I had to report it. Her father was a big shot customer. We had to let her go, charge her. I mean the whole bit. They had to make an example, you know, no exceptions, that sort of deal." She paused for another healthy gulp.

"The really dumb thing is she could have made five times whatever she tried to grab just by volunteering for some overtime hours." She drained her glass, and a slight drop ran down her chin. "I felt really bad for her."

"Sounds like your couriers must be pretty busy," he said and refilled her glass.

"Yeah. You know," she turned her head to look at him with glassy eyes. "You know, Tony, I should call her, see how she's doing."

"If you think it would help."

"Nah," she said and took a large swallow from the refilled glass. "I'm the one that turned her in. I had to, I mean, and I'm glad I did. The little brat. She jeopardized all of us. She put the count off by a hundred or two hundred, Jesus Christ. I mean, what was she thinking? Still, in the end, it was a stupid kid thing to do. We've all done dumb things," she said and took another long sip. She looked over at Beau with a glassy stare as her head weaved slightly from side to side. By now, she wasn't just drunk, she was absolutely plastered.

"So, you were telling me about the couriers," he said, topping up her glass.

"I was? I thought you wanted to hear about Lutherans and Catholics. Ha. Ha. Ha. Just kidding. One of our biggest customers is a church diner. Who would have thunk it! Get this. It's called The Last Supper Diner. Isn't that cute? Some church from like way out in Wilmer or Saint James owns it. All these old folks can't figure out whether it's Catholic or Lutheran, so they all eat there. It's pretty cool. These little old white-haired ladies giving you another cup of coffee. We get free passes at the bank every year. I know some of the ladies there, so I always get real good service."

She took another gulp of wine, dribbled some down her dress, but didn't notice.

"Mmm-mmm, know what? I'll take you there. I get a free pass, and they give me real good service."

After working seven days a week at his own place, he was having a tough time coming up with somewhere he would rather not be than The Last Supper Diner at the state fair.

"Do the couriers get free passes?" he asked, figuring he would give it one more try.

"Nah, they just pick the stuff up and run," she slurred, not looking at him. She waved her glass in his direction.

He refilled it and waited.

"They don't get to know the customers the way we do, and most of them don't even talk to us. They're pretty uptight. Except for this one guy, Billy. He's really nice. I mean, Billy at least says hi. The other guys all act like they have a stick up their butt. You know how people who carry guns are? Always walking around like they're really tough." She took a heavy gulp and rested the glass on her stomach. She stretched her legs out and examined her red toenails.

"How often are they there? Do they just come at the end of the day?"

"End of the day! You kidding? There wouldn't be room to breathe in the vault if they just came at the end of the day. End of the day! Ha!" She attempted to half-sit and immediately slumped back down, oblivious to the red wine she spilled down the front of her dress.

"Haven't you even been listening? They come every other hour, you goof. Only we have them scheduled, so it's at twelve after on the even hours and twenty-five after on the odd hours. You know, in case robbers are watching or something."

He casually jotted down the times she had just provided.

"Well, you have all those dye packs and things I see on the cop shows, right? Maybe tracking devices or something in there with the money?"

She turned halfway toward him, speaking as she moved. "Tracking devices? Man, where did you get that idea? We don't have tracking devices. God, we barely have enough room or time just to get all that currency into trash bags. Besides, the courier is coming to get them, so why bother to put a dye pack in there? Not that we have 'em anyway. Oh, brother," she giggled. She drained her glass and set it on the desk, almost knocking it over in the process.

"All done." She swung her body around. Her wine-soaked skirt was hiked up onto her midsection, exposing a silky blue thong as she struggled to sit upright.

"Hey, Tony, I need to pee," she said and attempted to brush some hair from her face.

He came from behind the desk to give her a hand.

"Come on. You can use my private bathroom right here around the corner." He pulled her chair back and helped her struggle to her feet.

"Whoa." She gulped and worked to focus her eyes. She took a deep breath, steadied herself placing one hand on the desk and the other on the green chair before she staggered off toward the bathroom door.

"You okay?" he asked.

"Be right back. No peeking. Unless you really want to," she giggled. She stepped inside the bathroom and then locked the door behind her.

He cautiously opened her purse and pawed through all sorts of keys and small containers to find her billfold. He quickly wrote down the address from her driver's license, returned the wallet, tossed the purse back on the couch, and retreated to his chair.

He needn't have hurried.

In the small white-tiled bathroom, Cindy sat on the toilet and rested her head against the side of the cool porcelain sink. She was thinking, *If I could just stay here for a little minute more, I would be all right. Just a minute or two to let some of the alcohol run through my system, and I would be fine.*

The sink felt so nice and cool against her face. She could feel the floor slowly begin to move from under her. She closed her eyes, thinking this is kind of fun before quickly concluding things were moving a little too fast. If she could just slow the wall down behind her, the rest would be pretty easy.

Beau waited at his desk. It wouldn't be the first time he had deliberately over-served a woman, but there seemed to be something different here. God help me if I'm developing a conscience, he worried.

Twenty-One

"A Leonardo DiCaprio impersonator. That's what you came up with?" Osborne yelled into his phone, incredulous. "I'm returning from dinner now. I'll have Milton dispatch him if he's still onstage when we arrive. I would advise you to encourage his hasty departure." He glanced over at Serpentina, sitting opposite him in the rear seat. "I've got what's her name, Snakey here. She'll dance. No, no, the one with the tattoo. Yes, Serpentina, that's right. And remove that DiCaprio character before I arrive. Good God!" he exclaimed and disconnected.

Milton glanced in the rearview mirror as Osborne wrestled to maintain control. He'd seen it a few times before. When the irrational greed for a dollar overcame all common sense. He noticed Osborne's slight twitching, the rapid blinking of the eyelids. Milton gripped the steering wheel with his throbbing right hand, focused on the road ahead, and hoped the moment would pass.

"It seems the best they could do on short notice was a transvestite Leonardo Di Caprio look-alike who would only strip down to a thong. The few customers in the place have departed. For God's sake, am I the only sane person? Milton," Osborne leaned forward as Milton drove, "once we arrive, you will go immediately to the stage and unceremoniously remove this individual if he-she has not yet vacated the premises. At least that wench, Sassie, and her unemployed camp followers have left. We'll just see how dancing in the breadline suits their fancy."

He sat back and inclined his head toward Serpentina. "My dear, I'm going to need your talents onstage tonight. It seems we have a bit of a booking snafu."

"Tonight? But for how long?"

"Just the remainder of the night."

"The remainder of the— but it's barely eleven."

"Excellent, you've learned to read a digital clock. Surely, you don't expect Milton or me to venture on-stage. Obviously, I can't entice new talent to come in at this hour of the night. Come, come, it's time we put all those surgically enhanced attributes of yours to work, my dear. Now, relax," he said, touching her hand with a moist, sterile towelette. "Your shift will conclude no later than four, and I shan't need your services until much later in the morning. There, perfect, problem solved."

Twenty-Two

It was just after four when Beau jerked awake at his desk. He'd fallen asleep in his desk chair. The candles had burned out at some point in the middle of the night, and a mound of melted red wax had dripped onto his desk. It took him a moment to get his bearings. But he knew something was amiss the moment he spied Cindy's purse on the couch. Was she still in the bathroom?

In response to his question, he heard a roar from behind the bathroom door, followed by a sputtering female cough that echoed from inside. A forlorn little voice seemed to echo from deep inside the porcelain bowl.

"Oh. My. God."

He silently crept to the door, heard her cough a few times, and the toilet flush. The water refilling the tank had always been loud, and it masked all sound from in-side the bathroom. He took a step back in the event she opened the door.

"Oh, oh, araugh," she roared again, only this time with not quite as much authority.

He was tired. All he wanted to do was go home and crawl in bed. Maybe just give her a little more time, he thought. He tiptoed back to his chair, snuggled down, and closed his eyes.

Cindy was gasping in little tiny breaths, hoping that might help keep her stomach calm. She was sure it was empty. She'd filled the toilet with a lovely shade of pink three or four times now. At the moment, she really didn't care what Tony thought. The way she felt, she'd be dead before sunrise anyway.

"Oh God," she groaned again, but nothing of sub-stance came up. Stick with the little short breaths, she told herself. She knelt in front of the toilet, held her hair back, and wished she was home so she could sleep in her own bed. She vowed to never to drink red wine again. She laid her head down on the toilet seat and closed her eyes.

Maybe an hour later, Beau got up from his desk and gently knocked on the bathroom door.

"Just a minute, be right out," a soft voice replied. She sounded as if it had only been three or four minutes instead of four or five hours. The toilet flushed again, and then the sink tap ran for a few minutes.

"Oh, shit," Cindy whispered louder than she intended. She attempted to focus on the horror scene staring back at her in the mirror.

Eventually, the door opened. Beau took a few steps back to give her plenty of room.

"Oh good, you're still here. How perfect," she said, not sounding at all sincere. Her hair dropped limply to her shoulders. Her complexion had a pale, pasty pallor, made more frightening by her swollen, bloodshot eyes and the smeared mascara across her cheeks. Any hint of lipstick had long since disappeared. Her wine-stained slinky dress was askew and appeared torn at the hem.

"Oh, relax, you look fine. We've all done it," he lied.

"Passed out on the toilet seat in a bar? Wake up at sunrise after puking my guts out in your office on our first date? No, Tony, we have not all done that. I'm unique in that vein, trust me," she said, sidestepping Beau. She cautiously picked up her purse and took a deep breath before she turned to face him.

Even hungover and an absolute mess, he found her beautiful. "Well, can I just say it's been an experience," he smiled and bent to kiss her.

"Oh, please, I'm just dreadful. Don't," she said and backed away.

He kissed her anyway on the cheek. "I don't think you're dreadful," he said and walked back to his desk.

"Oh, you poor, poor deranged man. Tony, I'm so sorry. You let me intrude on your busy work night. I wanted this to be so nice. You had this romantic dinner all planned, and I— I just ruined everything by getting falling-down drunk and throwing up all over your bathroom. If you never want to see me again, I'll understand. Look, I should go. I'm just making this worse."

"Wait. Before you go, Cindy, have one more drink."

She glared for half a moment before realizing he held a glass of water and some aspirin.

"Take these. They'll go to work, and by the time you get home, you can crawl into bed and wake up feeling a lot better," he laughed.

She took the aspirin out of his hand, popped them into her mouth, and chased them down with just enough water. She felt the water make a cold, hollow splash somewhere deep in her empty stomach. She waited a moment to make sure she didn't erupt again.

"Okay, thanks. I'm really, really sorry, Tony. You're so sweet, but I'd better go. Umm, do you know where my shoes are?"

He pointed to the floor in front of his desk, where her shoes had been dropped at a haphazard angle and rested beneath the green chair.

"God, how embarrassing," she mumbled. She stepped into her shoes and gingerly made her way to the door.

He caught up with her partway through the darkened bar and walked her to the front door. He felt sorry for her. The torn dress, limp hair, smeared mascara, no lipstick. She could use a shower, too. Now that he thought about it, *God, she was a mess.*

"Let me unlock the door for you here," he said as she cautiously stepped out into the bright morning sunshine and quickly covered her eyes.

"Ugh, shit. God, it's really bright," she muttered. She waved briefly over her shoulder without looking back. The bright light seemed to tear what little was left of her brain in two. She was too embarrassed to turn and look at him. She took a deep breath and made her way to the far corner of the empty parking lot where her car sat, looking abandoned and all alone.

Perfect. Let out of a bar at close to six on a Sunday morning. The last drunk. Just swept out with all the other trash, she thought. It was already warm and humid. The day had all the makings of being beastly— the perfect sort of weather to encourage a very bad hangover. At least, no one would see her looking like death warmed over at this hour of the morning. She gingerly made her way to her car, fighting to keep her stomach down.

Twenty-Three

Otto O'Malley was snoring in his recliner in front of the TV. It was tuned to the weather channel. In between squeaks and beeps, the forecast repeated the Twin Cities weather in a computerized monotone every seven minutes. He'd been out cold for a number of hours, clad in his bathrobe and USMC baseball cap. His feet were encrusted up to his ankles with the dried residue from an Epsom salt soaking and rested on either side of the blue plastic tray. A ring of chocolate residue from an ice cream bar encircled his mouth.

His feet hadn't hurt, but Otto soaked them anyway in an effort to ensure they would hold up for the ten-day combat tour they would receive during the state fair. A barely touched scotch and water sat alongside on an end table, and next to the drink, his trusty .45. He had set the alarm on his watch for five in the morning.

He snored loudly, dreaming he was back in Thailand, getting ripped off by pretty bar girls. Only this time, he had his briefcase with him, and he didn't want anyone to touch it. There was a car. A battered two-toned Fleetwood, dark blue with white spray paint all across the roof of the car. The car was parked in front of the Bangkok bar. Somehow, three rough-looking guys were all hanging out of the driver's window and waving at Otto sitting inside the bar. They were staring at his briefcase, and he wondered how they knew it contained his state fair money. He remained in the bar. The sight of three men hanging out the driver's window of the Fleetwood frightened the pretty girls away. Somehow, he had the sense that he didn't have to worry about them yet. But the thought was out there, somewhere on the distant horizon.

He woke, stretched, and turned off his alarm a minute before it sounded. During the middle of the night, he had removed his feet from the Epsom salt bath. They were marvelously dry, and he felt ready to face another twenty-mile day.

He pulled on a clean Vikings jersey, number thirty-five, and got his pot of coffee perking before frying up some bacon, eggs, and hash browns. The weather station continued to beep and squawk in the background announcing the forecast, not a cloud in the sky and hotter than hell— another sunburn day.

A half-hour later, he was waiting at a stoplight on his way to pick up his first load of bacon and batter. Other than a city bus, there wasn't another vehicle around at this hour. For a brief moment, he toyed with the idea of running the light but decided, with the loaded .45 in the front seat, maybe that wouldn't be the best idea.

He looked over at the bar on the corner and absently watched a woman stumbling out of DiMento's, which for some reason suddenly reminded him of his dream about the girls in the Bangkok bar. The woman looked vaguely familiar, but he couldn't seem to place her. Whoever she was, she looked like she'd had a hell of night— pasty skin, hair messed, clothes disheveled. What looked like wine was down the front of her tight-fitting dress. He thought about the dream again and the car with the three guys all hanging out the same window. He was thinking she had stopped by one of his stands, that got him think-ing in terms of the fair, which got him thinking cash de-posits, and that's when he put it together— the bank.

That's where he had seen her. She was that teller from the bank. The one he always tried to talk with. The one who always seemed to turn the other way or was busy whenever he stopped in. Hell, she was just a regular old party girl from the looks of things. Which suggested to Otto that maybe, just maybe, there was an opportunity.

A horn blast from the car behind him suddenly brought him back to reality. It figured, only one other car on the road, and they couldn't wait five seconds. He stepped on the accelerator, left the car in the dust, and shot through the next intersection on a yellow light. Yeah, he could smell opportunity with that little bank teller. He'd have to look into that.

Twenty-Four

Osborne paced back and forth across his office floor while Milton kept his nose buried in the middle of the sports section. None of the dancers had reported for work that morning. What few customers there were downstairs continued to stare at an empty stage waiting for Sunday's Brunch and Buns to begin.

"What is the point of exceptionally clever promotion if none of your employees arrive for work? Just who do they think is going to entertain that rabble down there expecting to dine on scrambled eggs with a side order of female anatomy? I have a mind to fire them all. Let them see how comfortable things are in the unemployment line."

They were questions Milton hoped were merely rhetorical. He grasped the newspaper a little tighter. His right hand felt stiff and hot this morning. The bite wound had grown puffy and raw, sporting a broader purplish tinge and a constant throbbing that was beginning to attract his attention.

"Milton, go up to the Phone Farm. Have six of them head down there and dance while I get this situation straightened out. I can't have our customers arriving for a Sunday morning event and staring at an empty stage."

"Dancers? From the Phone Farm? Really? Are you sure? If they do go down and dance, it's liable to damage the club's reputation even more."

"Will you please cooperate? In case you haven't noticed, I'm losing money by the minute here, and no one seems to care. Will you please, please not think, Milton? Just do as I ask, for God's sake. How hard can it be? Besides, there isn't one of them that couldn't use the exercise. In fact, that might be just the ticket. Yes, offer them a break. Mention our new policy. We're encouraging a healthy workforce, and they should just go down and stretch and rotate on stage. There, problem solved. Off with you now, go, go."

When Milton returned twenty minutes later, he held no doubts as to the wisdom of Osborne's decision. About three minutes into Tracey from the Phone Farm stretching and rotating, all the tables in Cheaters had cleared out. He wasn't about to mention that Tracey was the only one who had agreed to go on stage.

"So? Did that do the trick?" Osborne asked, standing imperiously behind his desk, ready to congratulate himself.

Milton shook his large head, aware of an increased throbbing in his swollen, purple hand. The room was beginning to spin ever so slightly.

"Whatever do you mean? Cat got your tongue? Come on, man. Speak for God's sake. Speak. Do I look like a mind reader?"

"Everyone just ran out of the place. They all left. She was on stage for just a moment or two, and the place emptied out."

"Ran out?"

"Yeah, they ran out the door, left drinks on the table, food on their plates. There's still two guys sitting close to the stage, but I think they're just waiting for a taxi to show up. Otherwise, there's no one down there, well, except Tracey. The Phone Farm gal. Oh yeah, and the bartenders."

"Perhaps, they just stepped outside for a cigarette or a breath of fresh air."

"No, sir. I even looked out the door, hoping that might be the case. To put it bluntly, sir, they pretty much fled the scene."

Osborne seemed to deflate on the spot. He lowered himself into the chair behind his desk and pulled a drawer open. He took out a small elongated capsule, cracked it open, and inhaled deeply— smelling salts. After a half-dozen deep inhales, he tossed the capsule onto his desk. He sat up, and his eyes seemed to cross.

"Are you going to be—"

"Silencio, please. Just find me the phone number of that Sassie wench. It seems she's put me over a barrel," Osborne said disgustedly.

Twenty-Five

Every Sunday for years, DiMento's offered an all-you-can-eat Sunday brunch. Beau's father had started it, turning an otherwise flat business day into a lucrative event. In the process, it guaranteed he would have to work seven days a week and most likely sped up the arrival of his fatal heart attack.

Beau had been working the brunch crowd, bussing tables, seating folks, checking the buffet lines, and in general, glad-handing customers while asking about kids and grandkids. The brunch went on until two in the afternoon. Beau's eyes were continually checking the clock, almost willing the thing to move faster, so he could get home and squeeze in a decent afternoon nap.

A little past noon, he made his way through the all-you-can-eat crowd, thinking, Come on, clock, tick!

"Beau, you forget about purple pride?" Dickie yelled from a lounge booth. He was seated with a blind attorney, Andrew, another attorney named Victor, and their friend Weiner. They were all squeezed into the same booth. Wiener was crammed into the far corner of the booth and smothered by Dickie's massive form. With his shoulders squeezed together, Weiner looked like he might be fighting for oxygen.

Dickie appeared to be costumed in a gigantic pair of plaid shorts and perhaps the largest purple Vikings jersey Beau had ever seen. The jersey sported the number thirty-five. A good eighty pounds of Dickie's right side hung dangerously into the aisle.

"Oh, no," Beau groaned.

"You didn't forget again, did you?" Victor asked.

"Hey, guys," Beau said and grabbed Andrew's hand. "Hi Andrew, it's—"

"Yeah, I know, Beau. Hey, I'm only blind, not deaf. I recognize your voice. How's it going?"

"So, did you forget we've got tickets to the game, dipshit?" Dickie shouted.

"No, I didn't forget," Beau said and wondered, *'How in the hell could I have forgotten?'*

In Dickie's mind, the final preseason game had taken on a life of its own. One of those major occurrences in life by which time and events could forever be measured. Oh, that was before the final preseason game. Or, that was just after the final preseason game.

The reason was Dickie's third or fourth cousin, Jerry Cardy Jr. from the town of Chisholm, Minnesota. Cardy was making his debut as a rookie wide receiver for the

Vikings. And to hear Dickie, you would have thought he had personally coached the guy for the past twenty-two years. As if that wasn't bad enough, the local sports media came up with a name dubbing Jerry Cardy Jr. the 'Wild Card'. Dickie had taken up the chant to a nauseating level.

"The Wild Card is gonna deal us into the Super Bowl. The Wild Card is gonna run the table. The Wild Card is gonna stack the deck in our favor."

It went on and on until they all promised to go to the final preseason game for the Wild Card's debut. If only Dickie promised not to mention him for the two weeks preceding the game. The two-week timeframe had officially ended last night at midnight. Wasting no time, Dickie said, "Come on, Beau. Get your ass in gear. The Wild Card is gonna trump Seattle today."

Across the aisle, a grandmother surrounded by her extended family looked over with eyes shooting daggers. Two guys, probably her sons, smiled into their coffee cups.

"Let's hope so, Dickie. Let me just finish a couple of things here, and we can take off," Beau promised.

"Well, don't take too damn long. I want to get there on time. You know what a pain in the ass traffic is gonna be. Hey, while we're waitin', who's up for a couple more?" Beau felt the slightest twinge of impending disaster.

"Woo, hoo, hoo, purple pride, baby! Purple pride!" Dickie yelled out the window of Victor's Escalade as they drove west on I-94 into downtown Minneapolis. His hair blew in the wind, and he resembled some sort of giant dog hanging out the window with his snout jutting into the seventy-five mile per hour breeze. He was seated directly behind Victor, and the Escalade tilted heavily to the driver's side.

Dickie was yelling out the window to anyone they passed. Currently, two women in the far left lane. "Purple pride, you cute little things. You hear me, baby? It's the big man talking. Purple pride, baby." Dickie thrust his head further out the window as he slapped the outside of the car door with his gargantuan paw.

The woman in the passenger seat stared at Dickie in his gigantic purple jersey. His blond hair and chins fluttered in the seventy-five mile per hour breeze. She wore a look of utter disbelief, or was it just fear? Beau read the woman's lips. 'What a fucking idiot,' she seemed to say as their car quickly accelerated and left Dickie in the dust.

"Yeah, baby, woo, hoo, hoo. Wild Card, honey. Deal me in, baby. The Wild Card."

"Dickie, don't dent the damn door and, for Christ's sake, settle down," Victor cautioned. He put his blinker on and began slowing after bypassing four or five miles of bumper to bumper game traffic crawling toward the same exit.

"Wild Card," Dickie sang to the tune of *'Wild Thing,'* the old Trogs classic, pounding a semblance of the beat on the roof of Victor's car.

"Wild Card, you make my, err, ahh, um…"

Sputtering, not coming up with anything that rhymed, before beginning anew.

"Wild Card,

You make everything groovy.

Come on, come on, Wild Card."

"Okay, Dickie, that's enough now. Just settle down, big boy."

"Here," Andrew said, pulling a handicapped sticker from his pocket and thrusting it in Victor's general direction. "Hang this on the rearview mirror. I've got a card that will get us into handicap parking, so we don't have to pay. Just take the Fifth Street exit, then where the road T's, you make a sharp right and haul ass all the way across the main lot and into the blue zone. We can park right next to the stadium for free."

Beau wondered how a blind guy knew street directions.

"How about some brewskis, boys?" Dickie yelled over his shoulder. He was plowing through the crowd in the U.S. Bank Stadium, three paces ahead of Beau and company. He was like a runaway semi-truck clearing a broad path in his plaid shorts and tent-sized jersey as the crowd jumped to get out of his way. The four of them followed in his massive wake. Andrew held a white cane in his right hand. His left arm was loosely linked in Victor's. Wiener and Beau walked behind them and watched people's reactions as Dickie, attired in his number thirty-five jersey, steamed his way toward the nearest beer stand.

"Hey, thirty-five," some guy called, jumping out of Dickie's path. "Jerry Cardy, man. Minnesota proud." As if Dickie needed any encouragement.

"Eight beers," Dickie said and threw down a hundred-dollar bill. He inhaled an eighteen-ounce cup while he stood at the counter, never once taking the cup away from his lips.

"I'll carry Andrew's," Beau volunteered.

Their seats, compliments of Victor and Andrew's law firm, were on the fifty-yard line and six rows up.

"Dickie, you're in the end seat on the aisle," Victor yelled back as they filed into their seats. He nodded in an effort to ensure the wide-eyed woman in seat number six that everything was under control, at least for the moment.

The pregame ground director was searching the crowd for interesting camera shots. When he spotted Dickie, he shouted into his mouthpiece. "Oh my God. Camera one. Get a shot of the huge guy right on the fifty-yard line. See him, in the Vikings jersey, number thirty-five? Man, look at the size of that guy. You can't miss him."

"Yeah, yeah, I got him," the cameraman replied.

"Okay, main shot on camera one, it's all yours," he said and glanced around a wall of monitors in the booth.

The camera focused in on the white thirty-five of Dickie's jersey and then gradually pulled back for a larger shot just as Dickie drained another beer on television screens across the nation.

"That is one big boy," the cameraman shouted.

"Hey, Dickie, look. Up on the monitor. It's you," Weiner yelled.

Dickie followed Wiener's outstretched arm until his eyes rested on the monitor's twenty-foot image.

"Purple Pride," Dickie screamed, jumping to his feet. Multiple images of Dickie flashed all around the U.S. Bank Stadium on enormous screens.

"Come on, come on, Wild Card, you make… "

"No, Dickie, we don't need you on national TV singing that, okay. Come on. These are the firm's seats," Victor screamed.

"Yeah, okay, Victor. I know. I get it, so just relax." Dickie raised a meaty paw over his head and screamed, "Wild Card. Wild Card."

The sold-out crowd rose to their feet as giant Dickie images on a half-dozen monitors waved them on. "Wild Card. Wild Card," he screamed.

"Do you believe this shit?" Wiener yelled into Beau's ear.

"Well, they're certainly ready up here in Minnesota for football this afternoon," the voice-over said as the camera switched off Dickie's fifteen seconds of fame and refocused on a pair of sultry blondes chanting "Wild Card" to each other.

"Everyone's here this afternoon in Minneapolis at the U.S. Bank Stadium. And they're all screaming Wild

Card. That's a reference to rookie wide receiver Jerry Cardy, the Vikings number thirty-five out of the University of Colorado and a local Chisholm, Minnesota native. So, we wish Jerry Cardy and the Vikings all the best this afternoon, and we'll be back with the kick-off after this message. It's the Minnesota Vikings versus the Seattle Seahawks in today's final preseason NFL Sunday game."

Twenty-Six

"**Y**ou see that fat bastard on TV?" Mendel rolled halfway over to face Elvis on the bed. He sipped a warm beer from the night before.

"By rights, you ought to share that. You know, if you were any kind of a decent sort, you'd at least offer me a sip," Elvis reasoned, furious with himself for not checking under the bed for the unopened can.

"Share? Hell, you coulda grabbed it yourself. Seems like you just didn't have the brains to look around, Elvis, and now all of a sudden, that's my problem? I don't think so," Mendel said and loudly slurped a large mouthful.

Lucerne was in the bathroom, sitting on the floor up against the toilet. He kicked the bathroom door closed with his cowboy boot and continued his phone conversation. "So, what'd ya say you was wearing?"

Tracey giggled and looked at the readout on her screen. She'd already had him on for the better part of a half-hour. "I didn't say what I was wearing, Lucerne. What do you think I'm wearing?"

"I'm just not sure. Something skimpy, I bet. Right?"

"Well, Lucerne, honey, it's the middle of the afternoon, and the air conditioner is turned off in here, and my favorite color is red. That give you any clues, sweetie?"

"I love it when you talk to me like that, Tracey."

Tracey swallowed her Oreo cookie, grabbed another out of the open pack, and tossed the thing into her mouth. She brushed the crumbs off her T-shirt then said, "Mmm-mmm, well, Lucerne, come on now. You have to guess, or it just isn't fun for me."

Mendel rolled over, kicked the bathroom wall a few times, and yelled, "Hey, Mr. Shit-For-Brains. Get in here and watch the damn game with us. You can call your girlfriend at half-time. Get it, Elvis, his girlfriend?" Mendel laughed. "My dear Lord. Can she be that damn stupid?"

"Sounds like I'm gonna have to go and get these guys straightened out, Tracey. Sure has been nice talking to ya' all."

"You just be sure to call me back, Lucerne. I'm missing you already."

"Bye-bye, babydoll," Lucerne said and disconnected.

Tracey clicked on to her next call thinking, *This sure beat doing stretching exercises down on the stage.'*

Twenty-Seven

It was a painful first seven minutes of the game. Seattle marched down the field in increments of five and ten yards and scored a touchdown and an extra point. Number thirty-five, Jerry Cardy Jr., strutted onto the field for his first appearance as a Minnesota Viking. Dickie rose to his feet and got the stadium chanting once again.

"Wild Card. Wild Card," Dickie and the crowd roared in unison. Jerry Cardy Jr. began raising his arms in unison with Dickie and his stadium of followers. "Wild Card. Wild Card." The chant thundered around the stadium.

"Hey, hey," Dickie called and whistled to the beer vendor. "Any of you guys ready?" Knowing no one was more than halfway through their beer. "Better just give me two," he said. Things pretty much went downhill from there.

While Jerry Cardy was quick and had a definite talent for outwitting his defenders, there was one slight problem. He seemed unable to catch anything. It was on the third Viking possession that things turned from unpleasant to downright ugly. At this point, it was toward the end of the first quarter. The deficit was twenty-one to nothing. The Vikings had been pushed back to their own twelve-yard line. It was third and twenty-six. The play called for a screen pass to number thirty-five. Seattle was playing deep, more than willing to allow a few yards. Truth be known, Seattle wasn't really covering Jerry Cardy anymore. He'd already become a non-factor.

The signals were called. Everyone made their assignments with just enough of a performance to give one hope that maybe, just maybe, the Vikings had finally shaken their preseason jitters. The quarterback stepped into the pocket, looked around, spied number thirty-five wide open, and drilled him right on the numbers. Jerry Cardy, the Wild Card, hung on for once, broke a tackle, spun fully around, set his jaw, put his head down, and ran.

They were in pursuit— Seattle players to the left and right. Jerry Cardy, with no one to depend on but himself, kicked it into overdrive and ran like he'd never run before. He was vaguely aware of the roar from the crowd. He couldn't believe how quickly he had been able to cover the ground. There it was suddenly in front of him, the end zone. Time for some magic. He dashed toward the end zone, tossing the ball up into the air just as he was about to cross the goal line, anxious to free both hands so he could begin his practiced victory dance.

Unfortunately, after Jerry caught the pass, he had spun around a full one hundred and eighty degrees. Yes, he ran like he'd never run before, covering twenty-two yards, in the wrong direction. The worst was yet to come. He hadn't quite crossed into the end zone when he threw the ball into the air to begin his dance. Seattle's defensive end, Marcus Beedle, caught the discarded ball. Beedle stepped into the end zone directly behind Jerry Cardy, adding an additional six points onto what would later become one of the worst defeats in Vikings history.

Jerry Cardy was barely into his touchdown dance when the first purple Vikings jersey, number nine, slammed into him full force. That was just before he blacked out, thinking, *Gee, they sure pile on rough in this league.*

It took the referees and players from both teams to stop the blood frenzy as Viking players viciously attacked their rookie teammate. Cardy remained unconscious as they carried him from the field. The sold-out crowd rose to their feet again, only this time screaming for blood and showering the stretcher-bearers with plastic cups and burger wrappers. That marked the beginning of the end for Dickie. He grabbed the nearest beer vendor and handed him a crisp fifty.

"Stick with me," he said and began drinking beers as fast as the guy could open and pour.

"You guys want any beers?" he yelled from the bottom of another empty cup. He appeared oblivious to the catcalls and debris now beginning to be fired in his direction.

"Maybe we should just leave?" Victor suggested. The couple next to him stood and crawled in the opposite direction down the length of the row, excusing themselves past twenty-five fans rather than walk past Dickie.

"I don't think we stand a chance of making it out of here," Wiener said

"Oh yeah? Screw all of ya. You hear me. Screw all you bastards!" Dickie roared back to the stadium. Another deluge of cups and debris rained down in their direction as Dickie gave the finger to the stadium fans.

"Sit tight. Someone's bound to come and get us. They can't just leave us here. Can they?" Beau asked, then scanned the aisle hoping for police protection.

Security was coming down the stairs, and it wasn't usherettes. Beau counted ten large, muscular guys with five cops behind them. They were coming to escort Dickie out of the stadium, in fairness, for his own safety. It was at this point that Dickie turned, dropped his plaid shorts and custom-made boxers to the ground. He mooned the jeering stadium with three hundred plus pounds of broad, hairy, Dickie butt.

"This is for you!" he screamed, using both hands to give the stadium the finger.

There was a gasp from the middle of the stadium as people shielded their eyes in horror. The beer vendor, already fidgety from the insults and debris being hurled, poured a final beer. He grabbed his case and ran off with Dickie's change.

"Break to commercial, break to commercial," the director screamed into his mouthpiece.

The phalanx of security engulfed Dickie, swarming over him, keeping away from his massive rear end. They, not so gingerly, handcuffed him, pulled his plaid shorts up, and then glanced over as if to ask, "You guys want some of this action?"

Beau surrendered, placed his hands palms up, suggesting they didn't even know him. Dickie was escorted handcuffed up the steps and into the bowels of the US Bank Stadium, finally giving the fans something to cheer about.

"Did you know that guy?" Wiener yelled to the couple seated behind him.

"No, we thought he was with you."

"No, we've never seen him before," he said, hoping they'd pass the information on.

It was late in the fourth quarter before the Vikings finally managed to get on the scoreboard with a field goal making it sixty-three to three. Beau and company joined the mass exodus leaving the stadium in absolute disgust. They attempted to blend in as much as possible.

"So much for purple pride," said Wiener.

"Shhh. Come on, keep your voice down," cautioned Beau.

"We have to get him out of here," Victor said.

"Get him out of here? How? You plan on using a crane?" asked Wiener.

"No, I mean it. Look, this thing's going to be national. He doesn't need an arrest photo and all of that. He could lose his job."

"His job? Christ, we're lucky he didn't get us all killed!" Wiener whined.

"You mean we bust him out?" Beau said.

"Not like that. Andrew, will you represent him?"

"Against my better judgment," Andrew said.

Twenty-Eight

They entered the security area down in the absolute bowels of the stadium. It had that damp concrete smell that left one with the impression neither fresh air nor sunlight seldom ventured this close to hell. Beau's restaurateur's nose caught the hint of mold lurking just beneath the chemical air freshener. They waited patiently in an outer area for forty minutes before being ushered into a small security office.

There was a Minneapolis Police Sergeant on duty. He was seated at a chrome and woodgrain Formica desk, resting his elbows on the desk. The desk was bare except for a phone and one thin manila file. The file was labeled Ulmbacher, Hans, in handwritten red letters. The Sergeant read Andrew's business card and remained completely unimpressed. He glanced at Andrew, back at the card, and then glanced over at Victor.

"You're a lawyer, too, I suppose?"

"Yes, sir," Victor smiled and reached into his pocket to produce a card.

"No, thanks. That won't be necessary."

He was an older guy, late forties, Beau guessed. He had a grey crew cut, pale blue eyes, and a skin pallor that suggested he perhaps lived permanently below ground level.

"Um-hmm, did you gentlemen happen to be sitting in your firm's seats?" he asked Andrew.

"As Mr. Ulmbacher's legal counsel, it's my duty and frankly my concern that—"

"Look, save it, Clarence Darrow. This ain't the courthouse. Before you get too far ahead of yourself, let me remind you that your friend, Mr. Ulmbacher, was beamed across all fifty states on national TV. He was handcuffed in an effort to secure his own safety." He sighed, sounding very tired.

"His safety?" Andrew attempted to sound shocked.

"Prior to the arrival of our security people, he was filmed committing an act of indecent exposure. Indecent exposure in front of minors, I might add. I'm sure you two legal beagles are aware that's a level four sexual offense in the state of Minnesota. As you might guess, we are not exactly lacking witnesses."

Victor sighed.

"Now, quite frankly, I really don't care what happens to Mr. Ulmbacher." He drew out Dickie's last name, making it seem somehow obscene.

"I also don't want to have to transport him, fool around with booking and everything else tonight. I've got a sister living up in Chisholm, and I had it with that damn Wild Card nonsense weeks ago. Mr. Ulmbacher and I had a little chat."

"Without representation?" Andrew interjected.

Victor elbowed Andrew, mouthed the word "blind" to the Sergeant. "Excuse us, Sergeant, you were saying."

"Yeah, as I was saying. Once he had some time to cool down, I was able to have a chat with Mr. Ulmbacher. I'm going to cite him for indecent exposure, public intoxication, and we'll let it go at that, provided—" He shook a finger at all of them. "I don't see any of you in this stadium for the coming year."

"I'm prepared to remand Mr. Ulmbacher to your custody. But, I recommend you remain out there in the holding area for maybe another hour or two before attempting to head out of here tonight. His disgustingly fat rear end spread across the stadium screens won't be easy to forget. Unfortunately, it wasn't the only disgusting thing out there this afternoon. Right now, we've got an ugly crowd on our hands. If they catch sight of your friend, it would be like sharks to blood, a regular feeding frenzy. Frankly, I can't guarantee your safety if you decide to leave now. Good God, sixty-three to three. What in the hell?"

It was another hour before Dickie was released and able to join them. His eyes remained fixed on the floor. "Hey guys, thanks for hanging in here with me. I don't know what I'd do without you. Umm, did we win?" he whispered and looked up.

"Win? You gotta be kidding? No, Dickie, we didn't win," Wiener said.

"Any news on the Wild Card? Is he okay?" Dickie asked.

"I think right now, there are a couple of other items you should probably be focusing on," interjected Andrew.

"Yeah, 'spose so. Like I said, I really appreciate you guys hanging in here with me. Sorry if I caused you any problems." He stared back down at the floor.

"We just need to sit tight for a bit longer. Make sure things calm down out there before we try to make it home," Andrew said. "Now Dickie, neither Victor nor I can handle the charges against you. So you should get legal counsel and probably pretty fast."

"We can give you some names. Just don't say a word to anyone, and I mean anyone, including all of us, until after you've talked to your attorney," added Victor.

"Look, guys, I didn't mean—"

"Dude. No. Not another word."

They sat in virtual silence for another hour. Dickie occasionally shifted his massive bulk, causing the steel frame chair to creak. He stared at the floor for the next hour and never uttered a sound except for the odd sniffle.

"Okay, fellas," the Sergeant poked his head out. "You can go, but I'd head right out of town. Anyone recognizes you, we probably couldn't respond fast enough."

"Thank you, Officer. Wiener, Beau, you guys get on either side of Dickie," Victor said, then took Andrew by the arm.

They climbed up two different stairwells and a long ramp before they reached the main floor. The wide hallways were devoid of anyone except the cleaning crews pushing broad brooms sweeping up remnants of the day's disaster. They waded through the debris of a dashed afternoon, plastic cups, crumpled programs, and peanut shells.

A couple of the cleanup personnel pointed at Dickie as he waddled past. It was pretty hard not to notice him. He was still in his plaid shorts and wearing the enormous purple Vikings jersey sporting the number thirty-five. His eyes were downcast, and he clenched copies of his intoxication and indecent exposure charges in his fist.

Amazingly, they made it to Victor's car unmolested. Victor quickly drove out the Sixth Street exit, headed east onto I-94, and back in the direction of Saint Paul. No one spoke, and everyone seemed to want to get home and put some distance between themselves and the sordid afternoon.

"I hate Minneapolis," Dickie said softly as they pulled into Beau's parking lot. They were the only words he'd uttered in the past hour and a half.

Twenty-Nine

Cindy's alarm sounded at five Monday morning, kicking off her week from hell. Amazingly, given the fact she had spent virtually the entire Sunday in bed, she was still tired. She took comfort in the fact that the pounding in her head had stopped, and her tummy had finally stabilized. After a hot shower and a quick microwave breakfast of cheese pizza, she mustered the courage to face the day.

By five forty-five, she was on her knees, pulling out bag after bag from the stuffed night-deposit vault. She had to count and verify each deposit. Enter the deposit in the system. Next, she had to sort the currency for counting and banding. Once all that was completed, she had to pack it for transport to Central. All that had to be accomplished before the lobby doors opened promptly at nine. Once the doors opened, a dozen people swamped the teller area. From there, things grew to a nonstop roar. A continuous line of customers with overflowing bags of cash would be charging the teller windows until closing time.

By noon, the temperature was in the upper ninety-degree mark and climbing. The armored car couriers were sweating in the heat and humidity. Billy Truesdale stood at the rear of his armored car and looked dejected as his helper, Trevor, continued to complain.

"Oh man, this is like the Dark Ages meets convict labor. That's what this is." Trevor groaned as he hefted a trash bag out of the grocery cart and swung it into the back of the armored car. "Ugh, man, couldn't they come up with a ramp or something? I mean, if you want a ramp, I can design you a ramp, man."

Billy checked the bag off on the manifest then set his clipboard down on the massive rear bumper. He was afraid he might smash Trevor over the head with the clipboard if he held it any longer.

"Oh, Billy. I think I threw my back out. Man, this is barbaric. These bags must come in at about seventy-five pounds."

"More like fifteen. Climb in back there and move some of those bags out of the way," Billy said.

Once Trevor stumbled in, Billy closed the door and locked it. He pushed the grocery cart back to the bank and knocked on the door. Sidney, the bank officer, opened the door and wheeled the cart in.

Sidney was an exceptionally thin man. He stood just a whisker over six feet with wispy tufts of hair combed over a shining dome. What little color he had was pale and added to an overall frail appearance. His brown polyester suit coat, the bank uniform, hung shapelessly over thin sharp shoulders.

"Billy, you want some water or something? With this heat, diabetics like you and me, we gotta watch it."

Billy took off his uniform hat and wiped his brow. He looked up at the unrelenting, cloudless sky. Things were only going to get worse weather-wise. "Thanks, Sidney, but I've got some water in the chariot. Just in a lousy mood after that Vikings fiasco yesterday, that's all. You know they don't have to win all the time, but how about at least showing up to play? Good Lord, the neighborhood kids could have given a better showing."

"Oh, tell me about it, and that guy. Did you see him? That fat guy?" asked Sidney.

"You mean the Wild Card guy?"

"Yeah, that's the one. Where'd they dig him up?"

"Just one of the idiots attending the game," Billy said, a touch of yesterday's fury beginning to boil again.

"They must have hired that guy," Sidney said. "The size of him. I mean, that had to be a special order jersey. And getting the crowd to its feet, great fun until it actually came time to run a play. I told the wife, by the look of things, we might be going for some long Sunday afternoon walks this fall. That fat guy was a plant. He had to be."

"Gotta go," Billy said, feeling yesterday's frustration beginning to creep in. He pounded on the passenger door then climbed in once the lock clicked open.

"Everything okay?" Gary, the driver, asked.

"Damn Vikings," Billy responded.

"You kidding? Tell me about it. And that fat ass guy. What an idiot."

Thirty

Otto was in the process of making another run to the bank. It had been a strange day walking around from stand to stand picking up deposits. He had the sense people were staring at him, perhaps a little more than usual. It was after the third or fourth group of kids had given him the finger and yelled some names that he offhandedly mentioned it to one of the college kids working at his stands.

"Josh, what is it with everyone today? Man, talk about getting up on the wrong side of the bed. I've seen nothing but people looking pissed off. A couple of kids even gave me the finger. Is there something in the water?"

"You're kidding me, Otto, right?" Josh said. He continued to roll skewered slabs of bacon through a long pan of batter.

"No, I'm not kidding. It's just… There, did you catch that?" Otto turned excitedly in the direction of two sixty-year-old women walking away from the stand.

"See, see, they just sneered at me and shook their heads, like I ran over the neighbor's dog or something. I mean, what is it?"

All of his stands were built a few feet above the ground, and as Josh talked to Otto, he looked down on him by a couple of feet.

"You're serious? Not kidding?"

"Hell no, I'm not kidding. I'm gonna get a complex if this continues. Go ahead, enlighten me."

Josh continued to skewer thick slabs of bacon onto wooden sticks. He dipped them into the batter and set them into a wheel that worked as a sort of rotisserie. "You bother to listen to any of the game yesterday?"

"Vikings? Not really, tuned in for a minute or two, but they were down by something like fourteen points. Why?"

"They lost 63 to 3," Josh said, slicing open another twenty-five-pound bag of bacon slabs.

"You kidding me? So, why's everyone taking it out on me? What'd I do?"

"Otto, man, you got that number thirty-five jersey on. That's the guy who ran the wrong way and basically handed the ball to the Seahawks. He scored against his own team. Folks are still trying to get their lives back together after yesterday. They don't want to think about the Vikings, let alone Jerry Cardy, that number thirty-five guy. I gotta believe it's a pretty safe bet you are the only person in the state wearing a number thirty-five jersey today."

Otto made his way to his truck. Along the way, he was flipped off by a couple of cute looking co-ed types who'd given him the finger. He handed the kid in the parking lot another greasy paper plate of deep-fat-fried-bacon-on-a-stick, maple-flavored.

"Yeah, like thanks. Man, they suck, eh?" the kid said and nodded at Otto's jersey.

Once he arrived at the bank, Otto stood in the line for the teller he'd seen staggering out of DiMento's bar Sunday morning. It hadn't been the longest line, but hers was the slowest. Figures, Otto thought. All he wanted to do was get a sense of this party girl, and he hadn't moved since.

"Hi," he said, in response to the stare from a guy in the line next to him.

"God damn, Cardy. That boy's history. That takes some brass ones today." The man nodded at Otto's jersey.

Otto waited for what seemed like an eternity. He silently cursed the two women ahead of him who seemed to be taking their time. Eventually, he stepped to the window.

"Hi, Cindy," he said, reading the teller's name badge. A leer crept through the zinc oxide smeared across his face.

Only Porky would wear a Vikings jersey today, she thought. "How are you today, sir?"

"Fine, just fine." Otto leaned in so close to the bulletproof glass it fogged slightly as he spoke.

"You keep some late hours," he said, stepping back and giving her one of his all-knowing winks.

Oh, you absolute creep, she thought, counting his cash and piling it into stacks. "Yes, sir, special hours, we're open until six tonight," she said.

"Just wondered if you started early like that every day?" he half-whispered and snickered at his own crazy sense of humor.

"Mmm-hmmm," she said, counting twenty, forty, sixty, eighty, anxious to get him away from her window as quickly as possible.

"Go there often and do that sort of thing?" he asked.

Forty, sixty, eighty, hundred, four-thousand-six-hundred she counted, checking the amount on his deposit slip, crediting the cash. She shoved the grease-stained bag and the deposit receipt back under the glass. Making sure the receipt was at all times between her fingertips and the bag that had touched his sweaty body.

"Anything else I can do for you, sir?" She smiled and thought, *You are so gross.*

He wiped the sweat running down the side of his face with the back of his hand. He felt a tingle from the tip of his jungle boots to the top of his head as she spoke to him. He seized on her double meaning, 'anything else.'

"Well, now that you mention it," he said, posing. He placed a forearm on the counter and waited while she had time to examine his Donald Duck tattoo, U.S.M.C. boldly scripted just below Donald's rear. He nodded his head up and down, letting her know it was all right, attempting to buy time. He could feel his face blushing, and he began to sweat, waiting for her to ask about Deep-Fat-Fried-Bacon-on-a-Stick.

It didn't happen.

She repeated the refrain in her head, Gross, gross, gross. She heard her voice ask sweetly, "Anything else I can do for you?"

"I guess not. At least not here," he laughed. He winked, shrugged, waited for a moment before giving her a little two-fingered salute, and ambled out the door.

The woman waiting behind him approached the counter, shaking her head.

"Just a minute, please," Cindy said. She sprayed a can of Lysol over the window area and wiped it clean with a paper towel.

"Lord, I don't blame you one damn bit. And those dreadful Vikings!"

Thirty-One

"**T**ake us past the bank again," Mendel said to Lucerne.

They were on their way to a gun shop. Elvis sat in the backseat of the Fleetwood, worrying about the wisdom of breaking into a store full of guns. He slid over until he was centered between Mendel and Lucerne and leaned forward. He turned his head and fixed his good eye on Mendel sitting in the passenger seat.

"Why can't we just buy some guns?"

"Well, now that you mention it, Elvis, I think I can come up with two reasons. First, we're felons. And two, we're broke. I got me a sneaky feeling anyone who sold to us just wouldn't be that happy with our IOUs."

"You think they know that was us with the dead banker?" Elvis asked.

"The cops?"

"Well, yeah, for starters," Elvis said. He began a mental checklist of the various police departments and state agencies that had caused the three of them problems in the past.

"They probably don't know yet, dumb ass, but why chance it? All we're gonna do today is just look around a little. Get the flavor of the place. We can come back after business hours and take whatever we need. Simple as you please, we'll waltz right on outta there," Mendel said.

"What about just buying the guns from someone else? You know, one of them private party types," Elvis asked.

"Great idea. Why don't you tell me who in the hell we're gonna buy AK 47s from? Because I been thinking, and I can't come up with anyone. Not that we got any money, anyway. Hey, Lucerne. You know anyone wants to sell AKs to three broke felons who ain't got a pot to piss in?" Mendel growled.

Lucerne shook his head. He checked the rearview mirror and made the turn onto Como Avenue that would bring them past the bank building.

"Okay, Elvis, I don't know nobody. Lucerne here, he don't know nobody. So, you tell me. Who you know got all these AKs they want to sell?"

"Well, I—"

"They must be real good friends of yours, 'cause me and Lucerne, we ain't got a clue, man."

"I don't know nobody, exactly. I just think it's gonna be hard to grab 'em from a gun store, is all. Know what I'm saying, Mendel?" Elvis said.

"Maybe, you should wait and see how hard it is. You just might be surprised. Maybe they got AKs stored in a box outside, and we can just help ourselves. Maybe I'm working on a plan for us. Maybe it would be better to see what in the hell we're dealing with first, Elvis, before you go pissing all over a man's plan."

"Banks coming up," Lucerne said, hoping to calm things down a little.

"Okay, here we go. Pull up behind that pickup truck and wait for me. I'm going into this bank and look around." Mendel suddenly shouldered the door open before Lucerne had stopped. The door dragged and scraped loudly along the concrete curb.

Once Mendel was out, Lucerne said, "Why you get him mad like that? He just gets pissed off." He stared at Elvis in the rearview mirror.

"I'm worried for all of us, but I ain't afraid if that's what you're thinking. But to break into a gun store? Our luck ain't been the greatest lately, ya know. I mean, there's folks with guns in gun stores, get it? I just don't think it's gonna be the cakewalk Mendel says, that's all."

"I think he'll see it ain't that easy, and he'll eventually forget about the AKs. Maybe forget about this damn bank, too. I don't get why we can't just go back to knocking off liquor stores and folks' homes like the good Lord intended."

As Mendel opened the door to the bank building, he was cut off by the same character he had labeled Porky Pig the other day. The stupid bastard was dressed in a Vikings jersey and jungle boots. He had all sorts of white cream smeared on his face like some deranged clown. Mendel caught the Donald Duck tattoo on the man's forearm. There was a vague, distant look in his eyes and sweat running down his face. He decided it might be best to give this nutcase all the space he needed, and so he stepped back.

Thirty-Two

Beau had gone to bed thirty minutes after he made it home from the Vikings game. He didn't have the courage to watch the news, afraid that he and the others were caught on film. Despite the exhaustion, he slept fitfully. He woke with a start a number of different times throughout the night. He was frightened by the recurring nightmare of Dickie dropping his boxers and screaming, "Wild Card." More than once, he woke in a cold sweat. Eventually, he crawled out of bed, showered, dressed, and drove to the coffee shop for his doughnut and latte.

Chrissie stood behind the counter, looking like she had been waiting for him all morning. She was spilling out of a T-shirt two sizes too small and shorts that looked wonderfully tight.

"Hey, Beau, was that you on the news last night with that fat guy at the Vikings game? Wow, I wasn't sure you'd even show your face today."

"Vikings game, me? No, I had to work and wasn't there, ever. Did they win?"

"Oh, man, I could have sworn that was you. They were showing this ginormous guy, and I thought that had to be you right next to him. Oh, gee, now, that's really weird 'cause I yelled out to everyone in the room. We were watching at my sister's, and I yelled out, 'Hey'," she raised her voice and yelled across the coffee shop, causing everyone to turn toward her, "I know that guy. That's my friend Beau next to that fat dude's ass.' Isn't that crazy? You know, like you could have been famous or something."

A number of people were staring over the tops of computer screens and newspapers. A few of them stared at Beau longer than necessary. They were probably scanning their memory, trying to place him. Beau smiled weakly, grabbed his latte and doughnut, and hurried out the door.

That was only the beginning. He had to walk past two newspaper vending machines, one for Saint Paul's *Pioneer Press* and the other for the *Minneapolis Star Tribune*. Both were running a full-color shot of Dickie and company at Sunday's game. The *Pioneer Press* ran with the headline 'Family Entertainment?' While the Star Tribune took the more subtle approach, 'Biggest Loser!' Pictured next to Dickie, in order of appearance,

Beau, Wiener, and Victor. Andrew somehow managed to get cropped out of both editions.

Beau stumbled in the lounge door, downing his latte, cramming the doughnut into his mouth, and wearing a shell-shocked look.

"Hey, Beau," Patti called, pouring a double for one of her morning regulars, "you're really famous. I saw you on the news last night. Oh and ah, nice picture in the paper. You made the front page in both papers, good job," she laughed. She wiggled her finger to draw him closer, reeling him in for more bad news.

"Hey, remember those two creepy guys from last Friday?" she said and flashed her little 'I'm-so-cute' smile.

He nodded blankly.

"Well, they're waiting for you again in your office, honey. God, I had to hide the paper from my kids, Beau. Like I told you before, I don't want them anywhere near a guy like you."

By the time he reached his office, his heart was pounding, and he could feel his blood pressure rising. He took a deep breath and opened the door. "Gentlemen, you're a bit early. Didn't we just speak on Friday?" As he walked behind his desk, he picked up a slightly me-dicinal scent and felt his face begin to flush. "So, what can I do for you this morning? How was dinner with your nurse friend, by the way?" He directed his comments to-wards Osborne, hoping to avoid Milton.

Milton kept his right hand against his coat. It was clearly swollen with a purplish tinge extending from his fingertips back up his thick wrist jutting out of his sleeve.

"Well, if it isn't the new Vikings mascot. Taking up a second job to make ends meet?" The swollen hand had apparently done nothing for Milton's sense of humor. He was wearing a light blue sports jacket over a rippled black silk T-shirt. With Milton's huge biceps and thick forearms crammed in them, the coat sleeves resembled stuffed sausages.

"That's one of the problems with public facilities like the stadium. You never know who you'll end up sitting next to. Now, my office, on the other hand, is private. I can appreciate the concern for your loan. But, like I told you Friday, I'm concluding arrangements shortly and intend to pay that debt on time, if not before. Anything else?" Beau asked.

"All of a sudden, you're a big media star, and you think your shit don't stink?" Milton moved maybe a half-step closer and cast a glassy eye toward Beau.

"Milton, please," cautioned Osborne. He brushed some imaginary dust from his pink tie. He wore a tan suit and a pale blue shirt today. The pink tie had apparently been chosen to match the rim of his eyelids.

"I think it's time for you two gentlemen to leave."

"Milton," Osborne commanded.

Milton quickly reached across the desk, grabbed Beau tightly by the collar, and effortlessly lifted him off the floor.

Beau gasped. He thought of kneeing the giant, but his desk was in the way. Milton pulled him closer, bringing Beau just inches from his face. The giant's eyes had a glassy look, and his breath seemed a subtle mix of salami and latrine.

"I trust you will endeavor yourself of our generosity. Remember, in the event of nonpayment. We can invoke the special extermination clause," Osborne calmly continued.

Milton snickered and tightened his grip on Beau's collar.

Beau fought for air. He couldn't swallow, his eyes bulged, his tongue began to grow too large for his mouth, and he panicked. He attempted to kick Milton but only succeeded in smashing his shins painfully against the edge of the desk.

In desperation, he swung his elbow up and caught Milton solidly just under the edge of his jaw. Milton's teeth cracked together as his massive head snapped back. His eyes rolled into the top of his skull, and he fell backward. He retained his grasp on Beau's collar, dragging him up and over the top of the desk. They both crashed onto the floor with a collective groan. Beau quickly rolled off Milton and sucked in precious air.

Milton slowly moved his head back and forth and blinked his eyes.

Osborne jumped to feet but not as quickly as Beau, who suddenly brandished an aluminum softball bat in his left hand. Adrenaline coursed through his body.

"It's early in the morning, and I've already had a really bad day. Your unexpected visit isn't helping. Now, get him out of here before I lose my temper," Beau shouted. He viciously swung the bat against Milton's swollen right hand just as Milton placed it on the corner of the desk and attempted to rise.

The blow knocked Milton back down on the floor. He roared in pain, rolled to his side, and curled into a fetal position, rocking back and forth. The right sleeve of his sports coat was ripped along the shoulder seam. His jaw was clenched, and he groaned painfully as he brought Beau into focus.

"I promise you—"

"Shut the hell up. I promise you. I'll take you out without a second thought if you two don't get out of my sight right now. So help me, God. Now, get him up and get the hell out of here. I don't want to hear another damned word." He shook the bat in Osborne's direction to make his point.

Osborne, red-faced and furious, glared through pink-rimmed eyes. He helped the groaning Milton to his feet, and together they left the office.

"Good day to you, sir," Osborne said without looking back.

Beau suddenly felt an incredible urge to be sick and hurried into the bathroom. Fortunately, nothing came up. He took a number of deep breaths and steadied himself. It was shaping up to be one hell of a day.

Thirty-Three

Sidney sat at his desk and stared at the rough-looking character standing out in the bank lobby. The man seemed to have a number of issues. He fidgeted and looked this way and that. He stepped in and out of various teller lines. Apparently, all in an effort to remain in the back of the line. Was it drugs, alcohol, some sort of psychosis, or all three? Just as Sidney was about to offer assistance, the man suddenly turned on his heel and walked out the door.

Where do all these loons go when it's not state fair week? Sidney wondered.

"Place is crawling with folks waving money," Mendel declared once he climbed back in the Fleetwood. "And no guards that I seen. There's one little room in back, but I don't think there's a guard in there. The room just lets you go into where them bank tellers is standing. I'm thinking they got all that money sitting in there just waitin' for someone like us to come and take it off their hands."

"No guards?" Elvis asked.

"I said no guards. Get the shit out of your ears, boy."

"If there ain't guards, why do we need the guns?" Elvis leaned forward again in the rear seat and suddenly felt stupid before the words had left his mouth.

Mendel's look gave him his answer, and he sat back, quiet for the remainder of the ride.

"Let's just go pay that gun shop a visit. Take a look, see what's waiting for us up there."

The OK Corral Gun Shop sat on the far northern edge of suburban Blaine. Not quite the end of the world, but you could see it from there. The clientele consisted of guys who hunted whatever was in season, plus survivalists, ex-military, or military wannabes like the owner, T.J. Flood.

T.J. wore a sidearm virtually at all times, a blued Sig Sauer 229 with a twelve-round .357 magazine, to be specific. He took it off when he was in bed with his wife, Miss Suzie. But the Sig Sauer rested right next to him on the nightstand next to the bed and within easy reach.

A Dolly Parton look-alike, Miss Suzie insisted on two things. First, even though her name was Marsha, T.J. was to call her Miss Suzie, after the old Creedence song *"Suzie Q."* She'd once partied with some of the Creedence roadies for two nights and a day as a teenager when they played Saint Paul forty years back. Not that she ever told T.J. about it. Second, T.J. was not allowed to wear the Sig Sauer into their bed, hence the nightstand repository.

T.J. himself was a rather slight man with soft hands, a whiskey tenor voice, dishwater blonde hair, and a waxed handlebar mustache. He had soft brown eyes magnified behind Coke bottle glasses. It had been his poor eyesight that kept him out of the service.

He spotted the Ditschler brothers through the tinted glass in the front door. Mendel, Lucerne, and Elvis piled out of their two-toned Fleetwood Brougham and walked through the cloud of exhaust fumes drifting across the parking lot.

"I don't think so," T.J. exclaimed and set down FM-175 Ranger, the Army field manual he had been re-reading. He stepped out from behind the counter and cut off the Ditschler brother's forward progress just as they stepped inside the front door. Mendel, Lucerne, and Elvis looked in desperate need of a shower. T.J. correctly assumed they were most likely penniless. A demographic he wasn't the least bit interested in serving.

"Good morning. May I see some identification, please?" He rested his hand on his holster, blocking their path and not really meaning the word 'please.'

"Just taking a look round see," Mendel grinned, exposing dingy teeth and spewing beer tainted breath in a misguided effort to win T.J. over.

"Sorry, gents. Not without a proper photo ID and a backup. House rules. We scan everyone's ID and keep a record. I'm sure you can understand, what with our inventory." T.J. calmly twisted the holster on his hip, causing the leather to crack, adding an authoritative emphasis to his statement.

Mendel's eyes rested on a long steel gun rack just behind T.J. holding exactly what they had come looking for, AKs. The ones with the folded plastic butt.

"Well, now. We ain't got that kinda time, busy as we are. Got us an appointment in a few minutes. Just wanted to pop in. Take a look 'round see, is all. But, if your idea of customer service is to treat good paying customers this way, I guess we'll just be heading out. Come on, boys. Ain't nothing here of interest for us and our hard-earned money anyway."

The three Ditschlers beat a hasty retreat back out the door.

T.J. watched through the tinted glass as they fired up the Fleetwood. Once again, a cloud of exhaust drifted across the parking lot while Lucerne revved the engine a number of times. Just as T.J. was about to step out the door, they drove off.

"Damnation, now what?" Lucerne asked. He circled the lot, laying down a larger cloud of noxious fumes before they sped off down the street.

"Course neither one of you two dummies was looking round, was you?" Mendel asked. "Yeah, I didn't think so. Hell, I seen what we need right there. No more than fifteen feet inside the front door. Right behind where that soft-shouldered bastard was standing. So, what we're gonna do now is knock us off a liquor store or two for a little walking-around money. One of these next nights, we'll just come back up here and take what we need. Simple as that," he said, snapping his fingers. He leaned back, closed his eyes, and proceeded to nap.

Thirty-Four

Beau's mother was using her no-nonsense tone the moment he picked up the phone and said, "Hello."

"You just listen to me, Anthony. Please, tell me your uncle Mario was wrong when he phoned me at seven o'clock this morning all the way from St. Petersburg, Florida. Apparently, you were on the news last night and *Good Morning America* this morning. Please, tell me that wasn't my son staring back at me from my morning paper with that Wiener person at the Vikings football game yesterday. And that dreadful performance by Anna Ulmbacher's son. Good Lord, I'm sure she's a proud mother right now."

"Hi, Mom," he said, attempting to get a half-moment to think.

"Now, you just listen to me. You are known by the company you keep, young man. You bear just as much responsibility for those dreadful actions as if you'd done them yourself."

'Damn Dickie!' he thought.

"What were you thinking, Anthony? Did you, in your wildest dreams, think that you could cavort around town like some sort of depraved ne'er-do-well? What are my friends going to think? Good Lord, I'll have to sell the house and move."

"Mom, you're not going to have to move."

"Don't you be too sure about that, young man. Now, you listen to me, mister. I've had just about enough of these shenanigans. Your father, God rest his soul, and I did not raise you so you could behave like some sort of common criminal. You will cease this nonsense immediately. Do you hear me? Immediately. This is exactly why you need a good woman in your life, Anthony. So you settle down and stop this foolishness. And you are going to apologize."

"Apologize? Mom, I didn't do anything."

"Listen here, young man. You're not so big that I won't take you over my knee and blister that backside. And don't you think I won't!"

He could just picture her, probably standing over a pot of spaghetti sauce on the stove, waving a wooden spoon as she spoke.

"Well?"

"Okay, Mom. I'm sorry. Look, unpack the moving boxes. I'll be over tonight for dinner."

"See that you are. And be prepared for a healthy serving of humble pie. There is a lot I intend to say to you, young man."

"Gee, I can hardly wait."

"Anthony, you will stop immediately. Do you hear me? I will not suffer that tone from you. Now, I will see you tonight, and do not be late!" Click.

Damn it, Dickie, he thought and dialed Dickie's office number.

"Hans Ulmbacher, please."

"Hello, you've reached the office of Hans Ulmbacher. I'm unable to take your call just now, and I will be unavailable for the next few days. If this is an emergency, you can press extension zero-one-one at any time. If you wish to leave me a message, please, press zero-one-five. Thank you and have a nice day."

Beau was not having a nice day. He pressed 015. What he got was a computer-generated voice that informed him, "This mailbox is full," before disconnecting altogether.

He had just hung up the phone about to get back to work when it rang.

"Hello."

"So, how in the hell is your morning going?" Victor asked.

"Well, let's see. I've been identified and accused by everyone, from a blonde at the coffee shop to my own employees. I assaulted some prick with a baseball bat, and my mom called and said she's so embarrassed she'll have to move. You?"

"About the same. Well, except for the assault thing. Do I want to know about that?"

"Just joking," Beau lied.

"Yeah, well, not funny the way things are going. My loving bride, Tasha, raced over to her mother's in hopes of getting the paper from her before she saw us plastered across the front page. She called the office to inform me we'd be talking about it when I get home. My own mother called me to say she didn't work two jobs to send me through law school so I could embarrass her on national TV. On a positive note, I got a call from my brother in Atlanta, who said he enjoyed it. Of course, I had to cut that conversation short since Mr. Ehrmann, the firm's senior partner called and wondered if I had time to chat with him for a few moments. Immediately."

"Jesus, what'd he say?"

"Let's just say we won't be using the firm's season tickets. Ever again."

"That damn Dickie."

"You can say that again."

"I just tried to call that giant piece of shit, but he's got his calls blocked. So, I can't reach him," Beau whined.

"Look, his bank is a major corporate sponsor. Word gets out that fat white ass beamed across all fifty states belonged to a bank employee. Dickie is toast," Victor reminded.

"You think they'll do that?"

"You kidding? Firing him would probably be a good PR move. I think it might be, shoot first and ask questions later. I've got to attempt to salvage something out of this morning, so I had better go. You playing poker Thursday night?" Victor asked.

"I plan to," Beau replied, thinking he couldn't possibly.

"See you there."

He hung up and set off to track down La Tondra and Celeste. Hopefully, they had picked up the Saab from that Bernice woman on Saturday. He found the two of them in the kitchen.

"Hey, Beau. Caught you yesterday on the television. Man, I've always wanted to do something like that. I thought it was really cool," Celeste said.

"What? Go to the Vikings game?" he asked.

"No. Moon all those people. You know that would be so awesome. Just hang it out there. This is what I think of you," Celeste turned to shove her fairly well-formed rear in his direction as La Tondra came up behind her.

"How'd it go with the car on Saturday, girls? Were you able to pick it up?"

"Sure did, sugar. It's back in the lot. We ended up talking with Bernice for a while, so we didn't get back until last night," La Tondra said.

"Last night? You mean, Sunday?"

"Yeah, well, we started talking, and then things sort of turned into a little bit of a party, and the next thing you know, it was Sunday afternoon. She's really out there, and she's got all these really cute cats, and she gave each of us a kitty, too."

'Sweet Jesus,' he thought, shaking his head. "Did you remember the keys?"

"Keys?"

"Yeah, for the car?"

"Check the pockets, check the pockets," Celeste said, turning around.

"How about you hand me the keys, and then I can pay the two of you, like we discussed. Deal?" he said.

"Oh, you're no fun," Celeste groaned.

Five minutes later, Beau was standing out in the parking lot, sweating in the midday heat and humidity, looking at the recent damage to the Saab that Celeste and La Tondra had conveniently forgotten to mention. The left front quarter panel was scraped and dented, the front bumper was hanging at an angle, and the left headlight was broken. Beau didn't know if he should scream or just drive the Saab home to his garage, pull inside, and sit there with the engine running.

Obviously, the girls had hit something. The crease extended beyond the wheel well and across the driver's door. The sideview mirror on the driver's side was gone. The good news was whatever they had hit appeared to have been an object as opposed to an individual.

He opened the car door and immediately recognized the heavy stale smell of dope, noticed the empty vodka bottle on the floor and the condom on the backseat. At least, they had been practicing safe sex.

He tossed the vodka bottle in the trash. He tore a stick off a bush and carefully removed the condom. He started the car just to make sure it still ran. He left all the windows down in an attempt to give the interior a decent airing and headed back to his office.

Thirty-Five

Otto had been wondering all day what line would work best with that cute teller at the bank. He decided it was better to keep the information to himself for a while. Maybe spring it on her at just the right time. A combination of a slight touch of blackmail coupled with her dreams come true all at the same magical moment.

The sun had been merciless all day, burning through the haze from the heavy humidity. He had long ago sweated through the Vikings jersey, and folks were still giving him the finger. His forearms, the back of his legs, and the back of his neck were sunburned an intense nuclear red. His ears had gone beyond sunburned and were now painfully blistered. His nose would have been the same except that he had the presence of mind to slather it with zinc oxide, giving him more than a slight resemblance to a clown.

He didn't really care. As a matter of fact, it never even dawned on him that he looked ridiculous. Hell, he'd always looked ridiculous. Just now, he was trying to decide if he should choose a particular Deep-Fat-Fried-Bacon for his favorite little bank teller. Or, would it make more sense just to give her a sampling of all the flavors and let her decide which one she liked the best?

He imagined her telling all her girlfriends, *'This really cool guy, Otto. I told you about him. He's the guy who invented Deep-Fat-Fried-Bacon-on-a-Stick.'*

'The regular?' someone would ask.

'The maple flavor?'

'The Cajun Bar-B-Que?'

'Of course, he invented them all...' she'd say then gaze off dreamily.

Yeah, that was how it would work. She could leave that teller job and come work for Otto. Why not? She'd get her own apron— one featuring the pig roasting in the sun and showing his butt crack.

'He invented this logo, too,' she could brag.

He continued to dream. Each night, once they got home, she could cook dinner after she fixed the pan of Epsom salts for his feet. They could eat in front of the television and check out the weather for the next day. He could load up the truck twice as fast in the morning because she could help carry the sacks of batter. She would learn the business from the ground up and free him up to invent more bacon-on-a-stick flavors.

He had sort of been mulling over the idea of a drink for the past year. Not exactly pork juice, but something that went with the whole theme. Sauerkraut juice might be a thought. Maybe experiment a while. A mint jelly shake or a gravy chaser had been rattling around in the back of his mind. She could begin doing some of the more mundane chores that were taking time away from Otto's creative endeavors.

He was waiting in her line again and thought he caught the hint of a little smile directed across the crowded lobby. He touched the .45 wedged in his belt beneath the sweat-soaked Vikings jersey. He looked around the bank lobby just to make sure it was safe for her. There's a new sheriff in town, folks. Otto O'Malley's the name, and I'm here to see that this pretty little girl stays nice and safe.

"Next," another teller called to him.

He blinked his eyes and wiggled his zinc-white nose as he came back to reality. He shook his head. "No," he said and pointed to Cindy. "She wants to talk with me."

Cindy looked up for a moment and thought, *What?*

He gave her a meaningful nod and subtly patted his jersey where the .45 was tucked, letting her know it was okay. She was safe. Sheriff Otto O'Malley was on duty.

Oh God, Cindy thought and slid the Lysol can closer to the window.

Otto opened his briefcase and took out two grease-stained, brown paper bags filled with cash. He crammed the bags into the cash well and pushed until they popped up onto the counter in front of Cindy. The bags left a greasy trail across the Formica counter. Cindy wrinkled her nose as the scent of rancid bacon began to fill the enclosed teller area.

"So, how's it going?" Otto said.

"Just fine, thank you," Cindy replied. She grabbed the bags as quickly as possible, thinking, The sooner I'm finished, the sooner he'll leave. The air in the teller area suddenly seemed to grow heavier.

"Yeah, that's right. I did it all. First year there was just the regular flavor," Otto began to ramble.

"Twenty, forty…"

"Then came the maple flavor. Later on, I developed the hickory. Folks raved about it. Said they'd never had so many choices. Of course, this year, there's my new Cajun Bar-B-Que. You guessed it. I invented them all, came right from here." He tapped the side of his head.

"Three thousand, twenty, forty, sixty…"

"Working on the drink thing just now, letting it percolate through. I'm thinking something unique. Say, I, ahh, caught you yesterday morning," he said, giving a little nod.

"Yesterday?" She wasn't tracking this conversation and didn't think she heard correctly. After all, yesterday was Sunday.

Here it was, he thought, moving in for the kill— their first moment. They would laugh about this years from now while she fixed him dinner or mixed his Epsom salts or, hell, even folded his laundry. He could feel the magic about to explode.

"Yeah, yesterday. Sunday morning. You get up early for a girl. Or maybe you were just coming home," he winked and grinned.

"Oh, my, God!" Cindy half-screamed. She was just loud enough, so the tellers on either side of her looked to see if everything was alright. They looked over just as the color drained from her face, and Cindy brought her hand to her mouth in absolute horror.

"Yeah." Finally, Otto had her full attention. He moved right up next to the glass, fogging it with his breath.

Cindy was in shock, not quite believing she heard him correctly. She leaned forward and grasped the counter for support.

"I was thinking," he half-whispered. He was so close to the glass that the white zinc oxide on his nose was leaving a smear as he moved his head slowly down toward the cash well. "Maybe, we should get together, you and me—just the two of us. You know? Sort of let nature take its course. What'd you think?"

She slid his deposit receipt into the greasy cash well, too stunned to reply. Thinking, *This couldn't be happening to me. It just could not be happening.*

Otto stood up straight, grabbed his receipt, and reached into his briefcase. He pulled out a pile of what looked like dog droppings on a grease saturated paper plate and crammed the whole mess through her cash well.

"Brought ya a little sample of all my flavors. Just a little thank you. Maybe a taste of things to come," he said and grinned idiotically. He picked up three pieces that had fallen off the plate and pushed them through to her, leaving another greasy trail. A half-inch crust of greasy batter had built up along the edge of the protective glass.

"Oh, thank you." Cindy shuddered and felt like she was about to cry.

He blushed even redder than his sunburn. "Don't you worry. I'll be back," he said. He suddenly snapped to attention and gave her his two-fingered salute.

"Hey, Cin, you okay? You don't look so good, honey," the teller at the next window said.

"Oh. My. God. Dog poop on a stick," Cindy said, carefully carrying the plate to the trash. She took a minute or two to calm herself, working to catch her breath and stop the pounding in her head before she returned to her window. She saw the streak of zinc oxide from Otto's nose smeared down the length of her window, and she wanted to crawl down on the floor and cry.

'Well, that seemed to go pretty well,' Otto thought, driving back to the fair. He imagined her bragging to all her girlfriends, "My new boyfriend, Otto, he invented these. You can go to his stands. He's got more than one. Make sure you mention my name."

He tried to figure her out. Was she a Maple, Hickory, or Cajun gal? The timing could not have been better. By the end of the week, he was going to have a lot of laundry.

Thirty-Six

As Osborne answered the phone, a reptilian sneer crept across his face. He wore a heavily starched pale pink shirt, a pink and blue striped tie, plaid boxer shorts, and tan knee-high stockings.

"Excellent, excellent, have her highness wait right there. Milton will be down to fetch her momentarily," he said, snapping his fingers to get Milton's attention.

"Milton, you oaf. Quit whining about that stupid hand. Go downstairs and fetch this Sassie. She's already crawling back to grovel at my feet for her petty little job. I've half a mind to slap the little vixen. If things were just slightly different, I'd throw that tie-dyed wench out in the street. Unfortunately, I have got to get the dancers back on stage. I'm losing money hand over fist with the Phone Farm dancing down there. Not to mention my declining 900 number revenues." He tossed a stack of disheartening financial reports onto his desk.

"I'll have to bide my time with Sassie, but her days are numbered. Milton, are you even listening? Get up. Come on. Let's not keep her waiting." With that, Osborne strode to the wardrobe and retrieved his trousers.

"Damn hand's killing me. Between that bitch's bite and that baseball bat yesterday. I think I should get it checked out." Milton held out his swollen hand for Osborne's inspection. There was a twinge of greenish-brown beginning to develop around the edges of the purple bite wound. The throbbing had gone from intermittent to nonstop.

"Your hand!" Osborne half-shouted. He buttoned the waist of his trousers, zipped his fly, and turned toward the massive beveled mirror on the wardrobe door. "You're worried about your hand when I'm about to be locked in negotiations with the very witch who's tried to ruin me and all because a simple beer bottle was surreptitiously placed in her shapely posterior. Enough! I simply won't have it. Now, get down there before this she-devil has a change of heart."

"I'm just thinkin' that—"

"Milton, really? Please, stop and listen to yourself. Thinking? You? Quickly. Now move along. That's a good man. Left, right. Left, right." Osborne adjusted his belt in the mirror as he continued counting cadence. He donned his blazer and tightened his tie in anticipation of Sassie crawling in and begging for her job back.

Minutes later, Sassie flew into his office.

"So, you've returned to the scene of your crime, Sassie," Osborne said, seated at his desk.

Her hair, a rainbow vignette going from white blonde at the crown to electric blue, cascaded down to her shoulders. He jutted his chin from behind his desk, trying to look intimidating while at the same time keeping a safe distance from the little tramp. God only knew what germs she carried. He moved his bottle of disinfectant to within easy reach.

"We can start by you calling me Ms. Sassie. For your information, this is my lawyer," she said and stepped aside as a short round little creature in a wrinkled, baggy suit followed her into the office.

The lawyer, a weasel looking little bald man, wore a look of complete exhaustion as he shuffled hesitantly into the office. He carried a worn leather satchel under his left arm. He needed a shave and probably a good night's sleep. Clearly, she'd paid in advance.

"My card," he mumbled in a voice that suggested sinus blockage. He laid his card on Osborne's desk with a trembling hand. He sniffled, pulled a crumpled handkerchief from his pocket, and wiped his nose.

Osborne quickly reached for his bottle of disinfectant and sprayed the plague-carrying card. He silently cursed Serpentina for not being on duty to deal with this situation. He picked up a pencil from his desk and used the eraser end to drag the card slowly toward him.

"Prescott Spaulding, the second," he read, glancing up first at Spaulding before looking over at Sassie for a moment. He settled his withering gaze on Spaulding.

"At your service, sir," Spaulding groaned.

"Would second be the same as junior?"

"I prefer the term second," Spaulding said, a slight tremble in his voice.

"I prefer not to waste my time. What is it that you want?"

"We only want what's fair here, Mr. Osborne. We want you to provide some heat on that stage down there. When the girls go home, it takes them two hours just to thaw out. No more bottles allowed on the edge of the stage, and we want you to sell beer in smaller bottles. Umm, just in case."

"Yes, to the smaller bottles. I can increase my profit there. No, to restricting bottles on the stage. That's despite the somewhat unappealing image your particular situation presented," Osborn said to Sassie. "We have a large clientele who drink heavily while being enraptured with your entertainment. No, to your request for heat. It will cost me money, and frankly, the cold temperature adds to everyone's overall performance." He cast an understanding eye in Prescott Spaulding's direction, looking for agreement.

"Umm, okay?" Spaulding looked hopefully at Sassie.

She sighed and shook her head. "You might just as well go home 'cause you ain't doing nothing here, and you ain't gettin' nothing else for doing it."

Spaulding seemed to deflate, and he suddenly looked even more rumpled, if that was possible.

"And, Osborne," Sassie said, "I'll take this to the ladies. But I gotta feeling they're gonna give you a big fat no. That's N, O. Looks to me like we just might have to come up with something else to get your attention." She swung her purse over her shoulder, turned, and walked out.

Spaulding watched her admiringly for three or four paces. "Ah, nice to meet you, sirs," he said, nodding to Osborne and Milton before running to catch up.

"Burn this!" Osborne directed Milton, using the pencil eraser to slide the offending business card across his desk. He furiously misted his desk and surrounding area with disinfectant spray.

Thirty-Seven

"For goodness sake, Anthony, what were you thinking? Your uncle called me at seven o'clock this morning. All the way from St. Petersburg, Florida." Beau's mother was standing at the ironing board, shaking her head and saying the exact same thing she'd said during every one of her phone calls throughout the day.

"Honest to God, Anthony, I'm getting tired of repeating myself."

He was just as tired of hearing it. He wished she would hurry up and finish ironing his jeans so he could get the hell out of there. Christ, you'd think the way she was going on that it had been his ass hanging out on national television instead of Dickie's.

"I don't know. I'm going to have to move somewhere. Lord knows if I can even find someone to buy this house after what's happened."

"Mom, Jesus Christ, it—"

"Now, you just listen, mister. I will not have that sort of language in my house, Anthony. Maybe that's just who you should begin paying a little more attention to. Your Lord and Savior, Jesus Christ. Instead of these, these bums you seem to want to cavort around town with. I've told you before, what you need in your life is a nice girl. Start to think of a family. That's— what's that sound? That horrible noise?"

"It's my phone, Mom. I'd better take this. Excuse me. It's probably work," he said.

"How do you get anything accomplished, Anthony, with all these interruptions you have in your life? Now, don't you go anywhere. I'm not finished."

"Tony?"

"Speaking."

"It's Cindy," she said, waiting a moment.

"Hi, Cindy, how's it going?"

His Mother's ears perked up as she continued to iron his jeans.

"Oh God, it's been one of those days. I never thought it would end. Did you ever have a day like that? It just keeps getting worse," she said.

"Yeah, I think I can identify with that," he said, glancing at his mother.

Cindy waited a long moment for him to say something else before finally forging ahead. "Look, Tony, I just wanted to apologize, again, that's all, for the other night. I'm really sorry. Anyway, I just hope you're doing okay, and I guess I'm interrupting something." She thought, *'He's probably on a date with some woman who won't throw up.'*

"Oh, no. I'm just at my Mom's. Can I call you later when I'm free to talk?"

"I'd really like that," she said and ended the call.

"Who was that, Anthony? Anyone I know? What can't you say in front of your own mother?" She continued to iron the same area for the sixth or seventh time.

"You don't know her."

"My God, what has been my crime in life? Well, I can only hope she's the nice girl I've been praying for all this time."

"Yeah, sure. Maybe, Mom." He took the folded jeans from his mother and placed them on top of his shirts and the Tupperware container of homemade cookies.

"Be a good boy. I'm praying for you, Anthony, and I'm praying for a nice girl," she called out the door after him.

He nodded, waved, quickly jumped into his car, and sped away. Cindy, he thought. *Maybe I can still end this completely dreadful day on an upbeat note.*

Thirty-Eight

T.J. checked his watch before he placed his book, *The Survivalist's Field Manual,* face down on the coffee table. He had been trying to read and steal furtive glances at Miss Suzie Q for the past two hours. Eventually, his glances had turned to stares. It was a little after nine forty-five, and he always drove past the OK Corral at this time to check the place out before returning home and climbing into bed.

"I'm going down to the Corral, Suzie," he said and bent down to kiss her on the forehead.

"Be careful, baby," she called vacantly, not glancing up from her reality show. They were in the process of cleaning a woman's teeth right before giving her a complete makeover, including a tummy tuck.

Damn mindless shows the woman watches, he thought. He pulled into the empty OK Corral parking lot. He enjoyed this time. It gave him a chance to get the

GTO out, go for a short ride, listen to the engine hum, and not worry about other fools on the road. The car boasted twenty-two coats of lacquer shimmering over the diamond blue finish. It was his pride and joy, next to Suzie Q, that is, a four-speed, positraction GTO.

He circled the building twice, just like he did every night, and drove home.

Thirty-Nine

Beau had stopped in at work. It was slow, even for a Monday night. He hadn't set two feet in the door before Tommy announced his entry, "Live from the Vikings Game. I give you… Beau!"

For once, he was glad there were only four or five people in the place. He quickly made a beeline for his office, turned off his computer, and ducked out the back door to go home. He had tried calling Cindy twice. Both times, his calls were dumped into her voicemail.

Now, he was camped in front of the History Channel. The Marines had just begun landing on Tarawa when his phone rang. "Hello," he answered, half-distracted, as he watched black-and-white footage of Marines working a flamethrower in the jungle.

"Hi, Tony?"

"Oh, hi, Cindy."

"Sorry, I missed your call. I was on the phone with Karen. She said she saw you."

"Really, where?" he asked absently. He was watching the Marines roasting a section of the jungle while he naively stepped into his own personal ambush.

"Well, I guess you're really famous. I had no idea, you…"

He bolted upright, tuned out the Marines, and thought, *'That damn Dickie! And began to dream of a number of appropriate punishments.'*

"… so you were right about that, I guess. You know, I actually feel better telling you this. I mean, it's like an incredible weight off my shoulders."

Tuning back in, he had absolutely no idea what she was talking about. Apparently, he had managed to do something right, hard as it was to believe.

"So, enough about me and my dirty little secret. You sounded like you were having a bad day when we talked earlier," she giggled.

"Sounded like you were taking a bit of a pounding, too."

"Oh God, with the fair going on, we're just jammed. Then, I get this gross little man who brings these things on a stick that look like dog poop soaked in grease. Oh, it was just disgusting. He smeared his nose all over the glass and tells me he saw me leaving your place Sunday morning. Gee, I guess that was just yesterday, but it seems weeks ago."

"I'd give anything to be weeks away from Sunday," Beau replied.

Cindy gave a nervous laugh but didn't go any further with that particular line of discussion. She was afraid he might be referring to her unforgettable performance.

"Look, I sort of feel like I still owe you a dinner," he said.

"Oh, no, no, you shouldn't feel that way. I owe you a dinner and— and more."

Beau filed away the 'and more' comment.

"Well, what I was going to suggest was that we meet somewhere, another restaurant. You know, someplace where I'm not jumping up and down putting out fires— not eating in my office. And we just have dinner. That way, if you don't like the conversation or the company, you can just leave."

"Oh, I wouldn't do that. Leave, I mean. I promise. I think I owe you for being so nice, and the more I get to know you, the more I enjoy your company," she said.

The Marines were in a night defensive position, and all hell was about to break loose, but her last comment, which he selectively heard as "I owe you more, I promise," jerked him back to the present.

"You know Vesco Vino down on Selby Avenue. They've got an outside patio area and great food. I could make a reservation tomorrow night for eight if that's okay."

"That would be wonderful, and I promise not to throw up in their bathroom. If you promise not to moon anyone," she laughed.

He cringed, and once again thought, *That damn Dickie!*

"Believe me, I promise."

"Great. Tomorrow night at eight, see you there," she said.

Interesting, he thought and panicked when it struck him. He was supposed to rob the bank. Not date one of the tellers.

Forty

Otto woke at his usual five in the morning. The weather station forecast was cloudless and hot, with humidity hanging right around the beastly range. He scratched his face in the mirror before stepping into the shower. He noticed he'd forgotten to remove the zinc oxide from his nose when he'd come home just six hours earlier.

He looked around the tub as he showered and thought of that bank teller. This place could use a bit of a woman's touch. She could clean the tub, the wall tiles, get the floors looking nice, dust, scrub, and vacuum. No telling how much a hard-working woman could transform this place after cleaning for a few days.

Just before six, he found himself waiting at the same light across the street from DiMento's bar and restaurant. There was no sign of her this morning. He continued to think of her while he loaded his truck and how nice it would be to have someone help him with the sacks of batter.

By ten o'clock, he had gotten the first load of ice delivered to his stands. He was walking to his truck with his deposits stuffed securely in his briefcase and wearing a Twins baseball hat. He had pinned a white handkerchief onto the back of his hat to shield his neck from any more sunburn. His face was a different matter. He'd slathered his skin with level fifty sunscreen and added a thick layer of zinc oxide on his nose and cheeks and around his lips for additional protection.

He literally glistened as he walked in camouflage cutoffs and a bright orange T-shirt touting the benefits of Gatorade. He waited in her line at the bank, nodding at the not so subtle looks he was getting from people around him.

"What's that smell?" a little boy asked his friend. They were standing with their mother in the line directly next to Otto.

"You farted," exclaimed the friend.

"No, I didn't. You farted."

"Be quiet, both of you." The mother yanked her son's arm and glanced nervously in Otto's direction.

"But he farted," her son protested.

"Another word, and we're leaving. Do you two hear me?"

"But he farted. Jeremy farted, and I can still smell it." The little boy giggled.

"It's you that smells," Jeremy giggled back.

"All right, come on, both of you. If we can't behave, we won't stay. Come on. I'm so sorry. You know kids," she said to Otto, then quickly herded the little boys out the door.

Otto hadn't really noticed that no one was lining up directly behind him. He had been busily working out how this first conversation of the day would go with his new-found love.

Cindy attempted to take her time with the two customers ahead of him. But there was only so much she could do to move slowly, and none of it seemed to be working. Eventually, he stood before her, looking like some scary clown from one of those frightening serial killer movies. He seemed to leer at her from behind the zinc oxide smeared over his face, and she was genuinely afraid to look him in the eye.

He placed his briefcase on the counter and snapped it open.

Oh, God. If he hauls out more of that dog poop on a stick, I'm going to scream, thought Cindy.

Otto pushed two large, grease-stained, brown paper bags stuffed with currency through the cash well. He slid his hand beneath the glass and into the teller area. He kept it there atop the bags, wiggling his pink fingers, so she knew it was all right to touch him.

She looked at the grease-stained paper bags, greasy pink fingers wiggling on top of the bags, and she moved the Lysol can a little closer.

He kept his hands under the glass as the moment grew painfully long. He reluctantly pulled them back. *God*, he thought. *She is really shy.*

Cindy snatched the bags in a motion so quick it was virtually unseen and began counting furiously. "Twenty, forty, sixty, eighty, one, twenty, forty…" Concentrating for all she was worth. She worked furiously to get this pink little man with the clown face and his sweat-encrusted T-shirt away from her window as quickly as possible.

"How'd you like that Cajun Bar-B-Que style? It's my newest," he asked.

"Mmm-mmm," nodded Cindy. "Twenty, forty, sixty…" She could feel an army of germs jumping off the currency and running up her arms. She planned to Lysol her body when this ordeal was all over. Maybe spend an hour or two in a scalding shower and burn her clothes.

He dropped his hand to his waist and raised his right eyebrow. He was ready to catch her glance, give the little lady a slight nod. Let her know she was safe while Sheriff Otto was in town, packing his trusty .45. He leaned his left arm on the counter, kept the eyebrow raised, waited for her to look up so he could give her the nod. Eventually, his eyebrow began to ache, and his cheek began to twitch. He cleared his throat and faced her full front.

"Thank you," she said, slipping his deposit receipt in the cash well before quickly withdrawing her hand in the direction of the Lysol can. She forced herself to look

at him, swallowed hard, and mumbled, "Is, is there anything else?" She silently prayed he would just go away,
taking the stench of rancid bacon and sweat with him.

"Which one was your favorite?" he asked.

"What?"

"Your favorite? Which one did you like the most?
You know, yesterday. All the treats I dropped off for you.
Did you take 'em home? Almost like taking a part of me
home with you. Don't you think?"

Cindy had thrown the entire bunch immediately into
the trash, and she replied meekly, "I liked them all about
the same." Meaning she wouldn't touch any of them if
her life depended on it.

Otto nodded knowingly, closed his briefcase, then
snapped to attention and tossed her his two-fingered salute before he strutted away.

As the next customer stepped forward, he wrinkled
his nose and said, "Hey, what's that smell out here? It's
like rotten eggs or something a lot worse."

Forty-One

"Shit! Will you look at that?" Lucerne said as another person entered the liquor store, and he sped off around the corner.

"Damn it. I'm telling ya. We go round this block much more, I'm gonna get dizzy," Mendel growled.

"Maybe just go in there and get it over with," Lucerne suggested.

"Now, there's just one hell of an idea. Me and Elvis going in there armed with a damn note. You got the note, Elvis?" Mendel looked over his shoulder at Elvis stretched out on the backseat.

Elvis licked a pencil tip and focused his good eye while he wrote on the back of an envelope. "Gettin' her done right now."

"What's it say?" asked Lucerne.

"Sez 'No funny stuff, just the money, and nobody gets hurt, please.' I figure short and sweet's all we're gonna need here."

"All right, I'm tired of dickin' around here. Let's just get it done," hissed Mendel. He jumped out of the car as Lucerne pulled back into the parking lot. Elvis had to scramble out of the backseat to catch up.

Once inside, they nodded politely at the kid behind the cash register and walked down a couple of aisles, trying to get the lay of the place. They grabbed a bottle of root beer flavored schnapps and a bottle of Wild Turkey. They lingered in the back aisle for a few minutes. Once the only other customer exited the store, they ran to the front counter.

"This all for you guys?" the kid asked, not sounding the least bit surprised at their combination.

"Just one more thing," Mendel said. He turned and nodded at Elvis.

Elvis began slapping the pockets of his jeans, desperately searching for his recently composed note. "Think I might have dropped it outside," he said to Mendel.

A nervous few seconds passed while Mendel stared at Elvis and said, "You are one dumb son of a bitch." He suddenly reeled back and hit the kid behind the counter squarely between the eyes, dropping him to the floor. Mendel reached over the counter and began pushing buttons on the register until the cash drawer popped open.

"Shit on a stick! Will ya look at this here? Damn, hardly even worth our time," he groaned and quickly stuffed the meager holdings in his hand.

"Grab them damn bottles and come on," he said to Elvis.

"How'd she go, boys?" Lucerne asked as he quickly pulled out of the parking lot and took a right at the corner.

"Just one little mix-up. Shit-for-brains here forgot his damn note!" Mendel glared into the backseat.

"What?" Lucerne half-laughed.

"Here it is. I found her right down here on the floor," Elvis said, holding up the envelope.

"Lot a good that does us now," Mendel said and turned back around to count their cash. "Can you believe this? Thirty-seven lousy bucks! How in the hell do they expect us to get anywhere's on this kinda dough?"

Forty-Two

At least the teasing had died down, and Beau enjoyed a comparatively normal day. Of course, Patti had given him a framed copy of yesterday's front-page newspaper photo. He was looking at it just now and shaking his head. He slid the frame into a desk drawer and pushed away from his desk to go home for a shower before his dinner date with Cindy. Still no word from Dickie, and that was just fine. As if on cue, the phone rang.

"Hey, Beau," Weiner said.

"Wiener, how've you been? I was gonna call you. But yesterday was so bad I never got around to it. I don't know if you spoke with Victor or Andrew, but they were in deep shit, too. That damn, Dickie."

"Yeah, I know. Isn't it great?"

"You're kidding me? Great?"

"No, I'm not kidding. Beau, I was signing autographs down at the job site yesterday. A couple of guys delivering pipe had me autograph the front page of the paper right under our picture. They think it's gonna be worth some dough. Hey, this Thursday, we're still on for cards, right? We could all sign a bunch of 'em, newspapers, I mean. I picked up fifty copies and, well, anyway, we could autograph these things and probably make some money."

"Are you nuts? I'm trying to get this thing as far behind me as possible. My mom told me she was gonna have to leave town, she was so embarrassed. That Chrissie at the coffee shop—"

"The hot blonde?"

"Right. She says she saw us and then announces it to the whole place. From there, the rest of the day just sort of went into the toilet," he said, remembering his baseball bat assault on Osborne's thug, Milton.

"Man, sorry to hear that. It's been great for me. I got a couple of dates out of the deal. A guy bought me lunch yesterday. I got a couple of beers from some guys last night. I kinda like this whole fame deal."

"Fame? You were sitting next to a fat guy who went out of control and mooned all fifty states. How in the hell does that make you famous? Or get you dates?"

"Never look a gift horse in the mouth, man."

"Are you telling me there are girls out there who want to date you just because some idiot you know has a gigantic fat ass? Gee, I can't wait to meet these women."

"Well, there might have been a little bit of embellishment on my part. You know chicks. I just suggested there might be the possibility of some sort of screen-test deal, maybe an international movie contract, that sort of thing."

"Screen-test. What the hell for?"

"You kidding? You don't watch any of those reality shows? Idiots like us are always getting these acting and singing contracts. They're making a mint, man. You think I'm not gonna ride this lucky break for all it's worth?"

"Lucky break?"

"Whatever. Listen, you hear anything from the big man? I tried leaving a message at his office, on his cell, and at home but couldn't get through anywhere. I think I might have a date lined up for him."

"No, I haven't heard from him. A date? Please, tell me you're kidding."

"Maybe he's just booked up with all sorts of offers. You know Hollywood, Beau. Man, some guys have all the luck. That damned Dickie."

"Yeah, I've said something like 'damned Dickie' a couple of thousand times just in the last twenty-four hours."

"Well, if you talk to him, have him give me a call. I'm not kidding. This chick really wants to meet him."

"What is she, nuts?"

"Yeah, among other things."

Forty-Three

Beau arrived at Vesco Vino early. Cindy walked onto the patio area just a few minutes later, surprised to see him already there.

"Hey, Tony. Wow. I thought I was early." She leaned across the table and gave him a kiss. She lingered a second or two longer than just a casual kiss.

He lifted a bottle of chilled white wine toward a glass. "Can I pour you a glass?"

"Oh, okay, but only one tonight. So," she said once he had finished pouring, "here's to hoping your day went better than yesterday."

"It did. A lot better. I just can't wait to get another day or two away from Sunday and that damn Vikings game."

"Yeah, I kinda know that feeling." She put her glass down and gave him a serious look. "Tony, I really want to tell you how awful I feel about my behavior Saturday night. It was inexcusable. You don't need to spend your Saturday night babysitting some loser who had too much to drink and—"

He cut her off by shaking his head and taking her hand. It was actually the first time he had really touched her except for a hello or good-bye kiss. Well, and pulling her up out of the chair in his office.

"Look, Cindy. I'd prefer not talking about it, okay? It happened. Just forget it, and let's start over. But I will tell you that I have a hellish day tomorrow. And this is the first and only bottle of wine we are going to have to-night."

"Sounds good to me."

He moved toward her, pulled her hands closer to him, and kissed her on the lips.

"Wow," she said, only half to herself before she pulled away.

They talked on about their day. She regaled him with tales of a weirdo customer making different appearances throughout the day with zinc oxide smeared across his face. She described his hat with a handkerchief attached to the back. Rolled her eyes as she mentioned the crusty orange T-shirt. Of course, she topped it all off with the rancid bacon odor offending everyone within range.

He told her about Wiener's phone call. He neglected to mention the Saab La Tondra that Celeste picked up. His getaway car. He didn't mention the gun he planned to get tomorrow so he could rob her bank.

"Do you take breaks during your day?" he asked, hoping she might have a schedule so he could plan accordingly and avoid her.

"Supposedly, I get a morning and afternoon break, but we've been so busy, I sometimes forget to take them. When I look up, you know, there's just forty-five minutes left, and I figure why even bother?"

The waitress came and took their order. She returned with a basket of bread, olive oil, and balsamic and set them on the table.

"You look really familiar. Are you someone famous?" she asked Beau.

"No, I don't think so," he replied, not picking up on the potential danger.

"Gee, I'm sorry. It's just that I think I've seen you before. Are you with one of the local TV stations?"

"No," he insisted.

"I bet you get that all the time," Cindy said teasingly.

"Only since Sunday."

"You're kidding. You think that's where she saw you?"

"Not just think, unfortunately, I'm certain. That damned Dickie. We'd all like to strangle him. Talk about going off the deep end."

Forty-Four

T.J. was attempting to finish *The Survivalist's Field Manual*. He was sloughing his way through the section on proper field sanitation, having just finished the section dealing with sucking chest wounds.

For her part, Miss Suzie Q was curled up in her favorite corner of the couch. She clutched a pillow and appeared deeply involved in a reality show where families changed mothers. The new mom would come in, get the bratty kids back in line, make them eat food they didn't like, and get the dump cleaned up.

"Well," T.J. said, looking up from the chart graphing latrine depth versus usage ratio. He stretched back in his recliner for a long moment before throwing the lever forward and catapulting out of the thing.

"T.J. honey, I swear you are gonna launch yourself right into that damn aquarium someday," she cautioned and refocused on the forty-two-inch screen.

She was watching a cute suburban daddy with beginning love handles. All the while thinking, *'They were nothing she couldn't burn off.'* He looked to be a pretty sizable guy, which appealed to her. More importantly, he was bringing the new mom coffee in bed. Yeah, this woman was doing more than just washing dishes.

"Gonna just run down to the Corral and check on things," T.J. said. He leaned forward to give her a kiss on the forehead.

"Mmm-hmmm." She moved her head slightly so she didn't miss any of the show. The daddy was cooking breakfast. He'd picked flowers from the garden and put them in a vase on the kitchen table. The little monsters, there were three, were nowhere to be seen, and that had Suzie Q convinced that this was really just a reality show about swapping.

"Careful, baby," she called.

T.J. nodded, grabbed his Stetson, adjusted his gun belt, and strode out the door.

Just three miles away, Elvis was more worried about screwing up his part of the caper than being frightened. Especially after losing the note at the liquor store that afternoon. He took a deep breath and concentrated on getting the job done. He was standing in the far back corner of a grocery store parking lot licking root beer flavored schnapps off his lips and lurking around the dumpsters where Lucerne and Mendel had dropped him off.

He held the brick he brought with him in both hands as he calmly walked across the parking lot toward the bank. Any window would work. Elvis figured it would be best if he smashed one of the windows at the rear of the building.

He glanced around for cameras but didn't see any, except for the three focused on the drive-up lanes. He checked his watch and waited until the second hand swept up to twelve. He gave another quick glance around, then tossed the brick and ran like hell. His ears were tuned for breaking glass. Unfortunately, all he heard was a loud thunk as the brick bounced off the window and into the shrubbery.

With his one good eye, it took him three agonizing minutes to find the brick in the dark. Eventually, he spotted the thing wedged in the middle of a large thorny bush that scraped and scratched at his arms. He finally wrestled the brick out from underneath the thick spiky branches. He looked around again for any pain in the ass passersby, cocked his arm, and rifled the brick at the same window, hitting it at exactly the same spot and meeting with exactly the same result. He heard another dead thunk as the brick bounced back into the bushes.

Elvis began to panic. He should have been back at the dumpsters by now, safely hiding in the shadows. He scrambled into the thorny patch again. His ankles and shins were getting scratched and torn by the spiky branches. His hand was worn raw and bleeding in a number of places. Once he found the brick, he stepped over to the building. Holding the brick in his right hand, he began to hammer on the large tempered glass window. On his third try, a web pattern rippled across the center of the window, crackling like river ice close to the shore. The fourth effort left a fragile concave impression. Finally, his fifth swing exploded the window, sending cubes of tempered glass showering over him.

An alarm went off, not a ringing bell alarm but an electronic whoop, whoop, whoop that was deafening. Elvis dropped the brick through the shattered window, stumbled back into the bushes, and fell. He somehow managed to crawl out of the bushes. But in the process of crawling out, he tore both knees on his only pair of jeans. Along with the deafening alarm whooping into the night, there was an explosion of lights around the building and across the parking lot, illuminating the half-acre site as if it were high noon.

Elvis had no option but to run and run fast.

Forty-Five

Meanwhile, Lucerne and Mendel had pulled into the empty OK Corral parking lot with the lights off on the car. Lucerne drove to a dark corner and parked out of sight beneath an overhanging tree. Mendel sat in the front passenger seat staring at the illuminated dial on his watch as the second hand swept to twelve. Elvis would be smashing the window now. According to their plan, they would wait an additional minute, allowing the police time to react to the bank alarm.

They sat there in the front seat of the Fleetwood, silently waiting in the dark, hearts pounding. Lucerne reminded himself to breathe as he stared at the long wooden handle on the eight-pound maul resting between them.

"Get ready." Mendel paused dramatically for a few beats as he watched the second hand sweep up toward twelve. "Okay, now!" he shouted, forgetting for the moment that Elvis had never, ever in his life, accomplished anything in a timely manner. "Come on, now, damn it!" Mendel yelled, looking over at Lucerne.

The engine cranked as Lucerne, in the excitement of the moment, pushed the accelerator hard against the floor, almost flooding the big engine. Suddenly, the car exploded to life, emitting a noxious blue cloud. The bald tires squealed, and the muffler rattled against the chassis as the Fleetwood's 260 horse powered V-8 rocketed across the parking lot before screeching to a stop six feet from the front door. A dark blue cloud of fumes wafted up against the front of the building and hung there in the heavy night air. As was his practice, Mendel sailed out the door before the car had completely stopped. The momentum caused him to stumble and slide across the parking lot pavement, tearing knees, elbows, and the palms of his outstretched hands.

"Leave the doors open. Leave the doors—" Mendel shouted as he went down.

"What?" Lucerne called out. Mendel's loud creaking door made it impossible to hear.

"Go, damn it, go!" shouted Mendel from the pavement as he stumbled to get to his feet.

Lucerne carried the eight-pound maul across his chest and charged through the noxious cloud of exhaust to where he thought the door might be. He swung the maul in a great arc, crashing through the glass. The force of the blow struck the thick steel hand bar on the inside of the door with the wooden shaft. The eight-pound maul had just enough torque from his swing to snap the ancient wooden shaft, sailing the weighted head into the darkness of the OK Corral.

It was a night for alarms, and this one was meant to sound like the dive warning on a submarine. A-ooo-a! A-ooo-a! A-ooo-a! It had been T.J.'s nod to the 'Silent Service.' Submariners.

Dim emergency lights flashed inside the store. The upper portion of the glass had shattered, but the lower three feet looked like a series of jagged glass fingers clawing up toward the center.

"Knock it out! Knock that shit outta there!" screamed Mendel. He was limping back and forth in an attempt to get his legs functioning again. As he screamed, he pointed wildly at the damaged door.

Lucerne began to swing the broken wooden shaft into the glass. Three, four, five swings to clear the right side of the door.

"Come on. Hurry up, man! You're taking too damn long," Mendel screamed.

"Damn it, will you just shut the hell up!" Lucerne yelled. He turned to face Mendel, bringing his swinging to a complete stop. "Just once, I want you to quit telling me what in the hell to do and let me think for myself. Lord help me, but sometimes I don't think ya got the damn patience to save your soul. Hell, the way I—"

Mendel roughly pushed him aside, cleared most of the glass from the left side of the door with his boot. He reached in and turned the dead-bolt lock, opening the door.

"Now come on, and for God's sake, shut the hell up!"

Lucerne's eyes went wide, and he suddenly froze, covering his ears.

"Come on, you big baby," Mendel screamed. He attempted to grab Lucerne by the shirt. Lucerne wanted none of it, shook himself free, and jumped back toward the car. Unable to wait, Mendel stepped alone into the dimly lit store. He saw the rack from the day before holding the AKs. What he had not seen the day before was the chain draped through each trigger housing and the heavy brass padlock at the end. He yanked viciously at the chain and realized in an instant that they were royally screwed. He struggled to lift the rack only to discover it was bolted to the floor.

"Lucerne, find the damn head from that maul," he screamed out the door where Lucerne stood still wide-eyed, with his mouth hanging open. "Come on, boy, move!"

Lucerne gingerly stepped into the building.

"Come on, damn it. Help me find the head for that maul!" Mendel yelled over the alarm. He was frantically searching around in the dim light, kicking piles of glass shards aside with his boot.

"Got it. There it is!" Lucerne yelled after a long moment. He had spotted the maul head beneath a rack of old

Soviet uniforms. He grabbed it off the floor and handed it to Mendel.

Mendel began to hammer the brass padlock. But the play in the chain provided just enough slack to neutralize his blows. He tightened the chain with his left hand, hammering with his right until the lock eventually sprung. "Pull that damn chain from the end," he shouted just as a shot shattered one of the emergency lights on the wall above his head.

As was his custom, T.J. had been monitoring the police frequency as he drove toward the OK Corral. The female dispatcher contacting squad 112 sounded cool and professional as she dispatched them to the bank to investigate an alarm.

Probably just a mouse, T.J. thought as he rounded the corner. Even with the windows up, the AC on, and all the static from his police scanner, he could hear the distinctive submarine "A-ooo-a" alarm. A moment later, he spotted a blue cloud hanging suspiciously across the front of the OK Corral and the faint image of a vehicle drifting in and out of the cloud.

There was only one way out of the parking lot, and T.J. fishtailed his GTO to seal it off. He was shaking badly and lost his glasses as he tumbled out of the car. By pulling the corners of his eyes back using his index fingers, he could detect a large blurry shadow that he guessed was the actual building and a hazy light that probably was the entryway. He rested the Sig Sauer on the hood of the GTO, pointed in the general direction of the light, and squeezed the trigger.

"What the hell!" Mendel screamed when the light above him exploded. "Jesus, come on. Let's boogie, man!" Just then, the remaining glass in the right side of the doorframe erupted. Something zipped past Mendel and slapped against the cinder-block wall behind him.

"Grab them boxes of ammunition behind the counter and fill this damn thing up," Mendel screamed. He tossed a 30-round banana clip over the counter as Lucerne desperately pulled boxes of ammunition off a shelf.

"You crazy? We ain't got that kinda time!" Lucerne yelled as another round pinged through the metal door frame.

"We ain't getting outta here except we shoot our way out. Unless you got a better idea. In which case, you can just sing out with it anytime," Mendel said.

"Shit!" Lucerne screamed and began shoving rounds into the banana clip. Once he had it loaded, he tossed it back to Mendel.

"All right now, we're gonna get our asses outta here," Mendel said. "You get behind the wheel while I keep 'em pinned down." He didn't wait for an answer but limped straight out the door, firing. Lucerne followed close behind, carrying an AK and an armload of ammunition boxes.

"Get in the damn car," Mendel screamed and let loose with another burst in the general direction of the GTO blocking their escape.

Lucerne tossed his weapon and the ammunition through the open door and slid behind the steering wheel just as a fist-sized hole erupted in the rear window. He threw the Fleetwood in reverse and sped off as the open passenger door swung wildly. He raced around the corner and screeched to a stop at the rear of the building.

"Get back here, you worthless son of a bitch!" Mendel yelled as another round pinged off the building behind him, and he quickly retreated back inside.

Lucerne hit the accelerator and screeched around the building, just as Mendel stepped out from the doorway and let go with a long burst in the direction of the GTO. Lucerne skidded to a stop. A pungent exhaust cloud engulfed the front of the building as Mendel jumped through the open passenger window.

"Go, go, go, damn it!"

Mendel, upside down in the passenger seat, pointed the AK out the window and fired blindly. Lucerne raced back around the corner and screeched to a stop behind the building. He backed up slowly, keeping the building between them and the GTO. He carefully crossed a raised patch of grass and quietly rolled into the parking lot next door.

T.J. crouched behind his GTO with the Sig Sauer balanced on the hood. He blinked frantically as he desperately tried to focus and waited for what seemed an eternity. Suddenly, he heard a rumble and caught a blurry movement out of the corner of his left eye. A large car seemed to jump to life and raced out of the lot and along the road behind him. He squeezed off one round just before he heard the unmistakable eruption of automatic fire.

Mendel hung out the passenger window aiming across the roof of the Fleetwood as they raced down the road. A "phut" sound cut the humid air as it streaked past his head at about the same time he saw a muzzle flash. He pointed his AK in that general direction and sprayed.

T.J. dove to the ground, covering his head with his arms, unaware his bladder had emptied. Rounds zinged through the air, pinging and tearing through twenty-two coats of lacquer and the diamond blue finish of his prized GTO. The side windows exploded almost simultaneously, raining chunks of safety glass all over, and still, the rounds kept flying. The tires exploded, hissing as the car lurched heavily to one side. Rounds stitched their way across the length of the vehicle, shattering both taillights and exploding the rear window.

Then, just as suddenly, it all stopped. T.J. lay still in a warm puddle with his arms covering his head.

Forty-Six

Beau and Cindy had a pleasant enough meal, chatting about everything and nothing. Beau had the distinct impression that whenever he was about to broach a more personal subject with Cindy, the waitress seemed to be hovering. Finally, he told her he'd call if they needed anything. He was busy signing his receipt and had just placed the credit card back in his wallet when she returned with two other staff members in tow.

"Sir, I'm really sorry, but we just know you're someone," she smiled, handing them both an unordered glass of wine.

He reflexively looked the other way, attempting to shield his face. As he did so, she said, "Hey, wait a minute. You're one of those guys. From the football game. Isn't he?"

Her two compatriots looked at her.

"You know. Those guys from the Vikings game. The really fat guy who mooned everyone. You're one of those butt guys. Right?" she said. Disappointed recognition seemed to wash over her two accomplices.

"Sorry, ladies, too late." Beau put the wine glass to his lips and drained most of it. He pulled Cindy's chair out from the table and made a hasty exit.

"My God, I don't believe it. You're one of the famous butt guys from the Vikings game," Cindy laughed. "Nice reputation."

"Infamous is more like it," he groaned.

"Well, I think you're very nice, all the same," she said and kissed him. Her lips lingered for a long moment until a passing car honked, forcing them apart.

"Umm. Thanks," he said.

"The pleasure was all mine. Hey, my car is right over there. So sorry to be a party pooper, but I've got another early day tomorrow. Can I call you? Or even better, you could call me."

"Yeah, I'd like that," he said, walking her to her car. "Umm, sorry you had to leave your glass of wine back there. You know, I don't live too far from here. Just down the street, actually. You want to stop over for a glass of wine? I've got an early day tomorrow, too. You don't have to, you know. No pressure. I just thought if you felt like it maybe—"

"Sure. I'll follow you," she said.

Over the course of the three-block drive, he ran down a mental checklist of everything he'd need to make the night complete. He'd learned long ago to be ready. Clean kitchen, clean glasses, clean bathroom, clean towels, clean sheets, and a clean toothbrush.

Following his car, Cindy was reminding herself this was not a good idea since she had to be at work early in the morning. But, she was good at lying when she had to be. She promised herself she would only stay for one glass.

Beau knew from experience that one of the most difficult items of clothing to take off a woman was her shoes. Removing shoes signaled the possible start of things to come. If she dropped her shoes, they clomped to the floor. The potential noise might inhibit taking that next step. He eliminated the problem by simply slipping out of his shoes at the front door. Cindy did the same. Not giving the matter a second thought.

He quickly poured her a glass of wine to sip during the obligatory house tour. He innocently dimmed the lights in his bedroom before they moved into the bathroom, where she noted the toilet seat was down and the tub was clean.

"Here, look at this. I finally have a place for all the clean towels and washcloths," he said innocently, making sure she was able to see the half-dozen new, unwrapped toothbrushes he had on hand.

"Expecting a lot of company?" she asked, leaning against the door frame.

"More wine?"

"I don't know if I should," she responded.

Yeah, I've heard that before, he thought as he gently took her glass and walked back to the kitchen where Alan Jackson was singing.

"What time do you want to get up? I'll set the alarm," he asked two and a half hours later. He had been giving her a long back rub. He was still fascinated by the lacy tattoo scrolled across the small of her back.

They were naked. Cindy was half asleep, eyes closed, and enjoying the back rub he'd been giving her for the past fifteen minutes. They'd made love for the better part of the preceding hour.

"Five-fifteen," she murmured, not opening her eyes and sinking deeper into sleep.

Ugh, he thought, not losing the rhythm of the back rub.

Forty-Seven

Miss Suzie Q had fallen asleep on the couch. She was dreaming about the various projects she'd wanted done around the house. A plumber, an electrician, and a carpenter had been working at the house all day. They were all tan and very muscular. T.J. was working late and wouldn't be home for hours. The plumber was showing off his work, and he was carrying Miss Suzie Q into the bathroom, which was now large enough to accommodate all four of them.

Somehow, they all ended up in a giant Jacuzzi. The workmen still wore their tool belts. Bubbles were mounded up around Suzie Q, so they were all exposed, but they couldn't see her. They were taking turns filling her champagne glass. Miley Cyrus was playing, and the workmen decided they would stand up and dance.

Unfortunately, she woke up. It was sometime after three in the morning when she sat up wondering, What in the world? T.J. never let her sleep on the couch. She turned off the lights, filled a glass with water, tiptoed upstairs, and stood looking at their undisturbed king-sized bed.

"Dumpling? T.J.? Where are you, sweetheart?"

* * *

"I'd like to go over this one more time," a detective was saying to T.J. at just about the same time.

He was a thin-haired, leathery-looking man with more bags beneath the bags under his eyes. He had stale coffee breath that T.J. found impossible to avoid. They were in a grey, windowless cinder-block room. They sat staring at one another across a dingy grey Formica topped table.

T.J. removed his glasses. He'd found them undamaged on the front seat of the GTO amidst a mountain of shattered windshield. He rubbed his tired, burning eyes and repeated what he had already said a number of times. Only now, he was so exhausted, he groaned as he spoke. "Look, Detective, don't you think you should be out there trying to get these guys? I mean, you saw what they did to my GTO and to the OK Corral."

"Yeah, about the car," the detective checked his notes. "Tell me again, why you were there? Did they have something against your car?"

"Something against— They didn't have anything against the GTO. Who would? It was just there. I drove it there. I parked that way, blocking the exit so they couldn't make their escape. I was there in the GTO because that's what I do every night before I go to bed. I drive down to the Corral and make sure everything is all right. That's why I was there tonight. Just checking on things, and lo and behold, there was a robbery in progress."

"The Corral?"

"My gun shop, the OK Corral."

"So, you didn't think the police could handle it, is that it?"

T.J. rubbed his face in a combination of exasperation and exhaustion. "Apparently not, because no one arrived on the scene until ten minutes after these guys were long gone."

"There was an attempted bank robbery tonight, sir."

"Yeah, I heard it on my scanner. So, I end up in a shoot-out, sprayed down with an AK stolen from my shop. Meanwhile, you're out chasing a mouse running across the bank floor."

"Did you realize, sir, that you were discharging your weapon within city limits?"

T.J. closed his eyes thinking, *Those guys are already across the state line with the AKs.* He made a mental note to remove the "Support Your Local Police" sign from above his cash register.

Forty-Eight

Otto had thrown his sweat-encrusted Gatorade shirt in the trash and hauled the bag outside. He was in his recliner, wearing boxers, sipping a cold beer, clicking the remote until it landed on the weather channel. He set his feet in the Epsom salt bath and felt the stress and strain of the day begin to leave his body.

The same computerized version of a female voice promised more beastly heat for the remainder of the week. He woke one minute before his alarm went off. The sun was barely above the horizon. The glow from the weather channel illuminated the living room, forecasting exactly the same as when he drifted off to sleep, sub-Saharan temperature, subtropical humidity, Minnesota in late August.

He stretched in his recliner, then pushed the lever forward and splashed into the pan of Epsom salts, sending a wave washing across the carpet.

Today he chose a Twins jersey, a pair of pinstripe baseball pants he had cut off just below the knee, and his sweat-stained Twins cap. He pulled up white cotton knee-high socks and slathered on level fifty sunblock for added protection. He laced up his jungle boots and pulled on his Twins cap with the white handkerchief pinned to the back. He looked in the mirror and knew she couldn't help but find him irresistible.

By nine o'clock, he had already delivered the sacks of batter mix and slabs of bacon to his stands. He was almost finished with the first of the day's ice deliveries. He had ignored the crew at the ice company when they elbowed one another snickering.

He hoisted another bag of ice onto his shoulder and carried it to the stand. Josh was there dipping skewered bacon slabs into a pan of maple-flavored batter. The fifty-pound bag of ice was turning Otto's shoulder numb.

"Twins suck," screamed a pack of boys from across the street. They were pointing at Otto. "Hey, Twins suck!" they called before they took off skateboarding down the street, screaming, "Twins suck! Twins suck!"

"Hey, Otto. You sure don't seem to be having much luck in the fashion area this week," Josh said and laughed.

"There a game today?" Otto asked.

"Afternoon game, they're playing out in Los Angeles. Maybe they can pull out of this slump. Winning three out of the last thirteen doesn't really cut it," Josh said.

An afternoon game, thought Otto, perfect. Drop the deposits in the night drop slot until about mid-afternoon, so she doesn't see me. Once the Twins were ahead, he could walk up to her window and give her the famous Otto smile. He'd let her know Sheriff Otto was on duty. She would come around once she saw him, and the rest would be romantic history.

Forty-Nine

It seemed no more than a couple of minutes' sleep before the alarm jarred them awake.

Cindy snuggled against Beau as he gently stroked her back for a bit, both of them still half-asleep. Eventually, she opened her eyes and slowly realized she had to drive home, shower, and change into her work clothes.

By the time she got dressed, he was in his robe, holding a mug of coffee, walking her to the door, and asking for a third time if she wanted a travel mug. She kissed him lightly on the lips and gave a final wave as she climbed into her car.

He waved back and thought, That was certainly stupid. What the hell am I thinking? I'm planning to rob her damn bank. He attempted, unsuccessfully, to go back to sleep. After forty-five minutes, he climbed out of bed and spied Cindy's black thong wedged down at the bottom of his sheets.

It had been his experience that women seemed to mark their territory. They would leave earrings, lipstick, a bracelet, some sort of article behind. Apparently, in Cindy's case, that article was her thong. He carefully folded her thong and placed it in a dresser drawer in the hope she'd return.

An hour later, Beau was ordering his usual latte and French doughnut from Chrissie. He was still thinking of Cindy's thong, absently humming the chorus from Dean Martin's *"Volare."*

"You're in a good mood and up early, or are you just on the way home from last night?" Chrissie half-laughed. She gave a little bounce, which always seemed to get his attention.

Beau smiled, nodded, and made some vague comment about a meat order.

"Hey, you okay? You're looking kinda strange." She snickered and gave him another of her special little bounces.

"Yeah, sorry. What were you saying?"

"Never mind."

He casually paid and left, completely unaware of Chrissie's suddenly cooling attitude.

He was so early this morning that he had to unlock the lounge door to let himself in. So early that he didn't have to contend with Patti smiling sweetly and telling him she didn't want guys like him around her kids. So early that he strode into his office to find it wonderfully empty. No Osborne or Milton to contend with. Life at this hour was good as he sat down at his desk, sipped his latte, and dreamed about Cindy.

Fifty

Cindy was down on her hands and knees, reaching up to grab the last of the night deposit bags from the small overnight vault. There had been so many this morning, they were piled a couple of feet up the slot, and she had to pull them out one at a time, yanking them down and out of the shaft.

"There, finally. I guess that does it," she said. She smiled and slapped her hands together like she was brushing them off. She looked at the stack Carol had piled on the cart. It would take them at least two hours to count and record all the deposits.

"Finally, I guess that does it? When did you get to be so happy about all this?" Carol said.

"What can I tell you? I'm just in a good mood. I had a great night's sleep."

She had racked her brain on the drive home and then on the way to work, wondering what she had done with her thong. She finally decided that Tony must have hidden it. It had been her experience that some guys liked to keep mementos. Cindy had lost earrings, lipsticks, bracelets, and, apparently, in Tony's case, her thong. Hopefully, it would serve as his excuse to ask her back.

"Now, what's wrong with you?" Billy Truesdale asked Trevor two hours later as he swung the last of the cash-filled bags into the rear of the armored car.

Trevor had been making noises all week, getting progressively louder as the weekend loomed closer. Billy had seen it before. Tomorrow, Trevor would be all doubled up, complaining of stomach pains. He would call in sick on Friday and say he was going to the doctor to get checked out. Coincidently, Monday just happened to be Labor Day and a holiday.

The doctor, Trevor's idiot brother-in-law, and a gynecologist, by the way, would prescribe four days of rest for Trevor and probably a muscle relaxant administered in a large beer mug.

The truth was, Trevor and his malpractice brother-in-law would leave town Thursday night and head up north to White Fish Lake. They'd fish for walleye and northern at sunrise and drink beer for breakfast, leaving Billy and his partner, Gary, to fend for themselves, hauling the deposits in the heat and humidity.

"Oh, man, I don't know what the hell is wrong. It's been bugging me since Monday, so it's not food poisoning. Just seems to be getting worse. I wonder if I should get this checked out."

Billy looked to Gary and then Trevor. "Maybe it's just that you're so full of shit, Trevor. You're gonna go fishing this weekend, and you're gonna leave us high and dry, again. Aren't you?"

Trevor suddenly did start to look sick. "No way, man, this time it's for real," he gasped.

"Yeah, sure it is. Well, do what you want, but don't try to con us. It's the busiest week of the year for this run. It's all we do. We're all busting our ass, and you want to go fishing, fine. That's okay, screw your buddies."

"I don't know, man."

Billy ran down a list of replacement helpers in his mind. The company was shorthanded as it was, and his worst fear was they wouldn't send anyone. Instead of getting worked up, he thought he might just sit back, listen to the Twins this afternoon and let whatever happens, happen.

"Ugh, this is bad, man," Trevor groaned.

Fifty-One

"This is exactly what I don't need," Osborne declared, slamming down the window blinds in his office.

Sassie had organized the striking dancers into a picket line. Clad in thong bikinis, they were marching back and forth across the entrance to Cheaters carrying signs— all to the delight of the assembled news crews and a gathering crowd of well-wishers.

"Doesn't anyone care that a businessman in this community is being strong-armed by these, these over-endowed trollops?" He looked out again and suddenly spotted Serpentina in her nurse's uniform carrying a sign.

"You traitorous little tramp. Look, Milton, for God's sake. I'm up here devoid of medical attention, and that ungrateful wench is down there picketing my establish-ment. And from the look of things, that ingrate Sassie has encouraged some of the Phone Farm to join her as well. Dear God!"

For his part, Milton had been feeling feverish and lightheaded. The discoloration from his hand had begun to work its way further up his arm. He had difficulty opening and closing his right hand. His hand and wrist appeared extremely swollen. Fat purple sausages now throbbed where his fingers used to be.

"Time for you to rise to the occasion, Milton. I'm in need of your assistance." Five minutes later, Osborne shouted, "Have you even the foggiest idea what in God's name you're doing?" Osborne wrenched the blood pressure sleeve from Milton's left hand.

Milton's swollen and discolored right arm hung limp and useless, unable to do anything but throb painfully at his side. His hand was beginning to take on a greenish tint, leaking puss as well as beginning to carry a bit of an odor. He had attempted to sterilize the wound by pouring a liberal amount of gin over it, but Osborne had accused him of reeking like a distillery, and that had been the end of that.

"For God's sake, Milton, what do you think you're doing?"

Milton hadn't the foggiest idea of what he was doing. The infection that yesterday made him lightheaded was now making him dizzy.

"And, please, keep that wretched hand away from me. I'm liable to catch something. And while you're at it, please do something about that smell. Your rotting is beginning to affect my concentration." Osborne lifted the blinds once more from his office window. He glanced down on the thong-clad protestors below and groaned.

"I can't believe those ungrateful wenches have continued this ridiculous strike. It's been three days, and the only thing that's improved in this situation is their suntan. Milton? What if I offered a rather attractive purse of maybe five hundred dollars? We'll advertise it on the marquee, hold a suntan contest tomorrow. Yes, not only a suntan contest but an amateur night as well. What an excellent way to replace them all," Osborne said, then dropped the blinds and walked back behind his desk.

Milton groaned and hoped the room would stop spinning.

"Yes, a five hundred dollar first prize. Oh, yes, Milton. I'll win. I'll show them. Try to picket my business, will they? We'll just see about that!"

Milton attempted to focus on Osborne, but the room began to spin again, and objects took on a bit of a blurry edge. The floor developed a slight rolling wave action, and he steadied himself against the edge of Osborne's desk. As long as he didn't have to drive anywhere, he might be able to make it through the day.

Fifty-Two

Cindy felt flushed. They were swamped with extra bodies stuffed in the vault. The sun blazed through the drive-up windows, and the air conditioning was now out. The temperature in the teller area hovered just over ninety. But she didn't care about any of that. It was already past the noon hour. She'd had a fantastic night, a wonderful morning, and she hadn't had to deal once with Otto O'Malley and his greasy cash today.

The baseball game came across softly on a static-filled radio in the teller area that afternoon. The good news was the Twins were actually ahead in the bottom of the ninth. The bad news was Los Angeles had at least one more batter.

Otto's ears perked up when he heard the Twins were ahead three to one. He had timed things perfectly. He sat in his truck and slathered on another glistening layer of sunblock.

"Oh, oh, looks like it's bacon buddy time," Carol snickered a few minutes later, alerting Cindy and the other girls in the teller area.

Cindy was in the middle of a count. She looked up and saw Otto absently waiting at the back of her line, the longest line in the lobby. She groaned inwardly.

Otto grinned back at her, looking positively demented. He nodded at her as if to acknowledge some intimate private moment they shared.

Oh, please, she silently prayed.

I knew it, perfect timing, Otto thought.

Everyone in the teller area paused to listen through the static of the portable radio as the announcer called the pitch. The batter swung, and the ball began arching skyward. There were already two on for the Angels, with two outs, at the bottom of the ninth. All the twins had to do was catch this fly ball.

"And he's going back, back, Benny racing, on the track, at the wall, jumping, and it's bounced off his glove and into the stands. Oh no. Unbelievable. A home run. The Angels pull out a win at the last minute with a final score of four to three. Incredible, but the Twins just can't seem to get it right. Another disappointing afternoon of Twins baseball," the announcer called out.

A collective groan rose from the tellers' area. Could it possibly get any worse? As if on cue, Otto stepped up to Cindy's window. He rested his sunburned forearm sporting Donald Duck on the counter directly in front of her.

"Well, I suppose you're wondering where I've been today." With the white cream slathered across his face, he looked like an escapee from a psychiatric ward. There was a strange sheen to his forearm, and she nervously thanked God for the four layers of tempered glass separating the two of them.

"I'm sorry. Would you mind stepping to the next window, please? I think I'm about to get very sick."

With that, she left her window. She determined not to return until Otto had departed. Eventually, he stepped to the next window with a look more vague than usual on his face. Carol quickly counted his cash and slid the deposit receipt through the cash well.

"Anything else I can help you with, sir?"

"Well, I hope that Cindy person is all right," Otto said, nodding to the empty area where Cindy had been standing minutes before. He turned and walked out the door shaking his head, thinking, *'Damn women, they get so nervous around a real man they don't know what to do.'*

Two kids on bikes rolled past and screamed, "Twins suck!"

"He's gone, so it's safe to come out," Carol called. She watched as Otto climbed into his pickup out on the street and drove away. Cindy stood for another minute just to be sure, sweltering in the bank vault as the digital counting machine, generating additional heat, slapped stacks of twenty-dollar bills into bundles of five thousand dollars each.

"Thank God, he just gives me the absolute creeps."

"Yeah, I don't blame you. Phew, bacon!" Carol exclaimed, sniffing her hands.

Fifty-Three

Beau's prayers had finally been answered. He was up in the attic of his mother's home in the middle of the afternoon. He could not believe he hadn't thought of it sooner. There was a gun in the attic somewhere. A pistol packed away for a thousand years. With any luck, he would find it.

"Anthony, what in the world do you need up there that's so important?" his mother called from down below.

"Ma, I already told you. I'm looking for something."

"I know that's what you told me. But what is it? You're going to be messing everything up. I just know it. Come down here now. I'll find whatever it is you need."

Yeah, he thought. *You haven't been up here since the 90s.* He hoped he could stall her for just a few more minutes. The heat was beyond oppressive. He had sweated through his shirt. Dark stains formed across his chest and down his back. He was opening boxes of towels and Christmas decorations that hadn't seen the light of day for at least a decade. There were photos of people he didn't recognize, an old army uniform, report cards, a box of toy trucks missing their wheels, his sister's wedding dress.

"Anthony, get down here now. I do not want a mess up there."

He knew from her tone she was near the end of her rope. The sweat ran down his face and dripped off his chin. Large drops splashed onto the contents of every box he opened. He wasn't bothering to replace the lids now. Quickly rummaging through each box, casting it aside, and grabbing the next one.

"Anthony, not a minute more. You get down here now, mister."

There it was in a shoebox from the Golden Rule, a store that had closed decades before he was even born. The gun, a revolver, was wrapped in an oily, white T-shirt. He unfolded the T-shirt. Even in this heat, the revolver felt cold to the touch.

"I'm coming up there, young man," she called, and he heard the ladder creak with his mother's weight.

"I'm coming down, Mom. Relax," he said. He carefully stuffed the revolver in his belt. He untucked his sweat-stained shirt to hide it and grabbed a photo album as he made his way down the ladder.

"What in the world were you thinking? Look at you. You're all sweaty, an absolute mess," she said and brushed grime from his shirt. Her hand narrowly missed the revolver jammed in his belt. "And what are you going to do with those photos? Don't you mess those up. I need those." She was a half-step behind him, barking directions as he carried the ladder all the way down to the basement.

"I just want to make a copy of one or two pictures for my office," he said, holding the album tightly against the revolver.

"Well, why did it have to be this minute? Did you leave a mess up there? I suppose I won't be able to find a thing."

"Mom, it's not a mess. Look, I gotta run. I'm gonna make a copy or two, and then I'll bring it back, okay?"

"Well, see that you do. I don't like the idea of you traipsing around town and forgetting that album somewhere. Or worse, one of those so-called friends of yours setting a beer bottle on it. The next thing I know, everything will be ruined."

He felt like pointing out the obvious. That the album had been in the attic for the last four decades suffering hundred and fifty-degree temperature swings, and no one was stupid enough to use it as a coaster for a beer anyway. Instead, he said, "I love you, Mom." He gave her a kiss on the cheek and quickly retreated to his car.

Fifty-Four

Back in his office, Beau examined the revolver. The oil-soaked T-shirt it had been wrapped in for the past thirty or forty years lay on the corner of his desk. He sat there with the cylinder open, spinning it, listening to the clicking. He worked the hammer back and forth, then carefully pulled the trigger. Everything seemed to be in working order when his phone rang. "Yeah," he answered, sighting the revolver at the floor lamp in the corner.

"Hi, Beau, Tommy, downstairs. Hey, someone here to see you. Ahhh, I'm sorry, sir. What did you say your name was?" A momentary pause. "Yeah, Beau, a Mr. Hans Ulmbacher to see you."

Beau sat up. That damn Dickie.

"Give him a beer and send him up," he said, quickly wrapping the revolver in the oily T-shirt and stuffing it in a desk drawer.

"Hey, man," Dickie said five minutes later. He walked in, sipping a mug of beer as if Sunday afternoon at the Vikings game had never happened. He had completely shaved his head. He was growing a mustache and goatee that made him look like an overweight version of Lucifer. He wore a dark suit, a blue shirt, and a loose tie. All of it splattered with food stains.

"So, Dickie, what's new?" Beau said, sitting back in his chair.

"Hey man, how's it going?" Dickie said. He took another sip from his beer before he set the dripping mug on top of the photo album.

"Don't set that there, you dumb shit."

"Oops." Dickie reached over to grab the mug. He caught it in mid spill sloshing beer across the cover of the album.

"That's my mom's album, man."

"Sorry."

"Where in the hell have you been, Dickie?" Beau shook the puddle of beer off the faded album cover onto the floor. "Christ, we've all been worried about you. And what's with the suit? I haven't seen you in one since high school graduation."

"Tell me about it," he said, rubbing his newly shaved head. "Can you believe what a federal case they're making out of Sunday? I've had to do this disguise deal so no one would recognize me. Hey, you dig the beard?"

"Yeah, great. You look like a demented devil. Where the hell have you been, Dickie? You still got your job?"

"Barely, that's the reason for the threads. I'm on like double secret probation and a whole bunch of other shit." He tilted his head back and stretched his three chins into one long fat chin.

"I can't even eat with the other employees in the cafeteria. They won't let me talk to other employees. I've been lying low in case someone recognizes me. Fortunately, we're so damn busy they can't afford to fire my ass right now. We're in the midst of switching over some systems, and they really can't do it without me. Well, unless they want to start over from scratch. Course, the bastards have banned me from ever attending another Vikings game as a condition of continued employment."

"My mom told me she was going to have to leave town," Beau said.

"God, I only wish my mom would leave. I catch hell at work all day. Then, I get home, and while I'm listening to messages of her bitching, she calls up to bitch at me some more. She's still really major league pissed off."

"Dickie, can you blame her? Jesus. You were on national news. The entire country was staring at your fat ass. My mom was complaining about it being on *Good*

Morning America. for Christ's sake. Shit, Victor's brother called him from Atlanta and gave him a hard time. Victor and Andrew are banned from ever getting to use their law firm's tickets again."

"No shit? And they're such great seats," Dickie said, not quite grasping the point. "Well, look, I'm sorry, man, I really am. I mean, I'm sure it's been a little tough on you guys—"

"A little tough? I gotta tell you, Dickie. I don't need this kind of publicity. I got a business to run here. I gotta deal with the public every day. I couldn't even get a doughnut and a cup of coffee without the woman behind the counter giving me a hard time."

"Hey, look. I know, man. Here's the deal. I'm going around apologizing to everyone. I'll go see your mom if you want."

"No, not that. Please don't."

"Well, anyway. I've seen Victor and Andrew. Of course, Wiener. You know how he is. Guess what? This is kinda cool. He's got some hot affair going with some kinky chick who got turned on by the whole deal."

Beau pondered that last statement and decided not to learn any more.

"Look, I know it's been tough, local news, the national news, talk radio, the papers, USA Today didn't help. I hadn't heard about *Good Morning America*. At least, it's sort of dying down on YouTube, for the moment anyway. This hasn't exactly been a picnic for me either," Dickie said, looking up at Beau, sounding sincere in his apology.

"It started Sunday night. By the time I got home, I had about a half-dozen messages from my mom. She was not a happy bunny. By then, the local news organizations and channel four, five, nine, and eleven had already called plus a bunch of radio stations. Did I leave anyone out?"

Beau groaned.

"I mean, how in the hell? That was Sunday night. When I went out the door on Monday morning at six, there were three live cameras waiting for me. So much for trying to keep a low profile."

"How'd they find out it was you?"

"Well, I figure so many folks know me just about anyone could have talked. Of course one of the rock stations had a contest to identify me. Guess their switchboards got flooded in the first few minutes. Hey, get this. Some guy sent an email. Wants to write a book about me. That was kinda cool. He seemed a little screwy, though. Another dude called and wanted to include me in a bunch of Ripley's Believe It or Not deals he was submitting, but you gotta pay him, so I said no. And another guy wanted to put my name into the Guinness Book of World Records. That could be kind of cool, but I took a pass on that one, too. What with them going ballistic at the office and all, I figured the timing might not be the greatest."

"Did Victor tell you we were trying to call you? We were all worried about you."

"Yeah, I know. Thanks. I just let the message box get full at work and haven't answered them. Probably, a good number of them are from my mom anyway. You know, more bitching. I'm using the extension next to me. Guy's on vacation, so if you need to reach me for the next week and a half, just call one-one-four."

"God."

"I talked to my attorney. He said I don't have to appear in court, just pay the fine and don't do anything like this again, like that's gonna be a problem. No worry there."

Beau nodded.

"Hell, even Jerry Cardy got my phone number from somewhere. Probably his old man. He called from the hospital right after the Vikings cut him loose. Left a message saying it was all my fault. Yeah, right, like I did something wrong. Well, I mean, yeah, okay. But I wasn't the one who ran the wrong way in the game. Wild Card. My fat ass."

"Dickie, anything I can do for you?"

"Naw, but thanks, man. I appreciate it. Sorry about your mom. Look, I just wanted to stop in, make sure we were still pals, you know."

"Hey, Dickie, we'll always be pals. You'll be at Wiener's tomorrow night, right?"

"Well, yeah, if it's still on. Hey, that's something positive, man. Did I mention Wiener says this chick named Lindsey or Ashley, or something has been on him the last two nights just wearing him out? She really got off once she found out he was famous and all.”

“Yeah, you mentioned that. So, there you go. It wasn’t a complete waste of your talent. At least Weiner got some benefit. Let’s just aim for something a little more subtle next time, okay?”

“Subtle. Yeah, that’s me from now on, man, subtle!” Dickie half-shouted.

“Calmly, Dickie, calmly,” Beau cautioned.

“Oh, yeah. Sorry, dude. Look, gotta go. I’ll let you get back to work here. See you tomorrow night, man.” He drained his beer then set the empty mug down on the photo album.

“Tomorrow night, Dickie, and remember stay calm.”

Fifty-Five

Lucerne was seated on the bathroom floor in the motel room half-whispering, so Mendel and Elvis wouldn't hear him on the phone. "What in the hell are you talking about, Tracey? Calm down. I can hardly understand you. You're talking so damn fast. What do you mean you're on strike? Didn't ya tell me you were a vice president? I thought vice presidents couldn't go on strike."

Oh, brother, Tracey thought. Still, there seemed something weirdly solid about this Lucerne guy. She could tell from his voice, the way he'd phoned her at least a half-dozen times a day. Every day for the past two weeks. She'd come to like his simple manner, the forceful tone in his voice. Perhaps suggesting a more sterling quality than the usual phone sex clientele she dealt with.

"Look, Lucerne, things are just crazy around here. I don't know how much more I can take. They had us dancing downstairs yesterday. That was a complete disaster. We organized our picket line late yesterday afternoon, and some folks from the TV news came around filming us. Maybe you caught it on TV." She paused, ready to explain why she looked a hundred and forty pounds heavier than the woman in the late-night television ad.

Lucerne wondered *why in the hell he would bother watching the news.*

Tracey waited a moment or two longer before she spoke, "Some of the girls are picketing right now. We're all taking turns. I'll be down there this evening after my shift," she confided, not sounding all that pleased about it.

None of what she said was making any sense to Lucerne. So he asked, "Well, why would they want you to dance? That part there, it ain't making a lick of sense to me." He envisioned a ballroom with a mirrored sphere spinning in the center of the ceiling. A bunch of musicians set up on a stage sitting behind little stands painted white with a black music note on the front of each stand. Tracey would be wearing white gloves that went up to her elbows, a long sparkly gown, and sparkly high heels. She probably had to run down a curving staircase from her vice president's job to dance with some old boss. He'd be a fat, white-haired guy with a white mustache wearing a black tuxedo, a monocle, maybe a top hat, and carrying a gold-handled cane. Once her dance was finished, she would have to run back up the staircase to do whatever it was vice presidents did.

"So, anyway, Lucerne, like I was saying, I don't know how much longer I'm going to be able to talk to you." She cringed at the memory of climbing on the stage wearing lingerie made for someone half her size. Some guy in the thinning crowd had yelled out, "Oh, no. Please don't."

Lucerne gulped audibly. "Tracey, I thought we had something here. I was thinking, wouldn't it be nice to meet, finally? We been talking every day for weeks. Seems to me it's sorta just like courtin'. Don't ya think?"

She shook her head in disbelief and reached for another caramel.

"Boy, that would be fun, Lucerne, but I just don't know how that's going to happen. Osborne's likely to fire the whole bunch of us the way things are going. And, to tell you the truth, I'm not so sure I even care. Maybe I'll just sit back and collect unemployment for a while and look at all my options."

"Don't you think that means we better meet and pretty quick? Before all that shit happens. Who's this Osborne fella, anyway? Is he your boss man?" Lucerne asked. He was conjuring up the image of the white-haired tuxedoed guy. "Maybe I could help straighten things out. I could talk to him, nice like."

"Lucerne, damn it! Lucerne?" Mendel yelled, banging on the bathroom door. "What the hell you doing in there, boy? Christ. We can hear ya moaning and groaning all the ways out here, you moron. Get your worthless ass out here. I gotta piss like a racehorse." Mendel pounded on the bathroom door a half-dozen more times.

"What's all that?" Tracey asked, tossing another caramel into her mouth.

"Oh, just my brother, Mendel. He's gotta piss is all."

"Huh?"

"Look, Tracey, I better let you go and get back to your vice presidenting."

"Sure, Lucerne, whatever, talk to you later, I hope."

The door burst open, and Mendel hurried in.

"God damn it, Mendel. Can't a man even talk to his woman for a few minutes without having to be interrupted by the likes of you needing to take a damn piss?"

"Your woman?" Mendel said, unzipping his jeans and ignoring his aim. "Your woman? Hell, you never even seen her, you big dummy. You ain't got the slightest idea what in the hell she even looks like."

"That's where you're wrong, Mendel. You are so damned wrong. Thinking you know every damn little thing. Hell, for your information, I seen a picture of Tracey. I just happen to know she's shy, has brown hair, a white phone, wears a black bra, and drinks champagne outta a tall, fancy glass. She's a vice president, and she's damn good at dancing, too."

Mendel strode out of the bathroom, zipping his fly. "All's I know is you're damn delusional. Now, help us get these damn weapons ready."

"You'll see," said Lucerne, thinking *I better make a plan to rescue Tracey from that Osborne fella while there's still time*. As they cleaned and loaded the AKs over the next two hours, it had become clear to Lucerne that he was going to have to do something where Tracey was concerned. The poor little thing, so shy she didn't even know how to ask him for help, and after all they'd been through. The late-night calls, the early morning calls, the mid-day calls. As a matter of fact, the late-night call he was placing right now.

"This is Tracey," Tracey said, adjusting her headset as she quickly swallowed the last bit of chocolate chip cookie. "I've been waiting for your call, Honey, just hoping it was you. You there, baby?"

"Course I'm here, sugar. Just calling to check-in. Make sure you're doin' okay is all," Lucerne said, grateful Tracey recognized his voice.

"Lucerne, is that you?" Tracey guessed. She had narrowed his voice down to three possible choices.

"Course, the one and only."

"I've been thinking about you, Lucerne. How nice of you to call back," Tracey said and reached for another cookie.

"I'll just bet you have. How're things goin'?"

"About the same. We don't know from one minute to the next if we've got a job. At least, the dancing is over for the time being." She choked down the cookie and reached for another.

"Well, that's good. I didn't like the idea of you having to dance with that old Osborne fella then having to run back upstairs and do your vice president stuff."

Tracey shook her head and wondered *what in the hell he was talking about*.

"So what are you up to, Lucerne?"

"I was gonna ask you the exact same thing. Funny how we're thinkin' alike, ain't it?"

"Listen, you won't believe this. Old Osborne is going to have a suntan contest tomorrow. Open to everyone. Guess it's his way of trying to break the strike."

"Since you're on strike, are you just taking a break from the picket line, or are you still doing your vice president stuff?"

"Actually, there isn't really all that much to my vice presidential duties. And I just lend support to the girls who're picketing. I'm not really on strike. I can't afford it."

Lucerne figured she most likely had elderly parents, a terminally ill child, or both. "So, you're okay, is what you're telling me. What the hell's with the suntan contest?"

"Osborne's trying to break the strike and get a bunch of new girls in here with a $500 prize. Then he'll offer them a dance contract, hoping they'll figure it's too good to pass up. The girls out on the sidewalk will be out of a job, and in a year or two, the exact same thing will happen all over again."

"And all this to hire some gal just 'cause she's got a good tan? Is he crazy, stupid, or both?"

Tracey shook her head in disbelief. Lucerne might be good, kind, maybe even decent, but he was sure dumb as a post. She grabbed two more cookies.

"He doesn't hire them because they have a good tan. He has a contest to see who has the best tan and offers prize money. He'll get all kinds of girls in here, and they all get the idea that dancing pays well, but it just never quite works out that way."

Lucerne was back to conjuring up his image of an old guy in a tux and all sorts of innocent women, tanned women apparently, being made to dance with the rich old bastard. With Lucerne's share of the bank money, he could maybe buy a double-wide. With a little luck, it would have one of those screened-in porches off to the side. They would have a picnic table where he and his brothers could drink beer, and Tracey could serve them fried chicken and live happily ever after.

"Does he still make you dance?" he asked.

"Just that one time the other day. But, like I told you, it didn't work out too well." She stuffed another cookie in her mouth.

"Hey, Tracey, did you tell me what you're wearing?" Lucerne asked.

"Finally, I was beginning to worry." She giggled. "What's your favorite color tonight, Lucerne?" She snuggled back in her chair, brushed the crumbs off the front of her T-shirt, and reached for another cookie. This might be a good long session.

Fifty-Six

Otto settled into his recliner and carefully placed his feet in the large pan of Epsom salts. He immediately felt himself begin to relax. He took a long swallow of beer and rested the can on the arm of his recliner. He looked around his living room at the growing piles of laundry and the dishes in the kitchen sink. He had a plan for that. He'd ask the bank teller out tomorrow. Give her a ticket into the fair. Maybe some sort of a half-price off deal at his stands. He'd set it all up so she couldn't possibly say no.

He had to play it carefully. Just get her over here with the idea that there was no pressure, and she could take her time doing the laundry and the cleaning. Maybe once she got him a beer, he could just sit in the recliner and nicely point things out. Save her some time.

As usual, he woke a minute before his alarm was set to go off. With the unrelenting heat and his unattended piles of laundry, Otto was forced to attire himself in an old North Stars hockey jersey. It was the green jersey with the capital letter 'N' on the front and a gold star. He was grateful for the protection the longer sleeves gave his arms. As usual, he had his face more covered than not with zinc oxide. The handkerchief was still pinned onto the back of his baseball cap.

A little before eleven, he was waiting in Cindy's line, working the old Otto magic, looking around to ensure the area was safe for her. He touched the .45 resting snugly in his belt beneath the hockey jersey.

"Morning ma'am," Otto said, giving Cindy his two-fingered salute. He slid another greasy deposit toward her. Cindy was afraid to look up. She worried about another nose smudge down the length of her teller window. She could feel her fingers growing slick as she counted his currency. The immediate area around her suddenly smelled like fried bacon— a lot of fried bacon.

"Ahem," Otto cleared his throat, stood up as straight as possible, waiting for her complete attention.

"Forty, sixty, eighty, nine hundred. Twenty, forty, sixty, eighty—"

"So, what are you doing when you're off work tonight?" Otto asked. He absently pulled up a jersey sleeve and exposed his Donald Duck tattoo, then leaned forward toward the cash well, so she wouldn't miss a word. "Thought it might be time for us to get together. Get a little more acquainted. Make it all kind of official, you know."

Cindy thought, *'This couldn't be happening. Please, don't let this be happening to me.'*

"Here, you can have this ticket. Gets you into the fair for free," he said and pulled a folded, sweat-soaked ticket out of his back pocket.

"Oh, no, that's not—"

"Here's a half-off coupon for my stands, too. All you could possibly eat. Like I said, half off of course, cuz, well, let's face it, we're an item. That's where you'll find me, by the way, at my stand. The one by the beer garden. Figured we could maybe grab something after that," he said, chuckling, as if 'grab something' might have an ulterior meaning. He casually tossed the coupon on top of the sweat-soaked ticket and gave her another all-knowing wink.

The coupon featured the sunburned pig with the shorts pulled down, revealing that deep butt crack. Otto folded his arms and nodded, ready to close the deal. "Like I said, we could maybe grab something a little later on." This time he accentuated 'grab something' with a sort of moronic leer from behind the zinc oxide.

Cindy remained speechless as her worst fears were realized.

"Thank, thank you," she stammered. She wrapped a Kleenex around her finger and dragged the greasy, sweaty little pile next to her can of Lysol.

"I, umm, I'm afraid I might be busy for the rest of the week but thank you anyway," she said, then bit her trembling lower lip, hoping she wouldn't start to cry.

"Only the beginning," said Otto, not taking 'might be busy' as her final answer. Obviously, the woman he'd chosen to do his laundry and cleaning was just a little overwhelmed.

Cindy was afraid she might cry. She blinked back the tears and forced down the hard lump in her throat. She stood there dumbfounded and stared at Otto with a glazed expression across her face.

"My, ah, deposit receipt?" he said eventually.

In her shock, she had forgotten the total and would have to count anew. "Oh, yeah, sorry," she said, sniffling back a tear as she started over. She counted as fast as ever and hoped she could hold the scream inside her until he was gone.

Otto stood there smiling, then looked over and gave a knowing nod to two women in the line next to him. Obviously, she was cleverly recounting his deposit just to get the extra few minutes together.

Cindy sniffled and continued biting her trembling lower lip as she quickly counted. She fought back the tears and, when finished, creaked out a timid, "Thank you."

"At your service, ma'am," Otto replied, then snapped to attention and flipped his two-fingered salute.

"I'm terribly sorry," she said to the next customer and ran off to the ladies' room.

Fifty-Seven

Beau was racking his brain, trying to think of a way he could pull off the bank robbery, not get caught, and still keep things going with Cindy. Thus far, he had come up with absolutely nothing.

If he could lure her away from the bank, or at least from her teller window, maybe, just maybe, he had an outside chance. Then, all he had to do was make his getaway, hand the cash over to Osborne, and be done with the whole sordid affair. He decided he would carry the gun unloaded to ensure no one, especially himself, got hurt.

He spun the cylinder and listened as the shells bounced across the top of his desk. A couple of the shells rolled around in a semicircle and came to rest against his mother's beer-stained photo album. He rolled the bullets across his desktop for over an hour, trying to think of a disguise, a mask, something, anything he could do that would allow him to pull this off. He was toying with the idea of dressing like a woman and had spent the past ten or fifteen minutes thinking about an appropriate breast size. He never did arrive at an answer. Instead, he decided to head over to the bank and check things out one final time.

Oddly, it was a short drive, and Beau held the door for some local character with clown white smeared over his face. The poor soul was wearing an old North Stars hockey jersey and grinning like an idiot. He watched as the obviously deranged little man walked away. Beau only hoped the man would be able to find his way back to the group home.

The heat in the small bank lobby was stifling. With floor-to-ceiling windows on three sides of the lobby, the sun beat mercilessly into the room all day, from sunup right through to sundown. Crammed with short-fused people dripping sweat all day long, the room rarely had a chance to cool.

He hadn't stepped five feet in the door before Cindy quickly glanced up and spotted him. He thought, *she looked a little pale and wondered if last night and their early morning had anything to do with it.* He waited in line for fifteen minutes. By the time he made it to her window, he was drenched in sweat.

"I just need two fives for this ten," he joked, sliding a soggy ten-dollar bill across the counter. "Hey, what the hell? You guys oil this? It sure seems slick." He rubbed his fingers across the counter and examined the oily sheen on his fingertips.

"It's the fair traffic. Everything gets kind of greasy," Cindy said, shaking her head to move damp strands of hair from her forehead. She pushed two five-dollar bills back beneath the thick glass window.

"Got time for a coffee or a Coke?" Beau asked as he attempted casually to inspect the teller area.

"I'd love to. Really I would, Tony, but we've just been jammed with customers all day, and I really can't take any breaks. None of us can."

"Not a problem," he said absently. He was busy examining the door into the area.

"You okay, Tony? You seem distracted." Cindy glanced around behind her to see what he was looking at.

"You sure you can't take a break?"

"I'd like to, but I can't." She shrugged, half nodding to the crowded lobby. The color seemed to return to her face. She leaned forward and half-whispered, "But, thanks for last night and this morning. I had a wonderful time. Really I did, thanks." She smiled.

"Yeah, that was a great little restaurant."

"I didn't mean the restaurant."

"Yeah, me too, thanks. You sure? Final chance, lady."

"I'd love to, but I just can't."

"Yeah, tell me about it. I held the door for one of your top customers on my way in." He laughed.

"Huh?" She crinkled her nose, not following the joke.

"Oh, that handicapped guy, you know."

"What handicapped guy?"

"The guy with the clown face in the hockey jersey. There a group home around here?"

"Yes, there is, and no, he doesn't live there," she said.

"Look, I'd better get going." He pocketed his two fives, oblivious to her reaction.

"Can I call you later, Tony?"

"Yeah. Please, do."

He took his time exiting the lobby, looking for a possible camera. Unfortunately, he spotted two. *This was going to be more difficult than he had first thought.* And, he still didn't have a plan.

Fifty-Eight

Milton's eyes were glassy. He was running a fever. His hand had stopped throbbing, but only because his entire arm had gone numb. He was beginning to drool slightly, and he reeked of the disinfectant Osborne had just finished spraying him again.

"We'll just see how that bovine rabble likes the idea of being upstaged by the crowds I'll have in here for the suntan competition," Osborne sneered. He was peeking out the Venetian blinds of his office window, making sure the police had arrived.

The police presence was, supposedly, onsite to keep order. Osborne himself had phoned earlier in the day to complain. Hoping they would arrest the protestors and cart the ungrateful wenches off to some dark hole. That episode had turned into a complete fiasco the moment the police had arrived in two patrol cars. Osborne, watching out his office window, had run downstairs to greet them, eager to point out the ring leaders.

"Thank God, you've finally arrived. You can start with this person here," Osborne said and pointed Sassie out to a large gawking sergeant. "She's the ringleader. Once you arrest her, that medical ingrate should go next." He indicated Serpentina in her miniskirt nurse's uniform. She had unbuttoned the majority of the buttons on her skimpy white garment, exposing an enticingly deep cleavage.

Hearing Osborne's directions to the officers, Sassie struck a pouty pose. In one fluid motion, she thrust her chest out, cocked her hip, and presented her wrists for handcuffs. All the while, batting her eyes.

"That won't be necessary." The sergeant laughed nervously as he ran his eyes up and down her figure. "Has this gentleman been bothering any of you ladies?" he asked.

Two officers stepped out of nowhere, grabbed Osborne by the elbows, spun him around, and pushed him up against the brick wall.

"Assume the position," a young officer yelled and kicked Osborne's feet apart. One of them shouted, "Careful, ma'am. We're not exactly sure what we're dealing with here."

Misty Morning put on a frightened look. She wore a blue baby doll nightie and false eyelashes.

"This is absolutely ridiculous. I—" Osborne attempted to turn and protest just before a hand forcefully bounced his forehead off the brick wall.

"Sir, I'm not going to tell you again. I want you to remain quiet while I search you. Are you carrying any needles or sharp instruments that will make me unhappy?"

"But, I haven't done anything," Osborne said.

"You wanna do this here or downtown? I don't want to hear one more word. Not one."

"Will you be doing that to the rest of us?" Natasha, a perky brunette in a bustier with matching French cuffs and a red bow tie, asked.

"No, not to worry, ma'am."

"Maybe we could work something out," she said and winked back at the officer.

Two officers quickly cuffed Osborne and placed him in the back of a squad car. They slammed the door and hurried back to the sidewalk to see about taking statements and, with any luck, search the strikers.

"Sarge, you think we better hang tight? Make sure this thing doesn't get out of control?"

"I'm already calling in for an overtime authorization. Nothing I don't think the four of us can't handle, at least for now," he said. He stood protectively over two of the girls as they applied suntan lotion to one another.

After giving the girls autographs and posing for a series of photos with the line of perfumed protesters, it was a good hour, possibly two, before the officers remembered Osborne in the back of a squad car. He had become slightly dehydrated. He was soaked with sweat, groggy, confused, and there was a large purplish knot the width of a brick running across his forehead.

"Sir, I'm releasing you for the time being, but I'm going to insist that you return to your office. You are not to converse with, touch, or in any way attempt to communicate with these ladies." One of the officers uncuffed Osborne's wrists and smiled at a striker wearing little red satin devil horns.

"Should you attempt to engage these demonstrators, I'll have you taken downtown and booked for disturbing the peace, harassment, attempted assault, and I'll probably throw in public nuisance, too. Any questions, sir?"

Osborne's head lolled back and forth for a moment before he nodded groggily. Two officers took him firmly by the arm and led him to the front door of Cheaters. They shoved him in the darkened entry and left him to his own devices.

Osborne looked down from his office window and closed his eyelids in response to the throbbing in his head. "The cows. I'll have each and every one of them walking in the unemployment line by tomorrow afternoon. I'll flood this place with new talent from my suntan contest, and they'll find themselves out of work. Milton, what about my loan to DiMento? We're supposed to see something from him within the next forty-eight hours. I trust you're ready to move?"

Milton's tongue was thick. His right arm had eclipsed into various shades of red, purple, and green. Osborne's words seemed to echo from some great distance as he attempted to focus through glassy eyes.

"Milton," Osborne called, standing over him and once again liberally spraying a heavy mist of disinfectant. "Milton. Damn it. I'll have to put you down if you continue in this manner. For God's sake, answer me, you ingrate. Speak. Speak."

Osborne's head throbbed after bouncing off the brick wall. Add to that the constant chiming from the ice cream truck outside. Milton was snoring in a semi-comatose state on the couch. It was all becoming too much to deal with. He sprayed Milton with more disinfectant. Eventually, he returned to his desk and reapplied an ice pack to his tender forehead.

Later, he peeked through the blinds, glanced down on the scene below, and was shocked to see someone had set up an iPod and speakers. Sassie and the rest of her ilk were dancing to the delight of clapping police and a growing mob of onlookers. Osborne slammed the blinds down, strode over to comatose Milton, and kicked him.

Fifty-Nine

"All right, I'm moving. Relax, will you?" Tracey shouted at a newspaper photographer in response to his scowl. He'd been wildly waving his arm, directing her out of the way.

He was hoping to get some decent shots of the thong-clad picket line, thinking there could easily be a Pulitzer in all this. His eagerness to get just the right shot had translated into a gentle but forceful effort to move the large, rather sweaty woman out of the way. He'd been in this situation before and knew exactly where it was going.

"Sorry, just trying to get this shot," he'd said, not in the least bit sorry.

Tracey struck a pose, shook her hair back over her shoulder, and said, "You could take my picture."

Like it isn't tough enough hanging onto readers, he thought. He pointed the camera and absently clicked in her general direction.

"Did you even take the picture? I didn't see a flash."

He glanced up at the sun beating down and thought, *'Why me?'* "I don't need one right now. There's enough natural light. Now, I gotta get these other shots, so if you'll excuse me." He crouched and thrust himself delightfully close to Misty Morning, applying suntan lotion all over a friend.

"Don't you want my name for the paper?" Tracey called after him. She waited a brief moment for a reply before she stepped up to the ice cream truck just as her cell rang.

"Hello."

"What'll it be this time?" the ice cream man asked.

His name was Morris. He'd lost track of how many ice cream treats she'd purchased today. Although, he could probably figure it out if he took the time to count the different colored drips staining the front of her T-shirt. He was thin, bordering on gaunt, with dirty, thinning, lackluster hair. He might have been labeled 'unattractive' were it not for a definite rodent quality to his face, which often caused him to be described as 'really ugly.' This, in addition to years of selling overpriced ice cream treats to whiney kids and unhappy parents, had left Morris with a noticeable twitch and a hair-trigger temper. He had parked his truck in front of Cheaters almost four hours ago, and business had been booming ever since. To

Morris's way of thinking, that, unfortunately, meant he would have to work even harder.

"Are you still out of banana fudge bars? Hang on, Lucerne," Tracey said. She pulled the phone away from her ear. "Well?"

"I told you before. You ate the last one around two o'clock," Morris twitched. "Pick something else."

"Oh, be quiet, you," Tracey giggled into the phone. She pointed and mouthed the words Creamy Dreamy bar to Morris.

"Jesus, do I have this, do I have that," Morris muttered, twitching involuntarily for a moment before reaching deep into his diminished cooler and handing her a Creamy Dreamy bar.

"Here. Now, you'll eat the last of these, too. So, don't come back here asking for another 'cause that's the last one. I ain't got another one. That'll be four-fifty."

"Oh, Lucerne, that's so nice of you." Tracey giggled. She slid four dollar bills and two quarters across Morris's little counter, tore the wrapper off with her teeth, and crammed a third of the bar into her mouth.

"Umm-mmm, you are so sweet, Lucerne. You've really been a big help. I can't thank you enough. I just wish there was some way to repay you." Tracey pulled the phone away from her ear and licked dripping ice cream off her hand and phone.

"Yeah, that would be fine with me," she replied, having no idea what Lucerne had just said. She focused on the large drip of creamy vanilla she was going to miss

if she didn't hurry. "Whoops, gotta go," she said, clicking her phone off. She attacked the large drop of ice
cream before it was lost to gravity.

Sixty

Otto entered the bank lobby, half-expecting Cindy not to be at her window. But there she was, busily shoving rolls of quarters to a woman who was just as quickly stuffing them into a bag. Amazingly, there was no line behind the woman.

Cindy rolled her shoulders and glanced up at the wall clock inside the sweltering teller area. She blew air up toward her forehead in a vain effort to cool her sweaty bangs. She was exhausted and couldn't remember if she'd even taken a break today. She zoned out, closed her eyes, told herself she could hang on and make it through the day. She could do it. She was almost there.

"Well, so, we finally get some time together. I was beginning to worry you didn't want to see me." Otto giggled.

Wrenched back to reality, her worst fears were confirmed. Otto grinned idiotically behind a mask of zinc oxide. "You can't have your favorite customer getting upset," he said. He propped his briefcase on the counter then looked around the half-full lobby before opening it. He snapped the two locks on the briefcase, pulled out a grease-stained paper bag, and crammed it into the coin well. His hand lingered, giving her plenty of opportunity to touch him.

Cindy took tiny little breaths to fend off the nauseating sensation. She grabbed the opposite side of the bag and avoided his twittering fingers. Otto held on tightly as she pulled on the bag until eventually, it tore open.

"That's okay. I got more, so don't worry," Otto said. He was trying to calm her down. Thinking, *It wouldn't do if she got this upset over little things. If this was the way she operated, she'd have his laundry screwed up in no time.*

"So, about what time do you think tonight? Closer to eight would probably be better for me." He figured, as long as she was getting all this half-priced stuff on their date, the least she could do would be to not show up until after his dinner rush.

Cindy suddenly felt lightheaded. Her stomach fluttered ever so threateningly. She swallowed hard, bit her lip to concentrate on the pain, and quickly began counting his greasy currency.

He continued talking as Cindy fought to close her mind to the outside world. She encoded his deposit receipt and shoved it through the shiny, greasy trail the paper bag had left.

"… 'Course after that, if you wanted, you could see how we mix up the batter, maybe put some bacon on skewers. You know, start to learn a little bit about the business. How we do things," Otto droned on.

"Huh?"

"Got a little something special for you again, more treats. Cajun-style this time!" He grinned. He pulled a stained paper plate from his briefcase and piled pieces of what looked like dog poop on a stick. He shoved and crammed the whole mess back into the coin well. The pile left a quarter-inch crust of grease and batter along the bottom edge of the protective glass.

"No, no, no thanks, please, oh please, no," Cindy half-whispered, afraid she was going to cry. She fought to swallow the lump in her throat. She pulled the saturated paper plate through the opening and shoved it off to the side.

"Thank, thank you," she managed to say.

"Tonight then, closer to eight," he said and snapped to attention. He gave her his two-fingered salute. "Tonight," he repeated and executed two crisp left facing movements before marching purposely out the door before she could respond.

She shuddered as he departed the lobby. A dark stain ran from his shoulders down the length and breadth of his back and transferred from his jersey to the back of the baggy cutoffs.

"Oh, disgusting," Carol exclaimed. She stepped over and swooped up the greasy paper plate laden with encrusted bacon strips and deposited the whole mess in a wastebasket outside the teller area.

"Like it isn't bad enough in here with all of us sweating our butts off. You sure attract them, honey!"

Cindy grabbed the Lysol can and sprayed down the counter area immediately in front of her. She wiped the area clean with a fistful of paper towels and sprayed more disinfectant for good measure.

Sixty-One

Otto was late collecting his receipts, but he didn't want to leave his stand. He was afraid Cindy would suddenly appear, and she'd get upset.

Typical, he thought, looking at his watch for the umpteenth time. Already a half-hour late for their date. I'll have to talk with her about that. Punctuality was important. He guessed she was probably spending time in front of the mirror, making herself look perfect the way they do, and the time just got away from her.

"You picking up the cash, Otto?" Josh asked.

"Yeah, I know, I know. I've got someone coming to see me tonight. I wanted to be here when she showed up so I wouldn't have to run around looking for her at the other stands."

"Her? You mean, you have a sister?"

"Naw, girlfriend," Otto said.

"A girlfriend? Really? No kidding? Wow, I'd like to meet her. God, I can't imagine," Josh said the last part under his breath. "I'm just a little surprised, that's all. You've never mentioned her before. How long you been going out?" For once, Josh had stopped working and was staring at Otto.

"You'd like her. She wants to learn all about the business. You know, once she's finally got the time, finishes her other chores and all."

"Other chores?"

"Well, yeah. She's got my laundry, cleaning, that sort of thing. You know, women's work."

"Laundry and cleaning? You mean to tell me she does your laundry and cleans? I gotta meet this chick. How long did you say you two been going out together?"

"Well, for a while now, sort of," Otto replied vaguely. He suddenly felt the urge to gather the cash from the other stands.

"A while?"

"Look, her name is Cindy. She'll be asking for me. So tell her to just stay put. I'll be back. I gave her a half off coupon."

"A half-off coupon? That's really nice of you, Otto."

"She's bound to show up any minute. Just have her sit tight."

Meanwhile, Cindy was attempting to calm down after her most horrible day at work ever. She turned her phone on just long enough to make one phone call. She had placed her phone on 'airplane mode' just in case that awful Otto character had somehow found her number. She shuddered at the mere thought before dialing Beau.

"Yeah," he answered on the fourth or fifth ring. He absently nodded toward Victor to deal him in. A moment later, he put his finger in his ear, got up from the table, and walked out the front door so he could hear.

"Hi Tony, it's Cindy."

"Hi, Cindy. How's it going?" His mind flashed to tomorrow and his desperate plan to rob the bank.

"I'm just taking it easy after another day from hell. Look, I just wanted to apologize for not being able to give you a couple of minutes today. It was really sweet of you to come by, but we were so jammed. No one takes breaks during this week. I just didn't want you to take it personally, that's all."

"Hey, ass wipe, you in or what?" Dickie yelled.

Beau shook his head and waved Dickie away.

"I'm sorry. What was that? I didn't hear you," Cindy said.

"Oh, nothing, just one of my associates. So, Cindy, if you don't take a break, do you ever get to step away from the counter. I mean, you must have to use the bathroom once in a while, don't you?"

"Sort of depends, I guess."

"You must grab a lunch, even if it's for a couple of minutes. Just wondering is all." He followed up with, "Don't worry. I'm not going to come over and see you or anything tomorrow. I'll be really busy, too." Hoping he had covered his tracks.

"We take really short lunches down in the basement. It's just the way it is during fair week. Course, the flip side of that is we get an extra vacation day to use later and a nice bonus for the week. But, believe me, we earn both of them."

"What time do you usually break for lunch?" he asked.

"Maybe about a quarter after one, once the other girls are finished. But, I still wouldn't have time to see you, Tony. It's just too crazy, and some days, like today, it was after two. I just had half a sandwich out of sight, stealing a bite from time to time. I never really even took lunch. So, it wouldn't be a good idea to plan on something like that."

"Well, I'd like to spend another quiet night together. Once both our schedules return to normal."

"Yeah, I'd really like that, too. Thanks, hope to see you soon," she said and hung up, feeling much better.

Sixty-Two

"What we're going to do is make a couple of dry runs. Practice getting the hell out of here," Lucerne explained. He was talking over his shoulder to Elvis in the backseat. They had the AKs loaded and ready. One in the backseat on the floor and the other resting next to Mendel.

Since Lucerne would be driving, he carried a .38 Special tucked into the waistband of his jeans. He had come to the conclusion that it might be better to get Tracey after they took down the bank instead of bringing her along. Neither Mendel nor Elvis would be able to see the wisdom or recognize the true love involved.

"See, it's just two and a half blocks to the freeway from here," Lucerne explained. "That's Highway 280. We take this back route, avoid the stoplight, the fair traffic, and anything else that might slow us up. Everyone, including the cops, are gonna be stacked up out there. Meanwhile, we'll race through the neighborhood. Some bastard is bound to see us leaving the scene tomorrow, but we'll be out of sight in less than half a block."

"We get down here, and the road comes to a T. So, the cops are gonna have to guess. Did we go north or south? Odds are we head north and link up with half a dozen roads in just four miles. That's why we head south over to I-94, cross the river, and get off on the Riverside exit." Lucerne neglected to mention this was in the general direction of where Tracey worked.

He smiled, imagining the look on their faces as beautiful, shapely, brown-haired Tracey hopped into the car, gave him a big kiss, and swung her gorgeous body around to introduce herself to his two speechless brothers.

"We hit this between say one-thirty and three-fifteen when traffic is at a low point. It's after any noontime headache and before the evening rush hour, so that gives us plenty of time. We run into any problems, and we're off this thing at the first exit," he said. He glanced over his right shoulder, floored the Fleetwood into the far right lane, and took the Riverside exit. "We can jump from here right back into Saint Paul, downtown Minneapolis, or the freeway heading south. There's a million places we can end up. Them cops will never be able to find us."

Early the following morning, Lucerne stood in front of the motel bathroom mirror and whispered his lines. He had been awake for hours, since just after midnight, and he'd been practicing what he would say when they picked up Tracey. "Hop in, sugar. Boys, meet my main squeeze."

He thought, once things settled down, maybe, they'd all go out somewhere for steaks. Show Tracey a good time right from the start. No doubt, she would be wearing something sexy. Tight jeans, maybe, a skimpy white top with a black bra, or maybe, she'd be in her sparkly dress and heels after just finishing up dancing. Either way, they'd have a good time. If Mendel and Elvis didn't like it, they could just come back here and play with themselves for all he cared.

Sixty-Three

Cindy rolled out of bed at five-forty. She had planned to stay in bed an extra ten minutes, but self-imposed guilt wouldn't let her. It was Friday, and that meant she almost had another week from hell under her belt. Good riddance to the whole affair for another year.

She let the hot shower run over her shoulders and down her back. She thought again about her brief conversation with Tony, hoping he'd be true to his word, and they would get together soon. She continued to think of him as she drove into work. She thought of him all the while she counted the night deposits with Carol until she came to that one deposit in particular.

Actually, she smelled it before she saw it. The deposit reeked of rancid bacon. The grease-stained nylon bag was stuffed so full she didn't think it was possible to cram any more inside. "Ugh, gross," she groaned, laying the greasy deposit slip on the counter.

"Oh, phew, that's the one from your bacon buddy." Carol sniffed the air. She had her own headache in front of her, counting out sticky currency from a cotton candy vendor.

"God, look, the bills just stick to me. I can hardly count it," Carol said, attempting to shake a bill from her fingers.

"Oh, this smells so bad. It just stinks. Did you see the day he ran his nose down my window? There was this gross smear right down the middle of the glass for the rest of the day," Cindy groaned.

"Yeah, I saw it. What's with those outfits he wears? He must have a thing for you, honey, because he always gets in your line. And, he does that little salute thingy. You better watch out. He's just crazy enough to follow you home some night," Carol said, not joking.

"Don't even go there," Cindy said, shivering at the thought. Otto, clown makeup all over his face, the handkerchief pinned to the back of a sweat-stained baseball cap, standing at her front door or peering in a window.

* * *

Otto pulled the recliner lever forward and launched himself out of the chair. He tossed his bathrobe over the back of the chair. He turned the sound up on the weather channel to hear what it would be like today, not that he really needed to check. More cloudless skies, heat, and heavy humidity. He showered, shaved, applied his zinc oxide, and grabbed the cleanest dirty jersey he could find on the floor.

There were stains left under the armpits from the last half-dozen times he wore it, but there wasn't a lot he could do about that this morning. He was in a foul mood remembering how Cindy stood him up last night. He'd have a talk with her and let her know he didn't appreciate being taken for granted. After the free pass and the half-off coupon, he had expected a little more in the way of gratitude.

He shook his head and looked around at all the dirty clothes. At least the Vikings jersey smelled more of rancid bacon grease and less of Otto. That seemed a plus.

Sixty-Four

Beau was still sucking some of the beer taste off his teeth when he walked into the coffee shop. Chrissie continued stretching and touching her toes behind the counter for two more minutes while he tried to make a decision.

"Beau, what could you possibly be spending your time thinking about? You go through the same routine every day, looking vacantly at everything. You always get the same thing, anyway. Here," she said, placing a French doughnut into a bag, "or do you want two? And, of course, I know, your latte," she said. She half-jumped as some of the hot frothy milk splashed on her hand. "Here, Beau." She pressed her chest up against the glass door on the pastry counter, reached across, and handed Beau his doughnut and latte.

"Keep the change," he said. He handed her a crisp five-dollar bill and walked off.

Chrissie shook her head, put the five in the cash drawer, took out a dime, and slipped it into her pocket. "Big tipper. Now, what can I get for you?" she said to the next person.

Beau hurried into the air-conditioned building. Even at this hour of the morning, there was that sense of unforgiving heat and humidity. He locked the office door behind him and placed his phone on airplane mode. He pulled his disguise, along with the revolver and the trash bags, out from beneath the cushions on the hide-a-bed sofa. The odds of walking into a bank with a mask and not attracting attention were a great big zero. So he had opted for a disguise.

I don't know, he thought, looking in a mirror at the black wig perched crookedly on his head. He pulled off the wig and bound the hair to form a ponytail. It didn't look half bad or, at least, as bad. He repositioned the wig on his head. Stuck the fake mustache in place and taped a Band-aid over the bridge of his nose. Once he slipped on the mirrored sunglasses, he began to think *there just might be an outside chance he could actually pull this off.*

He had been practicing with a number of different robbery notes. Some notes stated he carried a bomb, others a gun. Some notes made no mention of any weapon but just asked for money. He planned to bring a couple of trash bags, fill them with cash, and just get in and out of the bank quickly.

He stared at himself in the mirror for a long minute. He didn't recognize the freak staring back at him from behind the mirrored sunglasses. Hopefully, Cindy wouldn't recognize him either. His plan, such as it was, was not to say anything. Just hand the note to the teller and wait for the cash.

He reminded himself once more to wipe down the Saab for any trace of fingerprints. He made a mental note to be sure and wear gloves anywhere near the car from this point forward.

He knew if he thought about any of this at all, it would register as a very, very bad idea. So, he went mindlessly through the motions of laying everything out while checking and rechecking his watch every fifteen seconds. He ran down a quick mental inventory before dumping his disguise into an empty liquor box and carrying it out to the Saab.

He counted on substantial cash deposits being made through the noon hour. If he could time it so he would hit the bank when it was overwhelmed with deposits after the noon rush, he just might have a chance. Failing that, his backup plan was to dump the Saab. He planned to wear a second set of clothes underneath his disguise so he could run away undetected. Once back in his office, he would simply drown himself in the toilet before Osborne arrived with his goon to collect the debt.

Sixty-Five

Lucerne was at the end of his patience. Mendel and Elvis took their sweet time getting out of bed after a half-hour of rolling over and going back to sleep. Elvis had finally crawled out of bed, pulled on his jeans and one boot, and then crawled back into bed. The two of them eventually stirred to life once Lucerne threatened them with a bourbon bottle filled with cold water.

At breakfast, Mendel and Elvis had trouble making up their minds at Denny's. Elvis moved his lips as he read through the menu options. Everyone ultimately settled on the same thing they'd had every day for the past two weeks. The number three special with scrambled eggs and bacon for Mendel and Elvis. Pancakes and sausage for Lucerne.

"God damn it, I could have phoned in that order. You two fools burned twenty minutes of my life ordering the same damn thing you get every damn day," Lucerne groaned.

"Boy, what crawled up your ass this morning? Sounds like maybe what you need is a giant helping of that Tracey gal," Mendel said in a not too subtle tone.

It was at this point that the two women in the booth next to them got up, shot a disgusted look in their direction, and stormed out.

"Sir, I'm going to have to ask you to please keep your voices down," the assistant manager said to Lucerne a moment later. His yellow plastic name tag read 'Phil' in black letters right under his title of Assistant Morning Manager, followed by a happy face smile.

"Not a problem, Phil. Guess I'll just cool my ass outside in the car," Lucerne said. He walked out and waited in the car while Mendel and Elvis ate their number three specials before turning their attention to what remained of Lucerne's pancakes and sausage.

Back at the motel, they slowly loaded things into the car. Lucerne cut a length of carpet out of the motel room floor and wrapped it around the AKs so they could sneak them into the bank.

Mendel yelled at Elvis in the process of covering the holes in the knees of his jeans with duct tape. Elvis yelled back louder. The situation continued to escalate. Lucerne finally herded them into the car, where they continued to argue while he finished loading their belongings into the trunk.

It was close to noon by the time Lucerne dumped the last pile of dirty clothes into the trunk, and they sped off from the motel, owing over a week's rent. The temperature was in the upper nineties and climbing. The humidity was heavy enough that Lucerne had to run the wipers a couple of times just to clear the windshield.

"Close that window, Elvis. I got the damn AC on," Lucerne said. He adjusted the rearview mirror so he could give Elvis the evil eye as he turned onto the freeway ramp. As they sped down the freeway, the wind blew long wisps of Elvis's hair before howling out the fist-sized bullet hole in the rear window.

"I told you to close the damn window, Elvis. Come on, damn it. For Lord's sake, I can't hear myself think up here."

Elvis ignored Lucerne's request and continued to stare sullenly out the open window.

"Hey, dickhead, will you close the damn window? Christ almighty, you heard the man," Mendel yelled. When he got no reaction, he reached over the seat and swung a backhand at Elvis.

Elvis swatted Mendel's paw away and reached forward to grab a large tuft of hair, audibly tearing it out of Mendel's scalp.

Elvis's attack jammed Lucerne forward, and he fought to maintain control of the Fleetwood. He swerved back and forth across the lanes as cars around them honked and brakes screeched.

"Ahhh, you little bastard!" Mendel screamed and swung blindly. He connected with a right cross to Elvis's nose. The blow sent Elvis sailing back into the rear seat with his eyes crossed. Mendel wound up, ready to deliver another blow, but as he cocked a massive right arm, he caught Lucerne in the back of the head with an elbow.

"God…" was the only word Lucerne was able to utter before sideswiping a dark blue Toyota and sending it bouncing off a concrete barrier. The Toyota swerved back into traffic and set off a chain reaction of crashes. Lucerne caught brief glimpses of the debris in the rearview mirror while frantically fighting to keep the Fleetwood stable as it rocked from side to side. He pulled the .38 from his waistband and fired a round through the roof of the car. A small shaft of sunlight shone through the dime-sized hole in the roof of the car.

"God damn it. The next one of you bastards that so much as moves, I'm going to shoot your worthless ass off. Elvis put that damn window up, now!"

Elvis had the window halfway up before Lucerne had finished his request.

"And Mendel, sit down and buckle the hell up. Do it, damn it," he shouted and cocked the hammer back on the .38 for added emphasis.

"This is just one fine how-do-you-do. We're on our way to rob a damned bank." Lucerne glared at Elvis in the backseat. Blood was running from his nose and splattering onto his shirt. He'd already wiped his nose with the back of his hand once or twice, which only served to smear blood across the side of his face.

"Oh, Jesus, Elvis, lie down on the seat. See if you can stop that damn bleeding," he said. He shot another wicked glance at Mendel brooding in the passenger seat before moving into the far right lane and exiting the freeway. He noticed there was no traffic behind them. Not a car. He guessed correctly that the chain reaction they had set off shut down the entire freeway. He drove down the street, looking for a convenience store where they might get Elvis cleaned up.

Sixty-Six

Tracey thought *she might be feeling the beginning prickle of sunburn* as she waited at the ice cream truck. She knew Morris had just parked his ice cream truck here so he could leer at her and the other girls while they walked the picket line.

"Yeah, sorry," Morris grunted, not sounding sorry at all. "But, I'm all out of the Giant Gobblers. I just got the regular size left."

"Well, I guess I'll just have to get a regular size then. Won't I?"

"Fine, I don't care. You mind if I ask, you actually work here?" He nodded in the direction of the picket line where Misty and two other girls were climbing on top of a large air conditioning unit next to the building.

"Yes, I do," she said, trying to make herself heard over the crowd's catcalls.

"Frightening," Morris mumbled as he shook his head.

"Sorry, what was that?"

He twitched his head, eyes fixed beyond her to the air conditioning unit where Misty began to gyrate in response to clapping hands.

A T-shirt clad guy in need of a shave, a shower, and some serious dental work stepped behind Tracey and asked, "Hey, are you that broad that was in the paper?"

"Huh?" was all she managed to squeak out over a mouthful of ice cream.

"Yeah, you know, the headline read, 'Tons of Fun'. In this morning's paper? You didn't see it?"

"I have absolutely no idea what you're talking about," she said and stormed off.

"It's in the paper, the local section, your picture. Here, check it out," he called after her.

It was shortly after that she noticed people pointing at her, some of them giggling. It made her all the more hungry, and she'd gone back to the ice cream wagon twice, each time more ravenous than before. When a group of twenty-something guys asked to have their photo taken with her, she was finally convinced something was up.

"You kidding me, lady? You're famous. Well, sort of, maybe. Hey, show her the paper," one of the guys said.

She snatched the newspaper out of their hands. Her image took up a third of the front page above the fold.

There, under the heading 'Tons of Fun had by all!' was a picture of Tracey with her tongue aggressively attacking a dripping ice cream bar.

"I'm the laughing stock of the entire city," she screamed.

"Hey, look," shouted some shirtless guy in the crowd. He had a beer belly with red stretch marks. "It's that tons-of-fun broad. Hey, how about a picture, lady? Lick that ice cream and ditch that hat. I can't get your face." He crouched down and took aim with his camera.

She didn't remember much after seeing red and screaming. Fortunately, the police didn't cite her, and the shirtless photographer didn't press assault charges once Sassie and Misty offered to pose with him. Still, she had to phone someone to give her a ride, or the police promised they would take her downtown. She didn't know who she could call, and then it struck her.

Sixty-Seven

"Can you believe it? Perfect, an open spot right in front. Luck is with us, boys," Lucerne said, looking across the street as they drove past the bank. They were the first words uttered in the car since Elvis had come out of the convenience store restroom with toilet paper shoved up his nose and proceeded to sulk in the rear seat.

Elvis stared out the blood-splattered window, brooding. The clumps of toilet paper shoved up his nose to staunch the bleeding looked like birthday candles. His face around both eyes had begun to swell and grow darker by the minute. Lucerne hoped the combination of the black eyes, broken nose, and toilet paper might be just enough to disguise Elvis's appearance.

Other than a bloodied raw patch on the left side of his hairline about the size of a fifty-cent piece, Mendel looked none the worse for wear.

Lucerne swerved into the intersection and waited for a pickup truck to pass so he could make a U-turn and park right in front of the bank door.

Otto had determined that this time he would just wait to speak with Cindy even if she got called away. He was still mad she hadn't followed his directions and most likely wasted her entire night running around looking for him. He failed to notice the two-toned Fleetwood attempting to make a U-turn as he drove past and pulled into a parking spot right in front of the bank.

"That son of a bitch just grabbed our spot," Mendel yelled.

Lucerne leaned on the horn. As they drove past, Mendel lowered the window, leaned out, and gave Otto the finger.

Otto reached down and touched the .45 in his belt, secure the moment he felt the cold steel.

"Hey, that's okay, relax. We'll just park in the lot. It'll make it that much easier to head down that residential street when the time comes," Lucerne said. "Elvis, grab that carpet with them AKs, and let's get ready to rock and roll."

Lucerne's cell phone suddenly rang with its distinctive tone, Lynyrd Skynyrd's song, 'That Smell!'

"Yeah?" Lucerne answered with a questioning inflection. He glanced at Mendel and Elvis. Both wondering who would ever want to call Lucerne.

"Lucerne?"

"Tracey?" he asked, recognizing her voice as he hit the brakes. The Fleetwood screeched to a stop just as he began to back into the parking place. Elvis had just laid the AKs on the backseat, and they sailed onto the floor.

"Jesus!" Elvis whined. His voice sounded severely distorted between the broken nose and the wads of toilet paper.

"Hey. We're supposed to rob the damn bank!" Mendel roared as he pushed himself off the dashboard and glared.

Lucerne turned his back to Mendel, stuck an index finger into his ear, and half-whispered, "Tracey, you okay?"

"Did I catch you at a bad time, Lucerne?"

"Well, we're kinda busy with work right now."

"I wouldn't call unless it was an emergency. You know that. Don't you?"

"Matter of fact, I think this is the first time you've ever called me."

"Well, I need help, and I didn't know who else to call. You always said you'd be there for me. So I was thinking maybe I could take you up on your offer."

"My offer?"

"To help me if I ever needed help, Lucerne."

"Well, I'd be glad to help you, Tracey, just as soon as I'm done here. Shouldn't take too long."

Mendel glared and ran his hand back and forth across his neck, giving Lucerne the cutoff sign.

"Well, look, I have to get out of here. Could you pick me up?" she asked.

Lucerne felt his temper suddenly getting the best of him. "Is it that Osborne fella making ya dance with him again?"

"Not exactly, it's sort of tough to explain. Have you ever heard of Cheaters?"

"Cheaters? You mean that strip joint?"

"Cheaters?" Mendel and Elvis chimed in unison.

"Well, yeah, see that's kinda where I am right now. I have to leave pretty soon. In fact, right away," Tracey said. She glanced over at the young officer standing next to her, arms folded with a frown on his face.

"I'll be there directly, and Tracey, don't you worry none. I'm on my way," Lucerne said.

"I knew I could count on you."

"What?" Lucerne asked defensively, turning his phone off as he looked over at Mendel.

"Oh, nothing. I was just thinking, whenever you're finished with your little love talk, we could get back to the damn reason we're sitting here! Now, get your thick skull in the game, back up, and park this boat!" Mendel shouted.

Lucerne pressed the accelerator down before taking his foot off the brake screeching the tires. Just as quickly, he slammed on the brakes before crashing into the concrete curbing just an inch away. He sent the AKs back onto the floor again and hurled Mendel forward into the dash.

"Fast enough?"

Sixty-Eight

Billy Truesdale unbuckled his seat belt while Gary, the driver, waited for a dented, two-toned Fleetwood Brougham to move.

"Damn that little weasel, Trevor. He's probably sipping another cold beer, thinking he played us for suckers," Billy groaned.

"I don't know, Billy. It's almost easier just hauling this by ourselves. In half the time it takes him to complain, we got her loaded up and heading back to Central. Hell, the day's a little more than half over. We don't have to listen to idiot Trevor. We got a three-day weekend coming up. Somewhere in my immediate future, there's a cold beer just waiting for me."

"Mmm-mmm," Billy growled.

Five minutes later, he was talking to Sidney as they rolled a second grocery cart out to the armored car. Gary, standing guard on the shady side of the building, swung the rear door open as they approached. He helped lift the trash bags stuffed with currency into the back. They swung each bag back and forth for a brief moment before tossing them onto the top of the pile.

"See, what'd I tell ya, Billy? The two of us, with Sidney's help. Thanks, Sidney. We can get this thing loaded in half the time it takes that little dumb shit, Trevor, to tell us all the things that are wrong with him. Of course, he always manages to leave out the part about being an absolute idiot," Gary said.

"Yeah, you wonder what they're thinking," replied Sidney. "We got the same thing here. I could tell you a month ago who was gonna call in sick today before the three day weekend. Just like who ends up with bottle flu after the Super Bowl. Who do they think they're kidding? Say, little something extra today, boys," Sidney said and held out three cans of Coke.

"Man, that is a welcome sight. Thank you, Sidney," Billy said.

"Likewise." Gary nodded.

Sixty-Nine

Nothing seemed to be going right for Beau. When he negotiated the purchase of the Saab a week ago, he had neglected to ask if the air conditioner and windows worked. Had he asked, the answer would have been a resounding no. Unfortunately, in anticipation of the AC working, he had raised the windows. Now they wouldn't go down. He calculated he had lost about six pounds just during the drive to the bank, sweated them off while the temperature in the sunbaked car climbed to somewhere in the neighborhood of 'broil'.

The fact that he was wearing his jogging clothes beneath his disguise, plus the shoulder-length wig and mustache, caused him to sweat uncontrollably. Add to that the fact that he had on latex surgical gloves so he wouldn't leave fingerprints, and it all amounted to one big sweat fest.

He was sweating so much that the adhesive on his fake mustache failed. He'd thrown the thing out the door while stopped at a complete standstill on the freeway. At least, the car radio was working. From it, he learned traffic was backed up for miles due to some major accident that had shut the entire freeway down.

He had hoped to enter the bank in the middle of the noon rush, just get in and out quickly, hopefully avoiding Cindy in the process. His carefully thought out plan consisted of handing his sweaty note to a teller, grabbing a bag full of money, and running. Now, he was way behind schedule. As he drove around the armored car parked next to the bank building, he was preoccupied. So preoccupied, he almost ran into three guys carrying a small roll of carpeting across the parking lot.

"What the? Hey, you dammed idiot," Mendel yelled. He slammed his left hand on the hood of the Saab and glared into the driver's mirrored sunglasses. "Watch where in the hell you're driving, dumb shit."

"Man, you see that freak? Talk about burned out," Elvis said in his nasal tone. He carried the carpet covered AKs tight against his chest.

"Just keep moving, boys. Stay together. We're almost there," Lucerne said.

Get a grip, Beau thought. He coasted the Saab into a spot next to a dumpster and what looked like an abandoned Fleetwood. The temperature was ninety-seven, and the humidity level wasn't far behind. Climbing out of his suffocating car, it felt like air-conditioned comfort.

He held the empty revolver in his sweat-soaked waistband so it wouldn't drop down his pants leg and clatter onto the ground. Strands of rayon wig stuck to the side of his face. So much sweat rolled down his face that it was dripping off the tip of his nose. His shirt was drenched, and his jeans were soaked through.

"Dear God, please make this work," he whispered as he walked toward the door of the bank building.

Cindy had glanced up and caught sight of Otto parking in front of the bank. She was determined that this time she was not going to run away. She would let him walk right up to her, and when he asked how she was doing, she would face him head-on and do the only sensible thing. Lie. She figured mentioning a husband, and four sick kids in the conversation would take care of her problem once and for all.

Otto couldn't believe his luck. He was next in line to have Cindy take his deposit. He figured this would be the perfect opportunity to set her straight on a couple of items. Not the least of which would be following his directions. Gentle but firm, he reminded himself, gentle but firm.

Beau made his way into the bank lobby, convinced everyone was looking at him. He was afraid the excruciating drive in the Saab had brought him to the brink of dehydration. A few thousand strands of his cheap rayon wig clung to his sweaty face. The empty revolver in his waistband threatened to fall down his pants leg. He was trying not to bring attention to himself and prayed Cindy wouldn't recognize him. He slowly shuffled forward in the line, as far away as possible from Cindy. He just hoped the teller wouldn't scream when he handed her the note.

Lucerne, Mendel, and Elvis limped forward as one big clump in the line glancing nervously from side to side.

"I say do it, man," whispered Elvis. He had to gasp audibly because of the toilet paper crammed up both nostrils.

"Mendel?" Lucerne asked.

"Stay cool. Not yet. Just keep her cool, boys," Mendel cautioned.

Seventy

T hough longer than the other three lines, Beau's was moving substantially faster, and he suddenly found himself faced with his moment of truth. He quickly glanced down the length of the counter at Cindy. She was just finishing up with a woman, and the mentally challenged guy wearing the Vikings jersey was next in her line.

He took a deep breath, dug into the back pocket of his jeans, and handed his sweat-soaked note to the teller. He took a half-step back, keeping his hand on the revolver, lifting it ever so slightly. If she had any questions, a quick flash without pulling the thing out of his jeans would get his point across, hopefully. His heart pounded as she unfolded the note. She looked at it for a long moment before staring back quizzically into his mirrored sunglasses.

"I'm sorry, sir. The ink has run all over your note. I can't read it." She spoke slowly and distinctly, forming each word carefully as if he might have difficulty understanding. "Do you speak English?" she asked.

Otto stepped up to Cindy's window. He smiled, snapped open his briefcase, and reminded himself, *gentle but firm.*

Cindy smiled back at Otto and kept repeating to herself, a husband and four sick kids, a husband and four sick kids.

"Do it now, dudes!" Mendel whispered and grabbed an AK as Elvis let the carpet fall to the floor. He unfolded the stock, brought his AK up over his head, and fired a long burst across the ceiling. Ack-ack-ack-ack-ack-ack-ack-ack-ack. He paused for half a beat before stitching another burst across the top of the protective glass in front of the teller's windows.

"What the hell was that?" Gary asked, standing in the shade of the armored car. He listened to the engine idle while he finished his Coke. He was hoping the air conditioner would cool the front seat down before they climbed in and drove back to Central.

"That crap's been going on all damn week. If it's not the damn mid-day parade, it's some other bullshit, fireworks, or something from the fair," Sidney replied.

"Fireworks? In the middle of the day?" Billy asked and drained the last of his Coke.

"They probably set that shit off whenever they guess some fat guy's weight correctly," Sidney said, and all three of them laughed.

"Everyone down on the floor, now! Get your hands up where we can see 'em and shut the hell up!" Mendel roared inside the bank.

The customers caught in the crowded little lobby crouched down and thrust their hands in the air. Otto knelt down in the corner and pushed his briefcase behind him. He felt the reassuring grip on the .45 just under his jersey and glared. Cindy was in trouble, and it was time for Sheriff Otto to come to the rescue.

"You gotta be kidding me," Beau groaned as he dropped to the floor.

"Hey, burnout, you heard the man. Shut up," Elvis said. He took two or three steps in Beau's direction and pointed the AK at the tip of his nose.

By this time, Lucerne had entered the teller area via the door in Sidney's office. This wasn't a matter of concern to Sidney just now. He was still standing outside in the shade of the armored car, telling a joke to Billy and Gary.

"Come on. Fill 'em up. Fill 'em up," Lucerne encouraged the tellers, who were anxiously shoveling cash into his trash bags. Silent alarms went off as they pulled bills out from their cash drawers and hurriedly dumped the cash into the bags Lucerne held.

"You too, lady!" he shouted to the flushed-faced college girl counting currency in the vault. She had on cut-offs and a tank top. Her eyes were wide, and her lips were trembling.

"Me?" She pointed to herself questioningly.

"Yeah, you. Think you're special? Come on. Fill up this damn bag," he yelled and encouraged her by waving the .38 beneath her nose. She got the message and quickly started shoveling bricks of banded currency into the trash bag.

In the distance, Mendel thought he heard the wail of a siren. He looked nervously over at Elvis, who blinked back, hearing the same thing.

"Grab the freak," Mendel said to Elvis. He motioned toward Beau with his AK, then pounded on the glass to get Lucerne's attention. He nodded at Cindy and yelled, "We gotta get going, man. Right now. Grab her."

The whole operation took little more than ninety seconds, barely enough time for Sidney to get to the punch line of his Ole and Lena joke.

As Billy laughed politely, he glanced over at the drive-up teller windows. His first thought was *the girls were all stretching together until he realized their hands were raised.* The lobby looked empty. Three guys were running out the door with bulging trash bags and some pretty serious looking weapons. They pushed one of the tellers and some long-haired freak in front of them.

Billy cut his laugh short and pointed. "Ahhh, Sidney?"

Mendel picked up on the sound of scattering Coke cans as three figures dove over the hedge off to his right. They pushed the two hostages toward their car. They were almost to the Fleetwood when a round whistled past

Mendel's ear and left a softball-sized hole in their windshield.

"Christ!" exclaimed Lucerne as a second round hit the right front tire, and a hissing noise caused the huge car to lean forward. Lucerne turned with his .38 and fired blindly in the general direction of the bank. He caught the hint of a purple blur jumping behind a wide brick column and fired again in that general direction.

"Shit, man, where the hell is he?" shouted Mendel.

As if in answer, a shaking hand poked a .45 around the corner of the column and fired, shattering the rear window of the Saab parked next to the Fleetwood.

"Goddamn it!" Mendel roared and let loose with a burst of rounds raking back and forth across the front of the brick column.

Behind the column, Otto cringed. He squeezed his eyes shut as chips of brick and mortar shot past, and a cloud of red dust enveloped him.

"Hail Mary, full of grace. Hail Mary, full of grace," he screamed, too frightened to remember the rest of the prayer.

"Get to that damn truck," Mendel cried, changing direction and pushing Cindy and Beau toward the armored car.

"Elvis, smoke that bastard behind them bricks, damn it."

Elvis raised his AK and began firing bursts at the column, hoping to keep whoever was back there pinned down until they got away. "Ack-ack-ack-ack. Ack-ack-ack-ack. Ack-ack-ack-ack."

"She's running," Lucerne yelled as he climbed into the driver's seat. "Put them two in the back, man. Come on. Let's go!" he screamed. He pushed an illuminated green button on the dash marked 'Rear Door.' He heard an audible click, and the button immediately changed color to red as Mendel tore the rear door open.

Mendel pushed Cindy and Beau ahead of him as he shouted, "Elvis, come on, man. Get in here. Come on!"

Elvis walked backward toward the armored car, firing continual bursts at the chipped and scarred brick column.

"Ahh, Hail Mary," Otto screamed in terror from behind the brick column.

Mendel tossed the trash bags into the rear of the armored car, pushed Beau out of the way, and jumped in. He pointed his AK at Cindy, motioning her to follow him. Cindy quickly climbed in. Elvis dove into the rear of the armored car and motioned for Beau.

Mendel pounded his palm on the front wall of the armored car. "Drive, baby, drive!" he screamed as the armored car lurched forward. Beau did his best to hop into the back of the accelerating vehicle just as Otto, stunned and unable to hear anything, poked a visibly shaking hand around the scarred corner of the brick column and fired a final round.

The round whistled off the open rear door.

"Ahhh, Jesus!" Beau screamed and sailed into the rear of the armored car, landing on top of the trash bags.

"Pull that damn door closed," Mendel screamed at Elvis as they raced down the alley.

"Oh, my God," Beau groaned. His rear felt as if it were on fire from molten lava. A burning, slashing pain ran left to right across his backside.

"Son of a bitch. You just got shot in the ass!" exclaimed Elvis. He arched the eyebrow above his good eye and stared at the torn bloody jeans as Beau lay face down, groaning.

"Quit your bellyaching, you dumb shit. That's barely a flesh wound. Damn ricochet is all. Hardly a new crack in your ass!" Mendel said disgustedly.

"Oh my God, it really hurts," Beau screamed as his mirrored sunglasses fell off. The dive into the back of the armored car had pulled the long-haired wig down just above his eyebrows.

"Hey, what the hell's this shit?" Elvis shouted. He reached over and tore off Beau's wig, then leveled his AK at the back of Beau's head.

"What the hell?" exclaimed Mendel.

"Tony?" Cindy said, sounding even more incredulous.

"Oh, God, I've been shot!" Beau groaned.

"You're about to be hurtin' a lot worse if you don't start talking awfully damn fast. You some kind of undercover cop or weirdo or something?" Mendel shouted. He thrust the barrel of his AK between Beau's eyes. As the vehicle sped down the street, rocking back and forth, the barrel repeatedly bounced off Beau's forehead.

"Look, can't you see I'm dying here? I've been shot for God's sake," Beau whined.

"Shit, that's barely gonna leave an interesting scar. What in the hell do you think you're doing here?" Mendel scoffed.

"Oh, yeah, like I wanted to come along," Beau gasped just as a wave of pain raced across his rear.

"He's my boyfriend," exclaimed Cindy, moving in to get a closer look at Beau's wound.

"Hey, can you point that thing somewhere else?" Beau said. He looked up and crossed his eyes to focus on the barrel of Mendel's AK as it bounced off his forehead again.

"Check and see what's behind us. He ain't goin' nowhere's," Mendel said to Elvis. They could all feel the armored car gaining speed once it spun onto Highway 280 and began to race south.

"Oh, my God," Beau groaned as more searing pain raced across his rear.

"Are you okay, Tony?" Cindy gasped, gently tracing her finger along the puckered, bloody wound.

"Oh, please don't do that." Beau gritted his teeth.

"Nothing back there but cars, no cops," Elvis said, sounding a bit more relaxed.

"Good. Now, if we can just get the hell out of this thing, we'll be fine and dandy," Mendel said.

Lucerne merged onto I-94, heading west across the Mississippi River bridge and into Minneapolis. He took the Riverside Exit and accelerated in the direction of Tracey.

Seventy-One

"I'm sorry, Ma'am," the young officer said to Tracey. He sounded more exasperated than sorry. "We've asked you a number of times to, please, leave the scene before you cause another incident. We've allowed you to place five separate phone calls to this Lucerne individual. Maybe she just doesn't want to come and pick you up," he said, wondering who in their right mind would.

"Lucerne happens to be a 'he,'" Tracey exclaimed defiantly.

I doubt it, he thought. It was just his luck to have a crowd of women in thongs jumping up and down, and now, he had to deal with this.

"You've failed to leave the area as we have asked a number of times. Because of your actions, I'm afraid we are going to have to take you into custody. That is unless you leave immediately."

He was actually pleading with her, hoping he wouldn't have to end up booking her. Just now, everyone else was hanging around watching all the hot chicks screeching and jumping while they drenched one another with industrial size squirt guns.

"Look," he groveled, actually begging, as he watched Misty shriek and squeal after taking a full chest shot of cold water. "I'll let you phone one more time. But, if this Lucerne doesn't answer, you'll have to leave the area. You leave me no other choice. I'll have to place you under arrest." He just knew, the way his luck was running, this would be the one who sat down and refused to move unless she was carried out. God, they'd have to get a forklift.

Tracey listened to Lucerne's phone ring on the other end while the young cop was lost watching the distant, full-breasted reverie.

"Hello? Lucerne? Oh, thank God! I've been trying to reach you for the past ten minutes."

Lucerne had absently answered his phone while racing up the Riverside exit ramp. He glanced nervously in his side mirrors.

"Tracey? Angel, that you? Sorry baby, just a little busy is all," he replied, checking for a police pursuit. He couldn't recall a time when she had sounded so eager to talk with him. "You okay? You sound a little, I don't know, not shitty or pissed off, but more like worked up, sort of." He was doing his best to sweet-talk her.

"No, I'm not okay. They're asking me to leave. Telling me I'll be arrested if I don't go immediately."

"Arrested? They can do that to a vice president?" He pictured Tracey wearing her sparkling dancing gown, working with all sorts of files open on her desk, not wanting to dance or anything else except do her vice president's job. "Is it that damn Osborne fella again? Is he making you do dancing and shit you don't want to do?"

She was having a hard time hearing with all the whistling and cheering from the crowd. But, she did hear the words 'Osborne' and 'dancing'.

"Exactly!" she said. "Look, I was wondering if you weren't too busy, maybe, you could come get me. Give me a ride out of here. Right away, before things get any worse," she said, then glanced over at the policeman.

The young officer smiled coldly and pretended to check his handcuffs as an additional incentive for Tracey.

It sounded to Lucerne like Tracey was in one hell of a fix and in need of his help. Now. Frankly, he couldn't think of a better way to deliver it than in an armored car, with his brothers armed and carrying more money than God. Just cruise on up to Tracey, standing innocently and sweetly on the dance floor. It would make one hell of a big first impression.

"You at that Cheaters joint?"

"Yes," she said, wedging her finger tighter into her ear, hoping it might help her hear. The crowd was beginning to clap in unison, creating a beat. Two of the girls were dancing, driving the crowd crazy. The officer next to her suddenly began clapping in time with the rest of the crowd.

"I'll be at the ice cream truck. You can't miss it. It's parked right next to a big sign—"

She was suddenly hit by a misguided blast from a squirt gun that immediately switched off her phone.

"Huh? Hey, Tracey? You there, Tracey? Christ on a cross," he swore. He was only a few minutes from where she was. Quickly, he diverted the armored car along a side street for a few blocks before turning onto Hennepin Avenue and making his way toward Cheaters.

"Now, where in the hell is he going?" groaned Elvis looking out the back door of the armored truck.

"Doing just what he should," Mendel said, stretching out. He watched as Cindy gently patted and examined Beau's rear end. "He's got us off them freeways and into a quiet area. We'll ditch this ride, grab some other car, and get the hell out of Dodge. Cops'll all be guessing we're on the freeway somewhere while we just drive off into the sunset with all this money." He focused on Beau and Cindy. "We can leave dumbass and his nurse here locked in the back. I'll give you this much, son. You're liable to have one hell of a sore ass for a while. Best stay in that position for a couple of days," Mendel snickered.

Seventy-Two

"Come on, Milton, up, up, up, you ingrate!" Osborne continued to chide Milton in an effort to raise him off the office couch. All the cheering and whistling from the crowd assembled outside his front door without one of them buying so much as a bottle of water had simply become too much to take. Police or not, he was going to entice the assembled crowd inside with the tantalizing offer of his suntan contest. He pulled on Milton's arm, slowly, gradually, forcing the delirious giant to accompany him downstairs.

"Arghhh!" Milton growled heavily with a thick tongue. He staggered back and forth unsteadily as they headed out the office door. He drooled down his chin and stumbled, glassy-eyed, toward the staircase. The stairway seemed to toss from side to side like a rowboat in a storm. Milton grabbed the stair rail with his good arm, ran the side of his head against the wall for added balance, and began his stumbling descent.

"Quickly, Milton, hurry," Osborne chided and sprayed him with more disinfectant.

Lucerne could see a large crowd up ahead on the right and figured that was where Tracey probably was waiting for him. No wonder the poor little thing was frightened. From this distance, it looked to Lucerne like there was some sort of wrestling match. People were jumping all around. His blood began to boil just thinking what that son-of-a-bitch Osborne might be doing to his one and only.

"Damn traffic's looking awfully busy," Elvis groaned nervously through the toilet paper stuffed in his nose. Nothing looked familiar to him. Unhappy with the snail's pace they had suddenly adopted, he turned and slid down the back of the door. Beau's wounded rear end was pointed directly at him.

"Take her easy, E. He knows what the hell he's doing. You want him to race down the street and bring all sorts of attention and such on us? I'm telling ya, we're just blending in, that's all, just blending in," Mendel said.

"Hey, buddy, what in the hell is your deal? You got an awful lot of clothes on, and it's close to a hundred degrees. And what the hell was with that wig? You some sort of a pervert or something?" Elvis asked.

Mendel looked at Beau for a moment, shot Elvis a look, and then lowered the muzzle of his AK directly at Beau's head. "Best answer the man's question, son."

"Tony?" Cindy said. For the first time, she noticed the powder blue jogging shorts popping through the puckered seam running across Beau's rear end.

"Ahhh, God, my ass is killing me," Beau groaned.

"There's gonna be a lot more wrong with you besides a new asshole if I don't get some answers here pretty fast, mister," Mendel said, then bounced the muzzle of his AK off the top of Beau's head. "Now, I'm gonna ask you again. What in the hell are you doing in this getup?"

Elvis raked the barrel of his AK across Beau's wounded rear end.

"Ahhh-ahhh, God, please," Beau groaned.

"Hey, we're stopping," Elvis exclaimed, quickly scrambling around to peer out the corner of the window. "Jesus, cops, and lots of 'em!" he said, ducking down.

"What the hell?" Mendel exclaimed. He duck-walked over Beau, scraping a boot across his rear end before cautiously peering out over the bottom edge of the oval window.

"Ahhh-ahhh-ahhh," Beau groaned.

"Damn it. I told you I didn't like this one bit. I damn well told you," Elvis yelled.

"Shut up. Just shut the hell up, Elvis. Let me see what Lucerne's up to," Mendel shouted. He duck-walked back over Beau, scrapping the same boot across his rear end.

"Oh God, please," Beau pleaded.

"What are all them folks doing here? How in the hell are we gonna get out of here? What are all those cops—?"

"Will you please shut up, Elvis? I'm trying to find all that shit out, but I can't even hear my own self think with you babbling on and on. So, please, shut the hell up so I can figure this out."

"But—"

"Shut up," roared Mendel. He turned to the front of the vehicle and pounded on the wall with his fist.

Shit, thought Lucerne as his head felt the slight vibrations through the steel plate wall. He quickly returned a couple of knocks with his left hand, holding the ringing cell phone in his right. He desperately scanned the milling crowd for a light brown-haired woman looking like Tracey sounded.

Between the noise from the dancers' music, the crowd cheering, and whistling, Tracey couldn't hear herself think, let alone see Lucerne ever since that armored car had parked in the way.

"Move that damn thing, you moron," she screamed, red-faced. She waved a flabby forearm farther down the street, indicating where she wanted the armored car to move.

"Come on, answer your damn phone, Tracey," Lucerne swore and looked frantically across the crowd, wondering if Tracey was all right or if that Osborne guy had done something to hurt her. Maybe, Osborne found out Lucerne was on the way and just freaked. He began to scan the crowd for a white-haired guy wearing a tux-edo.

"Hey, you hear me? Move that damn thing, you jerk. I'm waiting for someone," Tracey screamed. Her eyes took on a wild look, and her face glistened scarlet.

"Jesus, what a nutcase!" Lucerne said under his breath and did his best to ignore the sunburned fat woman ranting on the curb. Tracey was supposed to be near the ice cream truck. He feared Osborne had already grabbed her, dragged her off, and was probably making her dance on that air conditioner. That's the way rich guys like Osborne operated. Find Osborne, and he'd find Tracey.

"Jesus H. Christ! Ya know where we're at? That stupid son of a bitch brung us straight to that naked lady dance place, the one his girlfriend works at. Cheaters," screamed Elvis, peering out the rear window.

"Cheaters?" Mendel responded, shocked.

"Cheaters?" Cindy said.

"Cheaters?" Beau whispered, thinking Osborne.

"Osborne, he's got her out there somewhere. I know it. I just know it!" Lucerne ranted. He ignored the faint pounding coming from the steel plate wall behind him. He was sure he could find her in a minute or two. Once he rescued her from Osborne's clutches, they could just drive away. "Back in a minute," he said, pounding on the wall. He was too preoccupied with Tracey to realize neither of his brothers would be able to hear him.

Tracey was enraged, knowing full well Lucerne would never find her with this big clunky armored car in the way. She stormed toward the driver's side just as the door opened, and the driver stepped down.

"What the hell are you doing? Move that thing. I'm looking for my ride here. He'll never see me with you parked there." As she sprayed spittle, it never dawned on her that drivers of armored cars typically didn't wear Lynyrd Skynyrd T-shirts.

"You're pretty hard to miss, Lady. Wouldn't hurt you to drag that fat ass of yours down a couple of blocks. Then, just keep on going," Lucerne said. He quickly moved into the crowd, pushing toward the makeshift stage— all the while, keeping a hand on his .38.

"Shit, there he goes. Lucerne, God damn it. I knew it. We are screwed, man, major league screwed," Elvis said, looking back at Mendel and shaking his head.

"You sure?" Mendel shouted, half-jumping across Beau. He once again dragged his boot across the wound in an effort to look out the window.

"Oh, my God!" Beau screamed.

"It's okay, Tony. It's okay," Cindy said, stroking Beau's hair.

"Will you look at that? Now, I'm gonna have to go and get that dumb bastard," Mendel said, leaning his AK against the wall. "Watch these two. I'll be back in one minute. Now you stay put, E. You hear me?"

Elvis nodded, his one good eye looking wild as Mendel pushed the release button and opened the door.

Once he was out, he stuck his head back in. "One minute, E. I'll get Lucerne. Just give me one minute, and I'll be back. I promise."

As soon as the door closed, Elvis peered out the corner of the oval window and watched Mendel disappear into the crowd.

Beau had always wondered what he would do if the time ever came to show some real cojónes. He swallowed hard, grabbed the empty revolver stuffed in his waistband, and thought, *My ass really hurts.* He shot a quick glance at Cindy, then rose to his knees and pressed the barrel firmly against the back of Elvis's head, forcing his face against the oval window.

"Ahhh, Jesus, don't, my nose, my nose. God, you're hurting me," Elvis pleaded.

"Don't move, or so help me!"

Elvis exhaled loudly through his mouth, drooling and steaming a portion of the window. "Don't you go shooting that thing, Mister. Just take her nice and easy."

"Lay down," Beau instructed, at the same time prying Elvis's hand from the AK and handing it to Cindy.

She grabbed the weapon, shouldered it like a pro, and calmly pushed the barrel into the back of Elvis's head.

Beau stared at her with a surprised look on his face.

"I've got four brothers," she said in response.

Beau tore his wig off, opened the door, and grabbed a trash bag full of cash as he backed out. "I'll get help. Anyone looks in here, tell them to get the cops."

Seventy-Three

"Hurry, Milton, hurry," Osborne said, half-pushing Milton down the stairs with one hand while spraying disinfectant along the handrail with the other. They were approaching the bottom of the stairs, and Osborne could see the milling crowd just beyond the door.

"Milton, get the door. Get the door," Osborne instructed, as he tugged his sleeves and adjusted the lapels of his sport coat. "Milton, will you get the door, please!" he yelled.

Milton weaved in Osborne's direction. He stared through glassy eyes before he turned, opened the large door, and crashed to the sidewalk like a collapsing chimney. He bounced twice before his body settled on the ground, wedging the door open.

"Oh, for heaven's sake, Milton!" Osborne scolded and stepped out onto the sidewalk.

Beau carried the trash bag stuffed with currency. His empty revolver was crammed into his waistband. Painfully, he hobbled around the edge of the crowd to the front door of Cheaters just as Osborne appeared in the open doorway.

"My friends, my good friends. Please come in and enjoy these tempting feminine treats in our air-conditioned comfort. Of course, free drinks to our first fifty guests," Osborne shouted.

Beau didn't notice Milton on the ground until he had stumbled over the body. "Jesus Christ! What's with him? Is he dead?" Beau asked.

"Oh, he'll be fine. Please, please, come in and— DiMento? Is that you?" Osborne asked. He scanned what remained of Beau's disguise, giving him an up and down inspection and looking genuinely confused.

"Yeah, it's me, Osborne. Here's your payment, in full, plus a bonus. Now we're even," he gasped, handing the trash bag to Osborne as another stab of pain slashed across his rear. "Ahhh, God!" he groaned.

Osborne snatched the bag from Beau's hand, opened it, and stuck his head in for a quick look. In the half-second it took to register what was in the bag, he wrenched it closed and, without another word, fled back up the stairs. Taking the steps two at a time and leaving Beau standing in the doorway.

Beau detected a commotion near the armored car. He turned to make his way back to Cindy just as a large, hairy, bearded giant with a Lynyrd Skynyrd T-shirt hovered over him. Beau recognized him as one of the bank robbers.

"Where's Osborne?" Lucerne asked, not recognizing Beau without the wig and mirrored glasses.

"He just ran up those stairs to the office at the top. You can't miss it. Feel free to go right on in," he offered.

Lucerne stepped over Milton and quickly dashed up the staircase.

No sooner had he disappeared from sight than police officers wrestled someone to the ground just ten feet away.

As they wrestled him to the ground, Mendel screamed at the top of his lungs, "Lucerne, you son of a bitch. Lucerne."

"Officer, officer, I saw one of them. He yelled at me and ran toward the building," Tracey said, tapping a police officer on the shoulder. They were gathered around a woman in a brown polyester outfit with her arms crossed, talking calmly at the rear of the armored car. A guy with bloody toilet paper crammed up his nose was handcuffed and being placed in the back of a squad car.

"Lady," the officer said to Tracey, "I told you before if you didn't leave the area, I was going to place you under arrest." He slapped a cuff on one of her sunburned wrists, forcefully spun her around, and cuffed her other wrist.

"But, I saw him. He climbed out of the armored car, and he went into the building. I talked to him. I told him not to park here," Tracey said as she was led away.

Osborne dashed up to his office and slammed the door closed behind him. The trash bag was stuffed with bundles of currency. He inhaled deeply, breathing in the sickly sweet smell of cash, and figured he had better get it safely tucked away. He was just cramming the last of the bag into the office safe when he heard a voice behind him.

"Osborne?"

He jumped, slammed the safe door closed with his foot, then turned around to look at a hairy giant in a sweaty Lynyrd Skynyrd T-shirt, pointing a gun at him.

"Changed your clothes, I see," Lucerne growled, surprised Osborne wasn't still wearing his tux.

"Clothes?"

"What? Lose that fancy gold-headed cane? So where's Tracey? What'd you do with her?"

Osborne raised his hands slowly. "I can assure you. I have absolutely no idea what in God's name you're talking about."

"You got one more chance to answer me, proper like, or we're gonna dance," Lucerne said, his face flushed, and his eyes glared, leaving no doubt he was serious.

"Sir, I can assure you, I know nothing of this Tracey person. I have a number of girls here. You're welcome to help yourself. Find one you like."

"That your game is it? You think you can treat a pretty lady like that? Make her dance with you? Take time away from her work? You do that to all your vice presidents?" Lucerne advanced toward Osborne.

"What on earth are you babbling about?"

"I'll show you what I'm babbling about!" Lucerne screamed. He suddenly picked Osborne up by the lapels and threw him through the window.

"The other one might be up there," a sergeant said just as Osborne crashed through the office window and dropped almost on top of Milton.

The police raced up the stairs and approached the second-floor office door with their weapons drawn using extreme caution. Lucerne sat calmly behind Osborne's desk with his feet resting on an open drawer. Both his hands were in plain sight.

"Come on in, fellas. Look, I ain't gonna resist no arrest or nothing. I got enough problems to worry about already. That special sitting there is loaded, and it's all yours," he said, nodding at his .38 resting on the far edge of the desk.

Seventy-Four

The hypo they gave Beau, and the subsequent medications knocked him out for the night. He was lying face down with the middle section of the hospital bed cranked up. He wore a hospital gown that exposed his wound to his mother, now sitting in the chair opposite his bed.

Cindy knocked on the doorframe as she entered the room.

"Tony?"

"Oh, God," Beau groaned.

"Well, it doesn't look so bad from here," she said, trying to make the best of the situation.

"You call him Tony?" asked Beau's mother, taking an instant liking to this girl. "You know we named him Anthony, after his father, my Tony."

"Oh, Mrs. DiMento, it's such a pleasure to meet you. I'm Cindy."

"Oh, you're the girl who was with him. He kept calling your name last night."

"Oh, God!" Beau groaned into his pillow.

"He saved my life," Cindy said. "Hey, Tony, look, you're the big headline!" She laughed as she read the headline, "Bar Man Rear Ends Bank Robbers."

"Oh, God!" Beau groaned again.

In the end, Beau was the only one who ever knew about his attempt to rob the bank. All questioners were overwhelmed by the fact that he had been shot, held hostage, and had ultimately overpowered one of the bank robbers, leading to the arrest and capture of all three Ditschler brothers.

Otto O'Malley was credited with, if not foiling, at least altering their getaway attempt. Police later discovered an unregistered Saab parked next to a bank dumpster and the Fleetwood. The vehicle was devoid of fingerprints, with the exception of an entirely perfect left-hand print belonging to Mendel Ditschler on the hood of the car. After careful consideration, authorities surmised that the Saab was to be used as a second getaway car.

Two months later, just before Halloween, Beau was standing at the bar watching Cindy sip a glass of red wine as she read him the latest article concerning the bank robbery trial.

"Noted strip club owner and reputed mobster, Declan Osborne, has been found guilty of being an accessory to the crime, as well as guilty of receiving stolen property from last August's botched bank robbery.

Portrayed as the mastermind of the comically ill-fated scheme, Osborne is currently awaiting sentencing while recovering from injuries received during his unsuccessful escape attempt out a second-floor office window. Throughout the trial, he denied any involvement in the robbery. However, four sets of circumstances seemed to outweigh his claims, and after thirty minutes of deliberation, the jury found him guilty.

The three Ditschler brothers, convicted of carrying out the actual robbery, fled directly to Mr. Osborne's place of business, the former Minneapolis entertainment club known as Cheaters.

Second, one of the convicted bank robbers, Lucerne Ditschler, testified under oath that after robbing the bank, he intentionally drove to Cheaters for the express purpose of meeting with Osborne.

Third, some of the stolen funds, in stacks of banded currency identical to those recovered from the stolen armored car, were found crammed into an office safe just moments after Osborne's attempted escape. These same funds were identified by the Minnesota State Office of Forensics as containing a residue of bacon grease and batter consistent with that used at a series of State Fair stands.

"I still say that bacon guy is really weird," Cindy said. She pictured Otto sweating in a jersey, zinc oxide smeared over the better part of his face, leaving a streak down the glass of her teller window from his nose. She shuddered before continuing, "Anyway, forget about him."

"Fourth, the funds discovered in Osborne's office safe were wrapped in a green plastic garbage bag identical to the bags used in the robbery. Fingerprints of the bank robbers, as well as blood and fingerprints from wounded hostage Anthony DiMento, were on the bag. When faced with this overwhelming evidence, Osborne claimed to have received the funds from wounded hostage DiMento.

Osborne's second-in-command and presumed go-between, local mob enforcer Milton Twiddle, was arrested and taken into custody at the same time as Osborne. Twiddle was convicted last week on charges of acting as an accessory to the crime. Currently awaiting sentencing, Twiddle is confined to a high-security prison hospital in Atlanta, Georgia, at the insistence of the United States Centers for Disease Control and Prevention."

"You know the part I don't get, Tony?" Cindy said, putting the paper down and looking at Beau. "Why did you take that bag of money with you? Why didn't you just start screaming for help like I did? I mean, my God, how dumb were those guys? There were about a thousand cops around. Why did they even stop at that place?"

Beau gave his practiced answer. The same one he'd given her since the morning she met his mom.

"I wasn't thinking. I just wanted to get those guys after they took you hostage. I was afraid they were going to get away."

He waited for a beat or two. Then, just as he was about to suggest they grab something to eat, she struck.

"So, okay. I mean, I get all that. But the wig, your disguise, the gun, what was all that about?"

"I told you a thousand times. I was going to ask you out. Pretend I was a different guy."

"But why would—"

Beau quickly kissed her.

"Why—"

He continued to kiss her, getting an electric charge, just like the very first time he'd kissed her.

"Let's get something to eat and then go home," he whispered in her ear. "See how things go from there."

The End

Thank you for taking the time to read Bankers Hours. If you enjoyed the read please consider leaving a review. Even if it's just a sentence or two it really, really helps.
All the best,
Mike

Check out the sample of Chow Down. It's the next book in the Hotshot series. Enjoy the read.

Sneak Peek

Chow Down

Second Edition

MIKE FARICY

One

Craig Cullen gripped the wheel tightly as he fishtailed off the paved road and splattered mud against the side of his BMW. He raced down the gravel road to the processing plant and skidded to a stop next to the black SUV parked in front of the building.

Terry Taggert slammed the rear hatch on the SUV, smiled, and thought, *'Oh shit.'*
"Hey, Doc, didn't expect to see you all the way out here." Taggert's eyes blinked and darted from side to side like a cornered rat.

"We have to talk," Craig said.

"Just delivering our first box of steaks. Want to take some home?" He almost had to yell to be heard over the noise from a hundred-and-fifty cinnamon-colored Chows barking in the kennels behind the building.

"Good God, no! Are you crazy? It's one thing to try and pass the pelts off as exotic fur, but steaks, my God!

You aren't really planning to go through with this insane scheme, are you?"

"What do you mean insane? You were all for it. You came into this with your eyes wide open. Hell, you even thought it was kinda funny. As a matter of fact, your wife, Marti, begged me to let you in on the ground floor, give you a little taste of the action. You sure as hell loved the old projected profit ratio on them fur coats."

"That was then, before—"

"What? Now all of a sudden, when things are about to happen, you're getting cold feet? A conscience? As far as anyone knows, we're just a little old import company, Doc, nothing more, nothing less."

"The coats… well, yeah, that was okay, maybe. But this meat thing, I mean, come on. Look, I want nothing more to do with your 'import company'. The idea of jail time doesn't really appeal to me."

"Does Marti know you're out here? Did you check this out with her?" Taggert asked.

"No! I don't have to check with her. I make my own business decisions, and I just want my investment back. We'll call it even. I'll just go away and not say a word to anyone. I promise."

"Hmm-mmm, well, as long as you promise, Doc. Not much I can say except sorry things didn't work out. Come on into the office. I'll cut you a check. You sure I can't talk you out of this?"

"I'm quite sure." Craig shook his head, relieved things had gone this well. He followed Taggert into the cinder-block building. The office was actually more of a grimy lunchroom, the counter littered with dirty coffee cups and empty fast-food containers. A table strewn with pornographic magazines stood at a haphazard angle to the counter. On one corner of the table, a cup of coffee steamed next to a land-line phone.

Tilted on the rear legs of a chair sat the rumpled figure of Luther Suggs, his psychotic face hidden behind a foldout and a two-day beard. He lounged in a grimy, blood-stained lab coat. A white baseball cap emblazoned with 'Chow Industries' was perched backward on his head.

"Luther, look who came to visit," Taggert said, his eyes darted from side to side, signaling there might be a problem.

"Something in your eyes?" Luther asked, looking up from behind the foldout.

"Let me see, Doc. We were gonna cut you a check," Taggert said, emphasizing the word check as he raised his eyebrows. He gave a palms-up gesture, suggesting Luther remove his size-twelve feet from the table.

"Mind if I use that chair a minute and cut the Doc here a check?"

"Huh?"

"Move, damn it."

"Oh, yeah, just reading an article here."

"Did I just hear the phone?" Taggert asked, inclining his head in Craig's direction.

"The phone?" Luther asked, now vaguely aware he might be missing something.

"I thought I heard this phone ring. Hello?" Taggert said, picking up the receiver. "Hmm-mmm… Oh yes, just a minute, he's right here. It's for you, Doc," he said, holding the phone in Craig's direction.

"Me, who would—"

Taggert slammed the receiver across Craig's left temple with a dull thunk. Thunk, thunk, thunk. He hammered until the receiver shattered across Craig's skull.

"Ughhh." Craig groaned and dropped to the concrete floor, pulling Luther's mug of scalding coffee down on top of him.

Taggert quickly followed with his loaded thirty-eight, hammering on the top of Craig's head. "Luther! Damn it. I could use a little help here."

Luther watched passively for a long moment, then reached down with a massive hand, grabbed Craig by his perfectly coiffed hair, and slammed his head a couple of times against the cold concrete floor. The third slam made a noticeably different sound, like a ripe melon falling off a truck.

"There, now he ain't going nowhere."

"It's about damn time. What did you think I was doing?"

"Sorry, man, I was busy."

"Take his keys and wallet and pull his car behind the kennel. Then dump him in the grinder. Grind him up a little at a time, so there's no trace. I doubt anyone knew he was coming out here. I was with that pain in the ass wife of his last night. She would've said something if she knew. I'll call her and set something up. Damn," Taggert said and rolled his shoulder, then kicked Craig's body for effect. "I think I tore a rotator cuff."

Luther grabbed Craig Cullen by the heels and dragged him across the floor, out through the door, to the processing area and the large stainless-steel meat grinder.

TWO

"Come on. I can't breathe! Oh, God. Dickie, I'm not kidding, get off me!" DJ gasped in a futile attempt to push him off.

Eventually, Dickie Mullins rolled onto his back and gasped for air.

"You know, Dickie, it's a good thing for me, I'm not picky about who I climb into bed with." She laughed, then crawled out of bed and put her glasses back on.

"No complaint from me," he said.

"Hey, what'd you do with my underwear?"

From his angle on the bed, Dickie watched the reflection in the full-length mirror as she crawled along the floor. In the relatively close quarters of his thirty-foot houseboat, there was no room to spare, and her bare hip made a squeaky sound as she brushed against the mirror.

"Oh, Jesus," she said, grabbing the errant garment from under the bed. She stepped into the thong and then stopped, thumbs hooked in the straps around her thighs.

She peered at the photo of his police academy graduating class. The light streaming through the small window cast golden highlights off her thick auburn hair.

"Looking for anyone in particular?" he asked.

"Yeah, my favorite arresting officers," she said, snapping the elastic across her hips. "Just looking. Hey, you were quite the stud back then. Oh, can you spot me twenty bucks? Oh, come on. Don't give me that look. If you're gonna make a Federal case out of—"

"Relax, there's twenty bucks on the dresser."

"Forty would go further."

"Twenty. Sure you can't stay?"

"Very sure. Look, I got an early day. See you around," she said, stuffing the twenty in a front pocket. She bent over Dickie and gave him a quick peck on the cheek before grabbing her cotton top and strolling out the door to the small deck area.

"Hey, put your top on for Christ's sake." He stepped out of bed, hopped across the floor and into his boxers.

"Good morning, Vernon," she said.

"DJ, always a pleasure." Vernon smiled, stared, and sipped some coffee from the deck of his boat next door.

"You know, Vernon, what do you think about an ex-cop who lives on a boat with a view of the city jail?" As she spoke, she gazed at the early morning reflection of the downtown buildings across the surface of the Mississippi.

"Real nice," Vernon replied, ignoring the river.

Dickie stepped out the door clad in Hawaiian print boxers.

"My God, that's too much to take in at this hour," Vernon said and covered his eyes.

"Dickie, put something on because you're scaring poor Vernon here. See ya later," DJ said. She pulled her top over her head, stepped onto the wooden dock, and walked toward the Wabasha Bridge.

"Dickie, Lord knows you sure as hell don't deserve it, but you're one lucky son-of-a-bitch," Vernon scoffed.

Dickie silently watched DJ climb up the marina steps and disappear before he went back inside.

His houseboat consisted of a room paneled in cheap knotty pine with a double bed, kitchen counter seating for one, a sink filled with dirty dishes, two cupboards, and a very small refrigerator. He poured a mug of coffee from the pot DJ had started and stepped back outside.

He sat on the tiny deck in a faded, folding aluminum chair. Every time he bent his elbow to sip some coffee, the chair creaked. He had almost finished the cup when he caught DJ's figure in the middle of the bridge, making her way to the downtown side. She was a computer geek who walked dogs for a living. It didn't seem to make sense, like just about everything else in his life.

He absently ran his hand across his midsection, where his t-shirt rode up, and his boxers wedged down, revealing an ample spare tire. He planned to lose twenty pounds last summer, get back into some semblance of shape. He'd have to lose closer to thirty now, starting tomorrow. Once he picked up the surveillance case from Darcy.

Dickie had been on a disability pension from the police department since 2013. Some guy coming out of a liquor store at high noon. Who robs a liquor store at noon on a Monday? The dirtbag came out, and his car wouldn't start. First squad on the scene calmly pulled behind the fool's car, blocking it. By the time Dickie and his partner showed up, they were just watching the show.

Some department shrink talked the idiot into giving up. The poor guy, dressed in a cowboy outfit with a black ten-gallon hat, sat in the front seat of his car with a six-shooter in his lap, crying.

They had him surrounded on one of the first nice days of spring. Sunny, warm, and the only question was what kind of paperwork would have to be filled out, an arrest or a coroner's report.

Eventually, the shrink talked the fool into tossing his weapon out the car window, which he did, unfortunately, with the hammer cocked. The damned thing discharged, ricocheted off a parked snowplow, and clipped Dickie's left hip before exiting his rear.

He was just minding his own damn business, thinking about how great it felt to be in the sun, warm, safe, and glad he wasn't the lead officer on this cluster when—BOOM! Just like that, quick as you could say, "What the hell!" Dickie ended up retired and on disability.

It wasn't long after that, once he had completed his correspondence course, that he had started his private eye gig. About a year after that, he got the brain fart to buy a bar and restaurant, the Emporium of Dance. It was a local meat market, for lack of a better term. Now, with the economy the way it was, he'd been working overtime just to keep it afloat. He glanced at the clock, six-thirty. He had an appointment at eleven, which gave him almost three more hours of sleep if he hurried.

He crawled onto the pile of leopard print sheets, reeking of spicy lubricant. A hint of DJ's perfume still lingered around the pillow as he fell asleep.

Three

"Knock, knock, knock, Sleepy Head, rise and shine!" a female voice, frighteningly familiar and way too cheery, called from the door.

"Come on. I brought you coffee. Mmm-mmm, here smell, Baby. Fresh black coffee, just the way you like it." The voice was suddenly next to his bed.

According to the digital, it wasn't quite eight-thirty, and Dickie could only hope he was in the midst of some strange nightmare and not really hearing his ex-wife's voice.

"Come on now, Baby. Open those eyes. Come on." She bent down, letting her blonde perfumed hairbrush lightly across his neck, chasing away the final vestige of sleep.

Dickie had always been convinced his ex-wife, Rae Nell, held on to his last name just to piss him off. She was the youngest of four sisters, Rae Jean, Rae Dawn,

Rae Lynn, and Rae Nell. They had been called the *Sun Rae's* by their mother, and by the time of his divorce, Dickie thought of them as the *Death Rae's*.

Rae Nell divorced Dickie six years ago in search of her *freedom*. Following the divorce, Dickie got the house payment, Rae Nell got the house, along with the *freedom* to pursue any get rich scheme that piqued her interest, which seemed to be most of them.

She sniffed as she stepped back to the kitchen counter. She picked up an oily hint of spicy something from somewhere.

"New aftershave you're wearing?"

"I don't suppose it would have done any good to lock the door," he groaned.

"Not really, Hon, you gave me a key. Remember? Besides," she said, snooping in the bathroom, "it's not like you have anything worth taking."

"Well, you'd know all about that, Rae Nell, since you already took everything. So what do you want?" Dickie said as he sat up in bed. He blinked in an effort to accept the brightness and rubbed whatever two scant hours of sleep might have deposited in his eyes.

"Oh, don't be such a sore loser. Here, just the way you like it, black, not too hot," she said, prying off the plastic lid.

"Mmm-mmm," Dickie groaned, then rolled out of bed and stumbled the five feet to the counter.

"Wow, there's a lot more of you to love, honey," she said, sounding genuinely surprised. She gave him the once over from head to toe before handing him the cup of coffee.

"Rae Nell, darling," Dickie said with an inflection, not quite suggesting warmth. "What in the hell are you doing here at this hour of the morning?"

"Well, aren't we just Mr. Crabby. A girl can't even bring you a nice cup of coffee without being yelled at."

"I didn't yell."

"Could have fooled me. For your information, Crabby Appleton, I was just in the neighborhood, and since I hadn't seen you for at least half a year, I was wondering how you were getting along, that's all. If you're going to be a poop, I'll just leave."

"Okay," he said and sipped.

"Honestly, Dickie, I just wondered how you were doing. Gee, I can't be concerned without you getting upset? What's that all about?"

"I'm touched you're so concerned, Rae Nell. I really am. But, you have to admit it's only right I'm a little gun shy. Let's see, there was that wrestler you were dating, you remember? You told him I was stalking you. That was great. He showed up at the Emporium of Dance with two other clowns the size of semi-trucks intent on wrecking the place."

"The Emporium of Dance? Oh, please, Dickie. It's a weekend meat market. You serve up one-night stands as the house specialty with a side order of too much to drink."

"Hey, Rae Nell, you don't have to describe what you did last night. I'm just a little leery about your so-called concern, that's all. We could discuss the stock-broker, you remember him? Had you selling stocks to me without a license, the inside tip on the clapper for computers. Clap it on, clap it off." Dickie clapped his hands.

"Remember? Securities and Exchange parked out in front of your house, attempting to serve you a subpoena. So you hid out here for a week and a half while I was vacationing out west. I come home relaxed and all jazzed from seeing Mount Rushmore, and you make me get a hotel room because you couldn't possibly be inconvenienced."

"Well, excuse me. I thought I was doing you a favor by giving you three more nights away from this scow! Besides, you were dating that underaged child, if I recall."

"She was twenty-four."

"Exactly."

"Then, there was that guy who was mad at you and your imported pearl business, so he took a baseball bat to my car!"

"That orange Geo Metro? That dreadful thing? Oh, really, Dickie, it belonged in the scrap heap, if you could even find someone to dispose of it. My God, talk about toxic waste. I can't believe the state even allowed that death trap on the road."

"It was a classic, Rae Nell, a classic."

"Classic junk is more like it, Dickie. It leaked, just for starters. Did you ever get rid of the bean bag you had for a passenger seat?"

"The passenger seat was reinstalled," he said, declining to mention the fourteen-inch gash slicing across the leather.

"Whatever."

"Well, we might discuss the shipping container of honey you imported from Thailand and had dropped off at the rear of the Emporium of Dance last summer. That was beautiful. I don't know the thing is coming, and they punch a hole in the container with a forklift before leaving it by my back door. I had to shut down for three days because the wasps and bees were so bad. Neighbors started a petition against me, and I'm still battling with the Department of Health."

"Yeah, that one was kind of goofy. Okay, I admit that," she said, shrugging. "Look, enough crying over spilled milk."

"Spilled milk, I—"

She held up her hand. "I didn't come here with fresh coffee, so I could get yelled at and listen to your attempts to start another fight. Honestly, I just wondered if you would like to come over for dinner tomorrow night. You know, see the old place. I mean, after all, you're paying for it. We could maybe just catch up. You know, touch base."

"Why? What do you need?" Dickie asked cautiously.

"Why do I have to need anything? Why can't I just do something nice without you complaining all the time?"

"Maybe, Rae Nell, because it's just that when you try to do something nice for me, I always end up getting royally screwed."

"Look, do you want to come over for dinner or not? You can leave as soon as we're done eating and get back to that Brothel of Dance place if that's what you're whining about. I'm sure you wouldn't want to miss out on all the haggling for price and services that's bound to go on."

"It's the Emporium of Dance, as you know. You promise I can leave after dinner and you're not going to ask me for any money? You're not going to ask me for any favors? You're not going to complain about…"

"Dickie, when did you get so cynical? I promise I won't ask you for any money. I promise I won't ask you for any favors. My God, I'm just looking to catch up, that's all. You're free to leave whenever you want. Jesus, I have to say, after extending the olive branch, I honestly thought I would get a little better reception than this."

"You sure?"

"Girl Scouts honor. Say seven-ish?"

He let out a long sigh, closed his eyes, reminded himself this was really stupid, then nodded helplessly.

"Okay, seven, but I'm warning you, Rae Nell. The first time you ask me for a favor, any favor, I'm out the door. Okay?"

"Okay, Crabby," she said, then gave him a peck on the cheek and quickly made her exit before he had a chance to change his mind.

"Hello, Vernon, you're up bright and early," Rae Nell said.

"Just enjoying the early morning views around this place," Vernon said.

Four

ickie cautiously backed his Jeep Wrangler into a parking space a half-hour late for the appointment with his accountant and friend, Fenton Larkin. His car had seen better days. The duct-taped windows leaked, and the interior was just a tad moldy from the summer rain. Earlier in the year, an irate stripper wielding a nail file had slashed a fourteen-inch gash across his refurbished passenger seat. The doors had a tendency to slam the unsuspecting before they had completely climbed in, and the infamous body had been reshaped a few years back by a boyfriend of Rae Nell's wielding a Louisville slugger.

He'd been seated in the lobby for a few minutes and was aggressively attacking either a chili or spaghetti sauce stain, he wasn't sure which, on the sleeve of his navy blue sport coat. Finally, Clairese, Fenton's secretary and receptionist, had enough. She charged out from behind her desk, armed with a towel and a bottle of club soda.

"You know, Dickie, you could just get this thing cleaned or, better yet, throw it away," she said, then grabbed his sleeve and poured club soda over the stain.

"Hey, watch what you're doing there."

"Oh, sorry, I didn't realize this coat never had anything poured on it. Give me this," she commanded, yanking his arm back in front of her.

"You could stand to get those trousers pressed too. Looks like you slept in them more than once. And maybe a shirt and tie instead of the golf shirt."

"You think maybe there could be something between the two of us, Clairese?"

"Nothing but distance."

"Want to think about it?"

"I don't see enough lowlifes in here every day? I need to take up with someone like you? I don't think so. Besides," she continued, snapping the wet towel at the golf shirt stretched tight as a drum over Dickie's stomach. "Someone like you rolls over on little old me in the middle of the night, they'd have to scrape me off the bed with a spatula."

"You could take tops."

"Please, I'm barely two hours past breakfast. Unless you want to see strawberry yogurt and All-Bran on that coat of yours, you'll think of something else entirely."

"Dickie," Fenton called from his office, "nice of you to finally drop in. Get the hell in here."

"Some other time, Clairese. Thanks for the wet spot on my coat."

Clairese just shook her head.

* * *

"Jesus, Dickie," Fenton sounded more frustrated than usual, "you had better start getting back into shape, pal, or I'm going to have to ask for cash upfront. At this rate, you won't be around to get my invoice."

"Just more of me to love." Dickie slapped his midsection.

Fenton peered back over the top of his reading glasses.

"You're an early heart attack just waiting to happen, my friend. Start eating right, start getting some exercise, or you become a liability. I'm not kidding here."

"Okay, okay. Did you get up on the wrong side of the bed this morning? Relax. I'm starting a new regimen tomorrow."

"It's always tomorrow, isn't it? Here," Fenton said, tossing a file in Dickie's general direction before turning back to his computer screen. "Things are looking pretty good, that is if your goal was to reach ground zero. You don't have any money to move around or protect, no working capital, no assets except for the Emporium, well, and that raft you live on. Basically, you're broke. I can't believe you're even keeping books. You taking cash out every night? Based on the figures you gave me here, you're not cutting it. Oh, hey, by the way, where'd you get that program?"

"Program?"

"Yeah, and you just answered my question. You have no idea, correct? Whoever you got doing your books has a nifty little program they're using. Just as a test, we ran it off some of our systems here. The thing just whistled through each and every one of them, spreadsheets, charts, ratios, whatever we wanted. Look, find out where they got it. I'd like to get copies in all our offices. It even worked on the overseas stuff."

"Yeah, my bookkeeper, DJ. I'll mention it to her. But back up a minute, I'm broke?"

To be continued...

Things are about to go off the deep end. Better grab your copy of Chow Down to see where it goes. I can tell you this much, it gets absolutely crazy. Just click on the link below to get your copy. It's FREE on Kindle Unlimited or costs less than a cheap beer…

Books by Mike Faricy

The following titles comprise the Hotshot series.
- **Reduced Ransom!** 2nd edition
- **Finders Keepers!** 2nd edition
- **Bankers Hours** 2nd edition
- **Chow Down** 2nd edition
- **Moonlight Dance Academy** 2nd edition

Contact the author:
- Email: mikefaricyauthor@gmail.com
- Twitter: @Mikefaricybooks
- Facebook: Mike Faricy Author
- Website: http://www.mikefaricybooks.com

Published by

MJF Publishing